FREEDOM'S LAST GASP

The Exodus Series

M.A. ROTHMAN

Primordial Press

Cover Art by M.S. Corley

Paperback ISBN-13: 9798633151329
Hardcover ISBN: 979-8-7774828-4-6

ALSO BY M.A. ROTHMAN

Technothrillers: (Thrillers with science / Hard-Science Fiction)

• Primordial Threat

• Freedom's Last Gasp

• Darwin's Cipher

Levi Yoder Thrillers:

• Perimeter

• The Inside Man

• Never Again

Epic Fantasy / Dystopian:

• Dispocalypse

• Agent of Prophecy

• Heirs of Prophecy

• Tools of Prophecy

• Lords of Prophecy

Special thanks go to:

Dr. Charles Liu, Professor of Astrophysics – I wanted to especially thank you for keeping me relatively honest from a physics point of view and also for giving this book its title.

I also want to thank Dr. Harold "Sonny" White, working out of the NASA Johnson Space Center, as well as Dr. Miguel Alcubierre for both inspiring key scientific elements in this novel.

And thanks to Marc Berte, one of the smartest guys I know who doesn't mind having bleeding-edge science discussions at 5 a.m. in the morning.

"Freedom is never more than one generation away from extinction. We didn't pass it on to our children in the bloodstream. The only way they can inherit the freedom we have known is if we fight for it, protect it, defend it, and then hand it to them with the well-fought lessons of how they in their lifetime must do the same. And if you and I don't do this, then you and I may well spend our sunset years telling our children and our children's children what it once was like... when men were free."

—Ronald Reagan

CONTENTS

CHAPTER ONE

"Ave Maria, gratia plena; Dominus tecum: benedicta tu in mulieribus, et benedictus fructus ventris tui Iesus."

The pope's recitation of the Angelus prayer was transmitted from Earth, across millions of miles of space, received by the mining colony, and echoed throughout the Chrysalis mental health hospital.

Terry Chapper paused in the hallway and bowed his head. Ranger, his German shepherd, mimicked his reverential motion while remaining alert. Terry, too, kept his senses razor-sharp. Seeing as he was currently covering a shift for one of the hospital's security officers, he had to—especially here in the green ward. This was the section of the hospital reserved for patients who were prone to violence, sealed off from the outside world by a minimum of three sets of biometric locks.

As the prayer came to an end, a middle-aged nurse hurried

toward him. "Terry, we've got a situation with Callaway. He looks like he's about to—"

"I got him," Terry said, giving her a reassuring pat on her shoulder.

He fast-walked to the east wing and found Josh Callaway in the hall. The former soldier was almost three hundred pounds of muscle, with a face that looked like it had been etched from stone. He was dressed like every other patient here—blue scrubs, footie socks, and a medical tag on his wrist—but he looked perfectly healthy.

Looks were deceiving.

Callaway was walking along slowly, brushing his right shoulder against the wall, and making hand signals that to most people would have meant nothing, but to Terry meant everything.

"Hey, Josh, buddy. Are you with me?"

Callaway didn't respond.

Ranger growled at Terry's side, and Terry snapped his fingers. "Sit."

The dog obeyed, his ears lying flat, and huffed with frustration.

Callaway's gesticulations grew more animated. The soldier was in another place, another time. Suddenly he bellowed, "Carbon Outlaw Five Four, Hawkeye Thirteen at three four!"

With the most authoritative voice he could muster, Terry replied, "Roger, Thirteen. Just got a call from three that LZ X-Ray is clear."

Callaway's eyes widened and he stared into space, seeing something that wasn't there. "Negative, Carbon Outlaw, I've spotted Charlie on the cliff rise of Chu Pong Massif. They're setting up an ambush. I'm four klicks east-southeast and have visual. LZ X-Ray is not clear. Repeat, LZ X-Ray is not clear."

Terry had studied Callaway's background. The soldier had never been off-colony, so whatever scene was playing through his mind was born of delusion.

"Copy that, Thirteen," he said. "Arranging with DASC to scramble fighters for LZ X-Ray."

One of Terry's backups came around the corner down the hall, a stun wand at the ready. But Terry waved the backup away.

"Arranging for dust-off at LZ Victor," he continued. "Medics are on the scene. You copy?"

The tension in the huge soldier's face eased.

Terry approached cautiously. "Sergeant Callaway, stand down. We're holding the position."

The patient pulled in a deep breath and let it out slowly. Tears rolled down his cheeks, and he blinked, his gaze returning to the present.

"I'm sorry, Terry." He wiped his eyes with the heels of his hands. "I lost time again."

Terry swallowed hard and patted him on the arm. "It's good, Josh. No harm done. Come on. Let's go get you refreshed on your meds."

"The sedative will keep him under for at least a handful of hours," said a blue-smocked nurse as she scribbled something on the holographic image of a tablet computer. "I'm impressed that you managed to penetrate his delusion. We usually have to stun him when he gets that way."

They stood at the entrance to Josh Callaway's room. Even in his sleep, the twitching of the man's fingers was a telltale sign of the traumatic brain injury that hadn't yet healed. Terry felt a connection to the damaged soldier and his struggles.

"Is he getting any better?" Terry asked. "What's his prognosis?"

The nurse made the tablet disappear with a swipe of her hand, then motioned for Terry to follow her to the nurses' station. "Well, considering the whack he took in that accident practically caved in the side of his head, he's doing fantastic. The nanites are doing their job. I figure in another month he'll be back to normal, though he probably won't remember a lot of what happened. That's the stuff that we usually can't get back, the most recent memories."

As head of security for the mining colony, Terry knew what had happened to Callaway, and it certainly wasn't an accident. The UN had sent over another spy, who had somehow gotten past most of the security checks. But he hadn't gotten past Callaway. The spy ended up ambushing him with a blow that would probably have killed a smaller man.

Terry vowed to never let another of those UN scumbags get past their perimeter. He just wished he knew what the hell they were looking for.

"Hey, Terry." It was Candace, one of the nurses, waving at him from the break room. "Up for a soda?"

He walked in and joined her. "Hey, Candace."

She looked past him to Ranger, who had stopped just outside

the doorway, an untrusting look on his furry face. "Hey, pup!" she said. "It's okay. I think I can find you a treat if you like."

Ranger wagged his tail, turned around, and walked backwards into the room.

"What in the world?"

Terry chuckled. "When I first got him, he was a bit of a mess. The vet said he'd been found in one of the deeper mines, his nose broken because he'd run into a glass door. I don't even want to say how many credits it cost to patch him up, but it was worth it. But as a result, he's not very trusting of doorways."

"Oh, you poor thing. I'm sorry the glass door gave you an ouchie." Candace knelt down and gave Ranger a dog biscuit. He ate it out of her hand, his tail a blur.

Terry patted Ranger as he licked up the crumbs that had fallen to the floor. Then he grabbed the dog's face, gave him a kiss on the top of his snout, and said, "Damaged goods or not, I wouldn't have you any other way."

~

Priya lay in bed, listening through earbuds to the recording of the last lecture she'd given, her alarm clock beeping all the while.

"Okay, folks. For those of you who weren't awake last week, I'll remind you that we covered the Seebeck effect and how it enables the conversion of temperature differences into voltage via thermocouples. As you know, we have decaying elements like Strontium 90 within these thermoelectric generator packs that power most of the handheld gadgets we own nowadays. By necessity, these long-lasting power packs contain strong beta

particle emitters that need to be shielded, and the sheer act of stopping the beta particles produces bremsstrahlung, a more penetrating type of radiation, which needs to be dealt with as well. Today, we'll cover how we calculate the thickness of the shielding needed and the different options we have..."

Every time she heard a recording of herself, she was surprised by how noticeable her British accent was. It bothered her, but not so much that she cared to do anything about it. She was far more peeved by the professor who told her she came off a bit snarky when lecturing. If that was true, she needed to deal with it. Long term, it was probably a waste of time, but she needed to play the game if she was going to get her PhD.

Her bedroom door opened and Aunt Jen turned the light on. "It's almost seven! You'll be late for school."

Priya had lived with her aunt since she was seventeen, just after her parents' untimely death seven years ago. Aunt Jen had no kids, had never wanted kids, but she'd volunteered to look after Priya, and for that Priya was grateful.

"I'm ready," she groaned. She flipped off the covers, revealing that she was already fully dressed.

Aunt Jen looked over her spectacles and sniffed disapprovingly. "Don't forget you agreed to walk over to the tube station with Mrs. Peete's little urchin. It's her first day at school and I'm sure she's waiting impatiently at her apartment."

"I'll be out in a second."

Aunt Jen retreated, leaving behind a hint of rose perfume that made Priya a bit nauseated.

She slapped the button on the top of her alarm clock, glanced at the mirror hanging above her dresser, and grimaced. Her thick mop of dark hair fell over her shoulders; it would need a good ten minutes of brushing if she was going to get all of those tangles out. Ten minutes she didn't have. She settled for roughly raking her fingers through her unruly hair, then she grabbed her bag and headed out.

It was a beautiful morning in South Florida. A breeze carried the scent of freshly cut grass and even a hint of the ocean, though the shore was a good ten miles away.

"Priya!"

She turned to find Anna Peete hurrying over to her. Anna was an adorable five-year-old with pigtails, a freshly pressed school uniform, and a backpack almost as big as she was.

The girl smiled. "I was worried you forgot we were going together today."

"No chance, Jelly Bean." The two walked hand-in-hand from their apartment complex toward the tube station. "Are you excited about your first day at school?"

Anna looked up at Priya with big blue eyes. "I'm okay," she said with a tremor in her voice.

Priya gave the little girl's hand a squeeze. "You've taken this kind of trip plenty of times. How about this? Let's test how much you know. If you're *really* ready for school, you should be able to pass this quiz. Want to try?"

"Okay, I'll try." The girl brightened a bit.

"Where are we, and where are we going?"

Anna pointed at the tube station sign. "That's easy. We're in Coral Springs, Florida, and I have to go to Mrs. Robinson's class at the David Holmes Space and Science Primary School at Cape Canaveral."

Priya frowned. "Hm. You're right, that was too easy. I'll have to think of a harder question."

Anna grinned.

They walked up the stairs to the tube station, passing a matronly woman carrying an armful of groceries, and as they reached the top, a hologram of a smiling recruiter wearing a lab coat with a government logo blinked into existence just ahead of them.

*"Welcome, neighbor! It's people like me who keep the tubes running efficiently and safely. Type *92-8374 on your SMS device to learn more about joining the team."*

"Okay, let's see how you do with this question," Priya said. "How far away is our destination?"

"Pfft. Still easy. Cape Canaveral is three hundred kilometers away. That's one hundred eighty-five miles."

They had arrived at the arrivals and departures platform, and Anna stepped up to a control panel. It lowered by about a foot so it was easy for her to reach, and she pressed her hand on the touch screen. The display automatically switched to her custom settings, and a woman's voice spoke with a British accent.

"Good morning, Anna. I'm Lexie, your tube assistant. You have authorization for four different destinations on your account. Where would you like to go?"

Anna turned to Priya and pointed at the screen. "See? It lists the distance to Cape Canaveral right there. It also says it'll take about fifteen minutes, so…" Her face scrunched up as she concentrated. "Our top speed should be right around fourteen hundred miles per hour, and we won't have any more than about a .3 G acceleration."

Priya smiled at her precocious neighbor. "That's amazing. Who taught you how to calculate acceleration like that?"

"Duh… it's not that hard. It's just delta v over delta t and then convert the value to G's." Anna tilted her head and frowned. "*You* taught me that. Ages ago." She turned back to the control panel. "Lexie, I need to go to school. Priya is coming with me."

"Two passengers for the David Holmes Education Campus at Cape Canaveral. Please confirm."

"Confirmed," Anna said with an exaggerated nod.

The sound of rushing air grew louder behind the metal doors to the tube. *"Establishing vacuum. Queuing request for transportation link between Coral Springs-North Junction and the main terminal at the DHEC-Cape Canaveral."*

Priya put her hand on Anna's shoulder. "See? You're an expert at this stuff."

"Ya, I guess. But it's still nice not going by myself."

"Link complete. The car is arriving in three… two… one…" With a loud hiss, the doors slid open, revealing an empty capsule with two well-padded armchairs inside. *"The car is now ready for boarding."*

They entered the capsule. As soon as they were both seated, the doors closed, and Priya felt the air pressure change.

"We are about to depart."

The automatic safety harnesses built into their chairs activated, wrapping a gauze-like mesh around their legs and chests. Priya knew the harnesses provided only an illusion of safety. The truth was, at speeds exceeding Mach two, if they ran into any kind of trouble, no harness could keep them alive. There wouldn't be enough of them left to scrape into a jelly jar.

That was how Priya's parents had died.

Without a whisper of noise, they departed the Coral Springs Station, their capsule slowly increasing speed. Their seats automatically swiveled in the direction they were accelerating, and in less than a minute they began slowing.

"Passengers, we are arriving at the main Fort Lauderdale switching terminal. Please remain seated. Your car will automatically be routed to the proper queue for high-speed transport."

A hologram of a safety technician appeared in the car. *"Welcome, neighbor! You're about to embark on a transport that will see you traveling across our great state at a velocity well in excess of the speed of sound. Some passengers may have moments of discomfort upon seeing the land streaking by at these rates, so be aware that all our cars are equipped with dimming portals if needed. And if for any reason you feel that you must interrupt this travel, please take note of the red emergency button on each chair. Hold it down for three seconds to request an emergency reroute. Are there any questions?"*

"No," Anna said.

The hologram shifted his gaze to Priya, and she smiled and shook her head.

"Okay, then. Relax, and you'll be on your way in forty-five seconds. Thanks for listening patiently, and enjoy your trip."

Priya looked out the window at all the other tubes converging on the switching station. Off in the distance, some workers in vacuum suits were using a plasma cutter to service a tube car that had been lifted onto a service gurney. Then their capsule started forward once more, gliding smoothly along a magnetic rail before switching onto a new queue.

"Do you know why it's always quiet inside the tube?" Priya asked Anna.

Anna shook her head. "I'm not sure."

"Sounds can't travel through a vacuum."

"We're in a vacuum? I didn't know that."

"Of course. These cars can only achieve such high velocities when they're in a frictionless environment."

Anna's eyes widened with understanding. "That makes sense. No air, so no wind to slow us down. And we're on a mag rail, so we don't touch anything the entire time."

"That's right. And do you know why sound doesn't travel in a vacuum?"

"Is it because..." The little girl pursed her lips, focused for a few seconds and then shrugged. "I don't know."

"Because sound is actually a mechanical wave, and waves spread by vibrating particles in the air, but—"

"And a vacuum doesn't have air!" Anna announced triumphantly, as if making a new discovery.

"Exactly right."

"Attention. Your car is next in line for departure. We are departing the Fort Lauderdale switching terminal in three... two... one..."

Priya was pushed back against her seat as the capsule accelerated. A screen at the front of the capsule showed their speed, and in just over a minute they'd broken four hundred miles per hour.

As Anna looked out the window, Priya settled in for the short trip, thinking about the cryptic email she'd gotten last night, and wondering what it meant.

The sender was a Colonel Jenkins, from a part of the military she'd never even heard of. He asked to meet her in the hallway just outside her Relativistic Quantum Field Theory class when it was over. How did he know what classes she was taking?

At first she was kind of intrigued, but now that she'd had time to think about it, the e-mail sort of weirded her out. Who was this guy? And more importantly, what did he want with her?

Sitting in a booth at Mama Tina's Diner, a hole-in-the-wall restaurant located just on the edge of campus, Priya's stomach growled as she scrolled through the menu choices. She settled on a dish her mother used to make.

"Priya!"

She hit submit on her order and looked up as Karen Tian, one of her physics classmates, came over from a nearby table, bringing her plate of food with her. She set herself up across from Priya.

"Hey, Karen," Priya said. "I thought you only came to this place during late-night cram sessions when all the junk food machines go offline."

Karen shook her head, sawed at whatever gravy-covered thing she'd ordered, and popped a bite into her mouth. "Nah, this stuff is also good for hangovers. And let me tell you, don't ever let anyone try and convince you that plum wine can't get you drunk."

"Order ready," announced the artificial voice of the elec-

tronic waiter. A slot opened in the device and a plate of steaming spinach dotted with cubes of cheese rolled out.

Holding her hair out of the way, Priya leaned down and took a deep sniff of the ginger, garam masala, and garlic.

"What's that?" Karen asked.

"Palak paneer. It's a traditional Indian dish. Basically a spinach puree with Indian spices and chunks of cheese." She took a spoonful and chewed on the rubbery vegan cheese. She wished she could find a place that used actual milk-based cheese, like her mom used to.

She pointed her spoon at Karen's plate. "And what's that?"

Karen sawed again at her steak-like object. "It's an old southern classic. Chicken fried steak with sausage gravy. A total salt and fat bomb, but it's great for that headache I'm trying to get rid of." She swirled her fork in the lumpy grayish-white gravy. "Can you imagine they actually used to kill cows and use real cream for this stuff? It's a miracle our ancestors didn't die of embarrassment, much less heart attacks. Just the thought of what they used to eat…" She shuddered.

Priya simply smiled. She remembered just how good the real stuff was, and her goal was to eventually find a way to get some. But she wasn't about to tell Karen about her private little heresy. She didn't need a lecture from someone who was barely able to keep up with the school's course material.

"Wake up."

The words were spelled out with taps on her scalp in Morse code.

Startled, Priya popped her head up and looked around. Nobody in the lecture hall was paying attention to her. They were all busy scribbling notes as Professor Darby droned on like the giant bag of hot air he was.

She whispered under her breath. "What the hell, Harold?"

A barrage of taps rained on her head, and she imagined her hidden companion wagging his non-existent finger at her.

"You shouldn't sleep in a classroom. What if something happens that you need to be aware of?"

"Give me a break. This QFT class is mind-numbingly remedial. Darby hasn't had an original idea since… maybe ever."

At the front of the hall, the professor droned on. *"An operator acting on identical bosons can be described in terms of N–particle wave functions, the first-quantized formalism, or in terms of creation and annihilation operators in the Fock space, the second-quantized formalism. This exercise is about converting the operators from one formalism to another—"*

"I can do this stuff in my sleep," Priya whispered. "So why don't you let me get back to it?"

Harold remained silent. Either he had no good retort or he was just being moody.

Harold was an AI, encased in a form that was much more advanced than anything Priya had ever encountered. It could shapeshift to physically mimic almost anything, including, as he was doing now, her hair and skin. He was also a family heirloom of sorts. Buried within him were memories of every Radcliffe from the Great Exodus until now.

But he'd been particularly grumpy of late. Sometimes Priya wondered if he'd been mimicking her in the personality department as well. Despite that, or perhaps because of it, she got along better with Harold than with just about anyone else.

The lecture came to a close, and the students began filing out of the auditorium. Priya hesitated to join them, thinking of the odd meeting scheduled for her in the hallway outside. It wasn't in her nature to shy away from confrontation, but then again, she didn't often have to confront unknown colonels with equally unknown agendas.

"Miss Radcliffe?"

Priya nearly jumped out of her skin. A tall man in a military uniform was standing right next to her.

This must be Colonel Jenkins.

"I told you you shouldn't sleep in a classroom," Harold tapped, still hiding in her rat's nest of hair.

The man extended his hand and gave her a crooked smile. "I snuck in while you were napping. Pretty ballsy to do in a level 700 class, but it fits your profile."

Priya shook his hand and silently fumed at Harold for not having warned her he was there.

"I presume you received my e-mail last night."

"I did, but—"

"I'll explain on the way."

The colonel motioned for her to follow as he took a step toward the exit. Priya had to jog to catch up; the man's strides were easily half again as long as hers.

Outside the Arts and Sciences building, Jenkins turned toward the north part of the campus.

"Where are we going?" Priya asked.

The colonel gestured toward a tall building ahead of them. "The Space and Science Museum."

The museum? Why? But Priya had a more pressing question.

"Exactly what branch of the military are you with? Your signature in the e-mail listed UNSOC, but I couldn't find a sensible definition for that online."

The colonel gave her a sidelong glance. "It stands for the United Nations Special Operations Command. We don't advertise, but let's just say we report directly to the UN's First Council."

Priya was not that into politics, but she knew the First Council was the top of the governmental food chain. Which meant that whatever UNSOC was, it was a serious thing, with access to some serious people who controlled some serious funding. And if she'd learned anything in her recent years of rubbing elbows with folks in academic circles, it was that funding was key to making any advances in the sciences.

At the entrance to the museum, the colonel flashed his badge at the guard on duty. The man nodded, walked them past a line of tourists, and buzzed them through a reserved set of turnstiles.

Priya started to ask another question, but Colonel Jenkins held up a hand. "Let's get to a secure area before continuing our conversation."

Priya pressed her lips together as she followed the man through the museum. To her surprise, her feeling of dread had vanished, replaced by a tingle of excitement. She hoped this was some weird recruiting strategy. She already intended to join the service after graduation, but if he asked her to join now, she might just say yes.

As they walked past old mockups of early space shuttles from the twentieth and twenty-first centuries, a synthesized voice came through speakers in the ceiling.

"On December 20, 2019, now known as 47.354 PE, Donald J. Trump, President of the United States, signed into law the formation of the United States Space Force. It would remain known as the USSF for decades, until forty-five years after the Great Exodus, on 45.30 AE, when the Space Force was moved under the purview of the United Nations."

Stardate 45 corresponded with the early twenty-second century. A time when the separate nations were in the process of merging under one umbrella government, led by the United Nations. It was also a period of global unrest. Priya's history classes had glossed over that period of Earth's history, but there was enough data on the web to glean the truth. There were riots, uprisings, general chaos. People resisted the change to a global government. That was understandable; change was hard. Some sources said that only the UN's imposition of martial law was ultimately able to quiet things down.

Priya followed the colonel past a scaled-down, but still huge, replica of a spaceship.

"On Stardate 151.23, UN Secretary-General Natalya Poroshenko signed the final approval for building Voyager, *humanity's first interstellar space cruiser. Details of its construction remain classified, but the design is said to be based on a nearly two-hundred-year-old schematic drafted by Dr. David Holmes himself."*

Jenkins ushered Priya through a door that read "For Military Personnel Only." They walked down a hall and stopped in front of an unmarked metal door with no handle. A uniformed military policeman stood next to it, glowering.

The colonel handed his ID to the MP, who ran it through a scanning device, handed it back, and snapped a salute.

Jenkins hitched his thumb toward Priya. "I've preauthorized Priya Radcliffe for a one-day pass. I'll be her escort."

"Yes, sir." The sergeant, whose hand was never more than a few inches from the sidearm strapped to his waist, turned to her. "Miss Radcliffe, I presume you have a CAC on you?"

Every student on campus had been assigned a Common Access Card. It was what allowed her entry into the various academic buildings. She dug hers out of her pocket and presented it to the sergeant.

He ran it through his scanner. When a green LED lit up on the device, he handed the card back to her and pressed a button on a black box attached to his belt. Something buzzed, and the colonel pushed the door open and gestured for her to follow.

She stepped through into a short, plain, unpainted concrete hallway. The door swung shut behind them, and Priya felt the air pressure change as it sealed itself closed. Her ears popped.

Then a door at the far end of the corridor opened.

The colonel started forward, Priya hurrying to match his long strides. "Getting permission to bring you here took more signatures than you could ever imagine," he said. "But remember: everything you see and hear from here on in is classified."

They passed through the open door into a huge room that looked like a hangar. At its center, a large metal frame was being constructed by dozens of remotely operated devices. Some were welding gangplanks between sections of the frame, others were spooling wires from one end of the structure to another. Camera drones flitted through the air, taking images from every angle.

"Do you know what you're looking at?" Jenkins asked.

Priya couldn't suppress the smile on her face. Over the years, she'd seen plenty of space shuttles and other space-bound ships. She'd seen takeoffs and landings, sometimes from quite close. But this… this was something very different. The structure in front of her was only a small piece of a much, much larger ship. A ship she'd just seen a replica of, back in the museum.

"I thought they were building this up in space," she said, her heart racing. "I mean, it can't really be—is this really a piece of Starship *Voyager*?"

"It is." Jenkins smiled and pointed from one end of the room to the other. "Priya Radcliffe, welcome to SAMER, the Starship Advanced Metallurgic Engineering and Research facility. This is the heart of Project Voyager." With a curl of his finger, he motioned for her to follow. "Let's introduce you to some members of the team."

CHAPTER TWO

Priya sat alone in Colonel Jenkins' office. As she waited for the colonel to return, she fiddled with three small cubes of metal sitting on his desk. They looked identical, but they were different weights. A desktop digital scale confirmed it.

"Harold, what do you think of these?" she said. "I wonder if it's possible that—"

"Be cautious." Harold tapped on her head. *"I detected a radio frequency transmitter activation nearby just as you began talking. You're likely being monitored."*

Priya's words caught in her throat. Why would anyone be listening?

Yet she trusted Harold. He was a gift from her parents, and though they didn't have a chance to share much about him before they were killed, they had told her two things: to always keep him a secret, and to always heed his warnings.

She pressed her lips together and tapped her teeth in a rhythm that the AI would detect. "Did I say anything wrong?"

"Anyone listening may naturally wonder who Harold is."

She winced and cleared her throat, then fiddled with the cubes again and let out what she hoped sounded like a self-deprecating laugh. "I swear, if anyone heard me talking to a cat that isn't even here, they'd think I'd gone mental."

"A cat?" Jenkins said with a wry smile as he walked into the office.

"What? Oh, it's nothing." Priya wondered if Jenkins had been the one listening. "I have a cat at home that I'm always talking to. Anyway, I was playing with these cubes and by habit found myself talking to Harold."

"Meow," Harold tapped.

Jenkins chuckled. "So, what did you learn by studying those cubes?"

Priya shrugged. "It doesn't take a genius to figure out they're different metals. The lightest cube weighs a third of a pound. Assuming it's solid throughout, and given it's about 1.5 inches per side, I figure it's aluminum." She picked up a second cube. "This one is almost a pound, so I bet it's some form of steel." She picked up the heaviest of the three and smiled. "But *this* material is something new. The heaviest metal, excluding the extremely rare ones, is tungsten, and a 1.5-inch cube of tungsten would weigh just over two pounds. This thing weighs almost five."

The colonel leaned forward a bit, his elbows on the desk. "What does that tell you?"

"Well, the highest elements on the periodic table are all

radioactive, with half-lives measured in milliseconds. Since this cube is cool to the touch, it's not obviously radioactive, and I doubt you'd have something radioactive sitting on your desk anyway. So I'm guessing someone has discovered a new island of stability. A nuclear shell construction that's stable and off the literal charts with regard to density. There's no other explanation I can think of."

Jenkins grinned. "Good. There's no pulling the wool over your eyes. Let's just say you're probably right. The details of the metal haven't been advertised outside of need-to-know circles, mostly because we aren't sure how to make it."

"What do you mean?" Priya frowned. "I'm holding a sample of it."

"Yes, but we didn't make it."

She was about to ask another question when Jenkins held up his hand.

"Before you even ask, I can't tell you how we've come into possession of it… at least not yet. We do know a lot about it, though. We've done an extensive analysis over the last century, and we know its atomic structure, the molecular bonds it forms, and its estimated half-life, which measures in the millions of years. More importantly, we know it's the toughest, hardest, and strongest material we've ever worked with. Ideal for the construction of *Voyager*."

Priya hitched her thumb toward the hangar. "You mean you're building with this stuff? Just that frame out there would have to be unbelievably heavy. How would you get that into orbit?"

The colonel smiled wryly. "You've caught me in a little white lie. I told you that that frame out there is a piece of *Voyager*—whereas actually it's more like a 3D blueprint for the actual ship. We build the prototypes to scale here on Earth, using more accessible metals, then we take detailed scans of them and have people in orbit build the real thing with that stuff." He pointed to the heavy cube, then leaned back. "But I didn't bring you here just to talk about metals."

He withdrew a sheet of paper from a manila folder and slid it over to her, along with a pen. "We're about to talk about some highly classified information. Before I can disclose it to you, I need you to read and then sign this. It's a pretty standard form. Basically, you're acknowledging that you're about to be disclosed on some compartmentalized military intelligence, and you'll be obligated to keep whatever you learn to yourself for the rest of your days. That means you can't talk to *anyone* about what you learn here, including your friends and family."

Priya lifted the paper and raised an eyebrow. "The military still does actual printed-out paperwork? It's the twenty-third century, for God's sake."

The colonel shrugged. "We wouldn't be the military if we didn't stick to certain traditions."

Priya read the document through to the end, nodded, signed, and slid it back across the desk. The butterflies in her stomach were dancing a jig as the colonel glanced at the paper and put it back in its folder. He sat back and stared silently in her direction for a few seconds. She wanted to jump up and scream, "Hurry up and tell me something, you bloody bastard!" But she maintained her composure and tried not to throw up.

"Let me start at the beginning," said the colonel at last. "I knew both of your parents. In fact, they were founding members of Project Voyager. Their deaths were a great loss to this team, and I can't even begin to imagine how it affected you. However, I've been keeping an eye on you from afar, especially since you joined the Academy. And I'm very, *very* impressed. Even though you're taking a heavier course load than most of your peers, you're sitting at the top of your class by a good margin. So, Priya, if you haven't figured it out already, I'm trying to recruit you. Normally we'd wait until sometime next year before reaching out to prospective recruits, but this is not exactly a normal situation."

That was exactly what Priya had been expecting, but she still felt a thrill of excitement to have it confirmed. At the same time her mind was whirling at the revelation that her parents had worked on this very same project. She'd known that they worked for the military doing science research, but they'd never taken their work home with them.

Jenkins continued. "Let me ask you a question or two. I know it was before you were born, but what do you think of the terrorist attack that occurred in The Hague against the UN's First Council?"

Priya sat back, surprised by the question. "I don't know that I've ever given it much thought. Of course I learned about it in school. The attack coincided with the first meeting of the UNFC. The year before, radicals protested the UN's greater role in how resources were coordinated globally." She shrugged. "I guess some didn't trust the new court system, the First Council, or perhaps any part of what had to feel to them like a very distant government. They were used to controlling everything themselves. I'd say that's understandable. Still, the protestors had to be mental. Violence wasn't going to help the situation."

Jenkins nodded. "Okay, and what about the attack seven years ago?"

A wave of emotion bubbled up inside Priya. She took a deep breath and let it out slowly before carefully choosing her words. "Seven years ago, the terrorists attacked this campus. A couple missiles were launched, but the Patriot laser defenses worked… for the most part."

Memories of the news reports replayed in her mind. The campus had been saved, but two of the missiles had been deflected. One of those missiles struck the tube her parents were traveling in at the time—directly causing their deaths. And yet their loss was barely a footnote in that evening's news reporting.

Her voice sounded small as she continued. "My parents died in that attack. I would have died as well, but I was sick that morning and so wasn't traveling with them." She took another deep breath and gathered herself. When she spoke again, she was stronger, more confident. "We don't even know for sure *why* we were attacked. Some news reports suggested it was because the campus symbolized the post-Exodus military complex. Others had even wilder speculations."

Jenkins leaned forward and stared unblinkingly at her. "Can you think of anything that would have made such an attack justifiable?"

"Are you bloody serious?" Priya's face flushed hot with anger. "There's no justifying the killing of innocents! If it were up to me, the scum responsible for those attacks would be tossed in a meat grinder and used as fertilizer." The blood drained from her face as she realized what she'd just said. "I'm sorry—"

"No," Jenkins said forcefully. "Don't apologize." He gave her a curt nod. "That's the fiery spirit your professors warned me about."

He tapped his thumbs on the desk, and his voice took on an ominous tone. "The news reports weren't necessarily wrong about the terrorists' motivations. They just didn't have the complete picture. In particular, they didn't know about this." He picked up the heaviest cube and turned it in his hands, the light from the LEDs above reflecting off the polished metal. "We call this metal Holmesium, after Dr. Holmes, who predicted the existence of this metal shortly before his death. He hypothesized its precise nuclear shell makeup almost sixty years before we first discovered deposits of this stuff at the Chrysalis mining colony."

Priya knew a little about Chrysalis. After Earth's position was set during the early years, planet Epsilon was deemed uninhabitable, but its moon showed promise. It took about fifty years of terraforming, but in time a mining colony took hold there.

"Is that why we established a mining colony there?" she asked. "Because of this metal? Holmesium?"

"Actually, we didn't know even know Holmesium was there until years later. But once we found out, well… as you can imagine, our plans for space exploration are now entirely dependent on that colony. Which is what has led to our current problems." He set the cube down on the desk with a loud thud. "Unfortunately, it appears there is a rogue element on Chrysalis. We aren't sure who, and we aren't sure how, but some group on Chrysalis helped put together the missiles that were responsible for both of the attacks we just discussed. The attack against the UN's First Council, and the attack that—"

"—That killed my parents," Priya blurted. Her stomach lurched. "Why are you telling me all this?"

"Miss Radcliffe," said a voice behind her. She turned to see an older gentleman stepping into Jenkins's office. His blue UNFC uniform was decorated with ribbons and medals galore. He gave her a nod before motioning for Jenkins to sit back down. "I'm General Heinrich Duhrer, first attaché to the UNSOC's anti-terrorism division, and I'm going to be blunt with you. We believe the terrorist element on Chrysalis is now planning *another* attack. One on a much larger scale than ever before. We've sent people to the colony to try to infiltrate this element, to root out the source of our problems—more people than I'd care to admit, in fact. Yet not only have we learned nothing, none of our people have returned."

Priya wished she could be anywhere but in this room right now. It took everything she had not to throw up on this man's brightly polished shoes.

"You're here for two reasons, young lady, neither of which has to do with your academic brilliance, though we all believe that will help. First, you're here because you have a powerful interest in finding out who killed your parents—and believe you me, it's someone up there." The general pointed to the ceiling. "And second, you're here because you're a Radcliffe. You may not appreciate the significance of that, and it may not even *be* that significant here on Earth. But it's significant to the people on Chrysalis. They're not like us; not anymore. They have very strong memories of the Great Exodus, and fond memories of the roles played by Dr. Holmes and the Radcliffes. That means they'll be much more likely to trust you. And therefore, you'll be more likely to succeed in your mission."

Priya frowned. "Mission? Are you asking me to spy on these people to figure out who wants to kill us?"

The general nodded. "Precisely."

Now Priya *really* wanted to throw up.

The general glanced at Jenkins before focusing back on Priya. "I must impress upon you the importance of this mission, Miss Radcliffe. Our government can't tolerate the attack on innocents like your parents, and we suspect their next targets are going to be much more public, bloodier, more destabilizing, and that's something our society won't tolerate. If we can't determine who is responsible, we'll have very few options other than wiping out the entire colony. In fact, this option is already being discussed at the highest levels. I believe I can delay those proceedings—but only if I can tell them someone like you is on board."

Great, thought Priya. *No pressure.*

The general continued. "If you manage to get us what we need, well … I can guarantee you any position you'd like once this is all over. Obviously, if I can't count on you to get on board, then I seriously doubt we'll find a place for you in future service." He turned to Jenkins. "Let me know what she decides."

The general walked stiffly out of the office.

Priya leaned forward, aiming for the trash can. She just barely made it as she threw up her lunch.

~

In the student meditation alcove, Priya shivered. She felt Harold slowly drifting from her head, down her neck, and under her sleeve. The only time he ever shifted shape was when she was upset, like she was now—and of course when there was no chance of him being seen while changing his form.

Despite all of her years of learning about materials science, she had only the faintest guesses as to how Harold managed to do what he did. He shifted and adapted as he slithered toward her lap, like a chameleon that could emulate not only color, but shape and texture. She'd seen him take on all manner of shapes —a metal spider with binocular-like eyes, a snake, a plant—but when she was upset, his go-to form was that of a kitten. That was what he was transforming into now.

The transformation process took less than thirty seconds, and when it was done she scooped the purring kitten from her lap and held it close. She didn't particularly care that this wasn't a real kitten, or that Harold was merely following some advanced programming directive to comfort her. Hugging the AI in this form helped. It helped a lot.

And right now, she needed that comfort. There were over three million people living on Chrysalis. She *couldn't* be the reason the UN would destroy them all. She just couldn't. As ridiculous as the whole thing sounded—her, Priya Radcliffe, a spy—she had to try. It was the only choice she had.

All she had to do was go to Chrysalis, earn some people's trust, and then betray them.

She buried her tear-streaked face into Harold's belly and cried.

CHAPTER THREE

"Listen to me, Captain. As head of security for the Chrysalis mining colony, the health and welfare of over three million people are in my hands. I won't grant you clearance until you've confirmed that all disembarking passengers have taken the mandatory cleansing procedures for Earth-based pathogens. If this is a problem, you and your passengers can turn right around and head back to Earth. You hear me?"

"No worries, Mr. Chapper." The pilot's Australian accent came through loud and clear in the air traffic control tower. *"It's being done. I've got someone doing the final sweep now."*

Ranger barked at the speaker as if to punctuate the message.

"Sorry to call you in on this, Mr. Chapper," said Gene, the on-duty orbital traffic controller. "But the guy was being a real jerk when I started going through the immigration checklist with him. Didn't want to give me straight answers. I figured I needed someone with a bit more authority to set him straight."

"First of all, call me Terry. We're on the same team." Terry looked at the young controller. The man was probably not much older than twenty. "Gene, how long have you been doing this job?"

"Six weeks. Just graduated two months ago."

Terry felt every bit of his forty years. "And one of your jobs is to ensure the immigration checklists are completed and verified by the ships coming out of orbit."

"That's right, sir. I mean, Terry."

"It's called assumed responsibility. You *are* the final authority on whether or not someone is allowed to land here. You got that?"

"But—"

"The *final* authority. When those pilots are in orbit or flying in from one of the outposts, it's you who calls the shots. Just remember that. That said, if there's ever a doubt or something doesn't seem right, don't hesitate to reach out to security like you did. Better safe than sorry."

"Mr. Chapper, confirmed. All one hundred seventy-six passengers who are disembarking have gone through the pathogen sterilization procedures. We're all good up here."

"Copy that. Handing you back to the controller."

Gene leaned in closer to the microphone. "Earth transport vessel *Stavropoulos*, this is Chrysalis tower, you're cleared for entry into Chrysalis air space. Lock on to beacon signal kilo x-ray tango."

"Chrysalis tower, breaking orbital trajectory. Lock on to beacon signal kilo x-ray tango. Earth transport vessel Stavropoulos.*"*

Terry leaned against the wall and looked up at the darkness of the night sky. "How do you like being in charge of all this?" he asked Gene, pointing at the miles of runway and support buildings.

Gene smiled. "I'm still getting used to it. There's a lot to do, but it's a nice challenge."

Terry chatted with the new controller for a few minutes. He made a point of getting to know everyone who was part of the chain of security. He knew from his days as a member of the Special Forces that since he couldn't be everywhere, it was important to gain the trust of others. They were all on the same team, and if everyone understood that, it made his job infinitely easier.

Through the viewing window, the *Stavropoulos* was an ever-brightening light in the sky. Gene checked the green-tinted hologram that showed a satellite view of the ship on approach, then leaned in toward his microphone. "Earth transport vessel *Stavropoulos*, this is Chrysalis tower, turn left heading two-seven-zero to intercept the localizer, cleared ILS runway alpha into Chrysalis, maintain two thousand five hundred feet until established."

"Chrysalis Tower, turning left heading two-seven-zero, cleared ISL runway alpha into Chrysalis, maintain two thousand five hundred feet until established. Earth transport vessel Stavropoulos.*"*

Gene swiped his fingers across the holographic image, switching through various views of the incoming vessel, before settling in on a view from ground level.

"How long before they land?" Terry asked.

"Looks like a smooth approach," said Gene. "I'd say they'll be wheels down in eight minutes."

"Make sure the ship taxis through the scanners."

"Will do."

Terry gave Gene a thumbs-up and left the young man to do his job.

Five minutes later Terry arrived at the orbital arrivals and departures terminal. At the entrance to the security viewing area, he looked up at a video camera. It beamed a wide-spectrum scanning laser across him, and the door opened with a whoosh of compressed air.

Inside, he was greeted by a two-hundred-and-seventy-degree viewing window overseeing the customs processing area. He flipped down his monocle and studied the miners who trickled into the staging area for departures.

"Chap, I don't get you," said Ian Wexler in his gravelly voice. "It's the twenty-third century, my friend. Why don't you get your eye patched up if it's not up to snuff?"

Terry tossed a smile at his old friend, an army buddy from back in the day. His vision was perfectly fine, but he let the assumption go unchallenged. Explaining the monocle was complicated. After all, it worked only for him.

"Anything caught by the scanners?" he asked, gesturing toward the miners.

"Actually, yes. My guys just pulled someone aside." He expanded his fingers, and a hologram popped up showing an empty room. The door opened, and a miner walked in with a duffel, accompanied by one of the customs employees.

"Mr. Tanaka, it's just a random check. Totally routine. We

need to go through your baggage, and I didn't want to do it in front of everyone."

"Okay, I guess. I just can't miss this transport. My wife is about to pop back on Earth and I need to get back home."

"Don't worry. We won't hold you up for long."

"Did they install the viewing window for that room?" Terry asked Ian.

"Sure. There's a one-way mirror at the end of the hall."

"Show me," Terry said, then pressed on his lapel mic. "Gene, allow the vessel to approach, but put a hold on them disembarking until I say otherwise."

His earpiece crackled with the sounds of an engine whining out on the tarmac. *"Understood. I'll have the marshaller hold the ship just off the arrivals gate."*

Ian led him down the unlit hallway to the window overlooking the room where the miner's bag was being checked. Through his monocle, Terry could see what others could not. The monocle beamed an enhanced image directly onto his retina, providing more colors and details than his other eye could discern. Some objects shimmered oddly when viewed through the monocle, but that was something he had gotten used to over the years.

"From the reading on the scanner, it's probably something small," Ian said.

Terry panned his gaze across the items being pulled from the miner's duffel. One of the benefits of the monocle was that its enhanced color patterns allowed him to identify the core materials in everyday objects. Although there was no manual for the alien tech he was using, with practice he'd trained himself to associate the most common materials with the color-enhanced patterns he was seeing.

"Mr. Tanaka, are you sure you didn't take any mining samples with you by mistake?"

"Of course not! I know the rules."

"I hope this guy didn't swallow whatever it is," Ian said with a frown. "He'll have a very bad day if that's the case."

As the customs officer pulled the next item from the duffel, Terry spotted the telltale color pattern of contraband. He snapped his fingers. "That! Ian, have him take a look inside those gloves."

Ian tapped his ear. "John, examine the gloves."

The officer felt along every inch of the mining gloves and shook his head. But when he swiped it against the detector built into the table, a red LED flashed. *"Mr. Tanaka, are these the gloves you used in the mines?"*

"Well, yes. I didn't think that was a problem."

The officer adjusted a gooseneck lamp attached to the examination table and put one of the gloves under a magnifying loupe. After a moment, he frowned. *"Sir, I'm afraid we've got some ore dust embedded in the fibers of your gloves. You do realize that this ore is an export-controlled substance, even in microscopic amounts. It cannot leave the colony. I'm afraid I'll have to hold these for your return."*

"Of course," said the miner, his eyes wide. *"I would never—I just didn't think about the dust. I'm sorry about that."*

Ian turned to Terry. "How the heck did you guess it was the gloves?"

Terry waved the question away. "I thought there was a

clothes change protocol when the workers entered and left the mines."

"There is. But apparently we need to work on enforcement."

They returned to the viewing window overlooking the arrivals gate, where Ian took a seat and leaned back with a smile. "You going to talk to our lady governor about her miners?"

Terry grimaced at the thought of talking to the governor. "I'd rather not."

He pressed the mic on his lapel. "Okay, Gene, you can give the go-ahead and let our visitors disembark."

"Roger that."

Terry turned back to Ian. "Keep your eyes peeled for anyone with a transmission tag. And flag anyone who didn't drink the contrast solution for further checks. If those UN assholes think they'll get another spy into our operation, they got another thing coming."

As the disembarking passengers entered the far end of the gate, they were limned with an orange glow and a holographic overlay that was only visible through the viewing window glass. Each person's overlay included all variety of stats, including the strength of the marking signal they'd ingested in their trip to the colony.

As Ian watched the arrivals, Terry walked to the window that overlooked the departures. Mr. Tanaka had rejoined the other miners, his duffel slung over his shoulder, minus a pair of gloves. The gloves were probably an innocent mistake, but that was why procedures were in place. That ore could not leave the colony.

Terry was more concerned with the arrivals. Every visitor to this colony had to be considered a threat. There would be no more Earth-based spies infiltrating his colony—not while Terry remained in charge.

His people's lives depended on it.

Harold shifted in her lap, exposing his fuzzy belly, and Priya absentmindedly scratched him with one hand as she tapped notes into her notepad with the other.

The engineer at the front of the classroom was warming to his subject. *"For braking systems that are less sensitive to temperature variants, we've resurrected a process from the twentieth century that involved a byproduct of the cashew nut, namely cardanol. The polymerization of the unsaturated side chain of cardanol, followed by cross-polymerization with formaldehyde, yields a cardinal-formaldehyde resin that works perfectly in the mining conditions we find in the depths of Chrysalis."*

Priya sighed. After accepting her mission, she had been inserted into the mining program at a tech school just outside of Arlington, Virginia. The military intended to have her enter the mining colony as an ordinary intern with no connection to the David Holmes Academy—and especially with no connection to the military. Just a student trying to gain credits for school. The approach made sense, but the classes were dreadfully dull, and she had six weeks of this to sit through.

The door opened at the back of the classroom, and a man slipped into the seat next to her. As Priya glanced over at him, she did a double take. It was Colonel Jenkins, in civilian clothes.

He looked straight ahead, avoiding eye contact, as he slid a slip of paper toward her.

Priya read the hand-scrawled message.

The security team wants to meet. Can you do it right after this lesson? I'll be at the tube station, waiting.

Without waiting for a response, the colonel got up and walked out, leaving Priya sitting uneasily through the remainder of the lesson on organic friction compounds.

Who and what was "the security team," and why did they need to meet now?

~

As Priya walked across campus, resentment built within her. She had agreed to this mission, but the more she thought about it, the less she liked how it had been presented to her. Either take a role as a military puppet, possibly saving millions of lives, or be blackballed from any future in the sciences.

That was no choice at all.

"Goddamned bastard," she groused, tucking her hands into the front pocket of her hoodie, where Harold nipped at her fingers.

Colonel Jenkins was waiting at the entrance to the campus tube station. Priya wiped the expression from her face as she jogged up the stairs to meet him.

As always, the hologram of a smiling recruiter blinked into existence. *"Welcome, neighbor! It's people like me who keep the tubes running efficiently and safely. Type *92-8374 on your SMS device to learn more about joining the team."*

Colonel Jenkins motioned for her to follow as he walked toward the station's control panel. He placed his hand on the touch screen, and a voice with a singsong Indian accent said, *"Good afternoon, Michael. I'm Mahesh, your tube assistant. You have authorization for all active destinations on your account. Where would you like to go?"*

The colonel swiped across several screens that Priya had never seen before. Clearly his access was much broader than hers. After a few taps, the disembodied voice of Mahesh returned. *"Two passengers for classified location code HF-392.5. Please confirm."*

"Confirmed," Jenkins said.

The sound of rushing air grew louder behind the metal doors to the tube. *"Establishing vacuum. Queuing request for transportation link between the Virginia Mining School campus and the terminal at HF-392.5."*

"Where are we going?" Priya asked.

"I can't say, but it's not too far. After we're done, you'll go home like normal."

"Link complete. The car is arriving in three... two... one..."

The doors slid open, revealing an empty capsule with two padded armchairs inside.

"The car is now ready for boarding."

When they were both seated, the doors closed, and the windows in the capsule all turned opaque. So—she was being prevented from even seeing where they were going on their trip. Harold oozed his way through a seam inside her hoodie and began wrapping himself around her waist.

"We are about to depart."

Priya closed her eyes, feeling the acceleration kick in.

Ten minutes later, the doors slid open.

They were underground, a first for any tunnel station Priya had ever seen. But she was beginning to realize that there was a lot more to this world than what she'd been made privy to. There were also no markings, no signs, no windows. This was definitely a classified location.

She followed Jenkins out of the station, which seemed to be located in a building with no obvious markings, signs, or windows. There was nobody in sight until they entered a distant hallway and passed several unmarked offices, some of which had people at their desks doing who knows what.

The lighting was dim throughout the building and the beige halls were a maze of identical corridors. How the hell anyone knew where they were in this place was beyond her.

Priya kept pace with Jenkins, who'd been eerily silent the entire time. "So, is there anything at all you can tell me about why I'm here? What's this security team about?"

"I'm sorry, I've been told not to say anything. In truth, I'm just acting as an escort. The UN intelligence folks don't always confide in the military on this kind of stuff."

"So, I'm guessing this is one of the UN's classified—" Priya stopped herself. "Never mind, you can't answer anyway."

They turned a corner and stopped in front of a door with a video camera. The door opened, and they stepped through into a large room that was part conference room, part medical lab. A long table sat at its center, surrounded by chairs, but the walls were covered with the sorts of charts and posters that were common in medical offices. At the far end of the room, a man in a dark suit was working at an ancient computer, the kind with an actual physical keyboard and monitor. The computer was attached to a reclining chair by a series of thick cables.

The man looked up, nodded at the colonel, then walked over with a smile.

The colonel leaned in toward Priya. "I'll be back when you're done," he whispered, and he departed the way he came, the door closing behind him.

The man stopped in front of Priya. "Welcome, Miss Radcliffe. It's good to have you in the dungeon."

"The dungeon?" Priya arched an eyebrow. "Is that what you call this place?"

"It's just a nickname. Fitting, though, as we're about five hundred feet under the streets of New York City." He extended his hand. "My name's Agent Ted. I'm going to walk you through the security procedures that we'll employ to maximize your chances of a successful mission."

Priya studied the man as she shook his hand. He was of Asian descent, maybe mid-forties, and spoke with a generic American accent. But it was his eyes that caught her attention. They were clearly implants, steely gray, the pupils growing and shrinking repeatedly as if he were scanning her for something. It was unsettling.

Ted gestured for her to take a seat at the table. He then retrieved a tray holding several vials and an injector, and sat down beside her. "Miss Radcliffe—"

"Please, call me Priya. I'm nervous enough as it is."

"There's no need to be nervous. This is completely routine, and besides, the agency wouldn't put a civilian in any real danger. Trust me."

"Agency? What is this place?"

"Well, that I'm afraid is classified." He smiled.

The agent's smile was eerie. Unnatural. Priya felt a shiver of uncertainty race up her spine.

He picked up the injector and one of the vials. "You're going to need some inoculations before you go. The colony is a bit backwards technologically, and they have some strains of diseases that we haven't seen on Earth for nearly a century. This one is for measles." He pushed the vial into the injector's carrying chamber and motioned to Priya's forearm. "Please roll up your sleeve."

She did as he asked and took a deep breath. As the agent pressed the injector against her skin, Priya felt the cooling sensation of a numbing agent, followed by a click.

They went through the rest of the vials, some for diseases she hadn't even heard of. When they got to the last vial, one with a red stripe running around it, Ted said, "This one is a tracking device."

Priya pulled her arm back. "A what? I didn't agree to a tracking device."

"It's harmless. It'll help us keep track of your movements, and—"

"No," Priya said firmly. "There's no damned way you're putting that in me. It's probably how the colonists detected the other people you guys sent, and now they're probably dead.

Radcliffe or not, I doubt they'd hesitate to shove me into a meat grinder if they figure out I'm spying on them. I'll take my chances without that thing in me."

The agent's pupils grew and shrank like spastic camera lenses. "I'll have to clear that with my superiors."

"You do that."

Ted paused, as if uncertain, then picked up a remote and pressed a button. A hologram of a woman's face appeared just above the table. She was older, but still blond, and on her face was a serious expression that brooked no argument.

"Let's discuss your mission," Ted said. "What do you know about the mining colony?"

Priya shrugged. "Not much. I know it was founded a handful of years after the Great Exodus by David Holmes, and its first governor was that woman, Margaret Hager." She pointed at the hologram.

"Anything else?" Agent Ted stared unblinkingly at her with his creepy artificial eyes.

"Well, there's some stuff that General Duhrer told me about, but I'm not allowed to talk about that. Apart from that, I know there's around three million people there, and... that's about it. It's weird, because the internet usually spews out tons of data about almost everything you can think of, but I searched thoroughly, and other than a bunch of stuff about the restrictive travel and immigration laws, there's almost nothing about Chrysalis online. No details, no maps, no anything."

The agent nodded. "Let's talk about the organization running things." He motioned to the woman's face. "As you noted, that is Margaret Hager. She was the American president during the

Great Exodus. And ten years after arriving here, when the terraforming of the Chrysalis mining colony began in earnest, she became its first governor."

He clicked on the remote, and the image changed to the face of another woman. The image was much grainier, obviously taken from a distance.

Priya frowned. "Who's that? It's hard to tell, but it looks a lot like Margaret Hager."

Ted nodded. "We believe that is the current governor of the Chrysalis mining colony. And yes, the two women look alike. In fact, there is an eighty-six percent match on key facial features. We have no genealogy data from the colony, but our intelligence tells us that the governorship is matrilineal. Which means that this woman is likely a direct descendant of Margaret Hager."

"Their people don't vote in their leader?"

"The colony is very secretive about some things, especially their leadership structure. We only know what I've told you, though we're always looking to enhance our intelligence. We also don't know why they would be trying to sabotage our society. After all, there's very limited movement of people between us and them and it's been that way for nearly a century. They don't allow tourism, and they limit the number of their people that are allowed to travel to Earth. The few colony citizens that come here do so typically for education purposes."

Priya pressed her lips together. "So you're sending me there with almost no information about anything? How am I supposed to find out who's responsible for the attacks? I'm just a student."

"You're more than that, to them. You're a Radcliffe. And over there, that'll mean something. Among the few things we do know is that the colony-borns practically worship Dr. Holmes and the Radcliffes. You'll be the first Radcliffe to set foot on the colony since the founding generation returned to Earth after Dr. Holmes's death."

"That's all well and good, but it would be nice if I could know a bit more before I risk my life trying to infiltrate the colony."

"And you will." Agent Ted rose from his seat and walked to the ancient computer with the keyboard, the one that was connected to the recliner. His fingers flew across the keys as they noisily clicked and clacked. "I'm adding a clearance marker on your identification record. It'll open access to files that will fill you in on all the intelligence we have regarding both the terrorists and the colony."

"Great. Can I access these files from home?"

The agent smiled that lifeless smile of his and shook his head. "These aren't that kind of file. They're deep learning files; they use transcranial magnetic stimulation to deposit working knowledge into your head. Given the seriousness of the mission, we can't leave it to chance that you'll absorb the necessary background information in the time you have before your departure."

He stepped over to the recliner, flipped up a dome-shaped object from its back, then returned to the computer. After a few keystrokes, a humming sound came from within the chair.

Priya looked at the recliner apprehensively. She'd read about transcranial magnetic stimulation, or TMS, and how it was supposed to help bring back memories that were lost due to trauma. But using it to inject new memories? That was unheard of.

"Is this safe?" she asked.

The agent laughed, and it almost sounded like genuine mirth. "Of course it is. We use it all the time in the intelligence unit, especially when we're trying to onboard someone into…" The agent stopped himself. "Let's just say it helps bring people up to speed much faster than they'd otherwise be able to do. Effectively we're depositing pre-formed memories into your head, accomplishing in less than an hour what would normally take six months of study." He gestured to the recliner. "Please, go ahead and take a seat in the chair. I'll explain as we go along."

As Priya rose and walked over to the recliner, the butterflies that were normally dancing a jig in her stomach died of fright, and all she felt was a hollow feeling of dread. Even Harold remained silent.

She sat down and sank into the cushions. At least it was comfortable. The chair's dome attachment hovered above her head.

"Okay, let's get started," Ted said. "Lean your head back, and don't move while the computer takes a few startup measurements."

Priya heard something whir. "What's it doing?"

"That's a MEG scanner. Short for magnetoencephalography—a neuroimaging technique for mapping brain activity. It'll help us get the information we need so that the computer can direct the data into exactly the right landing zones within your brain."

The dome lowered itself until it was practically touching her head, but not quite. The chair hummed with what sounded like a power plant's worth of energy.

"Good," said Ted. "Now just relax, and I'll start transmitting the information."

"Wait, what's this going to be like? Should I close my eyes?"

The agent chuckled as his fingers clacked on the keyboard. "You won't even sense it. The memories are simply being built within your neural cortex. Think about it this way. You know how to ride a bicycle?"

"Of course."

"I assumed so. But right now, are you thinking of all those memories and skills? Of course not. They're there if you need them, but when you don't need them, you're unaware of them. And even when you do ride a bike, the learned information is recalled without you having to actively think about it. These new memories will be no different."

The agent hit one more key. "There we go. This will take about forty-five minutes."

As the chair hummed even louder, and a cooling fan kicked in, Priya took a deep breath and tried to dismiss the voice in her head telling her this was a huge mistake.

~

"I don't need this crap," Priya grumbled at the underground tube station's control panel. She again placed her hand on the panel, and again the computerized voice with the New York accent said, *"This control panel is for the use of personnel with Section Z8 or higher access level."*

"To hell with you," Priya said.

It had been almost half an hour since Agent Ted had escorted her to the tube station from "the dungeon," and she'd been waiting for Jenkins to arrive ever since. She was literally trapped here without him, and her sore arm and growing headache didn't help her mood one bit.

Finally, the familiar sound of rushing air came from behind the metal doors to the tube, though there was no announcement of the incoming car nor any of the normal advisories. The doors slid open and Colonel Jenkins stepped out, once more in his military uniform. The doors slammed shut behind him the second he was on the platform, as if to prevent anyone jumping aboard.

"I hope you weren't waiting too long. Ready to head home?"

Priya frowned at his matter-of-fact manner, but she breathed away the snippy reply she was tempted to give. "Yes. Can you get just me to the Coral Springs, North Junction station? I'm exhausted."

"Of course."

The control panel graciously recognized Colonel Jenkins, of course, and within seconds, it had queued a request for a transport to Priya's home station. Priya just wanted to go home. This place gave her the creeps. Agent Ted doubly so.

"Are you okay?" Jenkins asked, giving her a look of concern.

"I'm fine." Priya didn't want to talk about it. It wasn't fair that he'd dumped all this on her. And the more she was learning about the mission, the worse she felt about everything and everyone around her.

"Link complete. The car is arriving in three... two... one..."

The doors to the tube slid open, and Jenkins motioned toward the capsule. "I'll catch the next one," he said, smiling.

Moments later, Priya felt herself pushed against the seat as her ride accelerated toward home.

CHAPTER FOUR

"General Duhrer's office, this is Valerie. Can I help you?"

The colonel leaned forward, resting his elbows on his desk. "Valerie, this is Colonel Gary Jenkins, head of—"

"I'm sorry, Colonel, I received your e-mail, but the general doesn't have any time on his calendar. If you have specific questions, please e-mail them and I'll make sure he's made aware of your request. Is there anything else? I have two other people waiting on the line."

"No," the colonel growled.

The line went dead.

"Damn, isn't she just a barrel of sunshine?" said Todd Winslow, sitting on the opposite side of the desk. "A full bird colonel and she blows you off," he snapped his fingers, "just like that."

Jenkins sighed and ignored the comment. With a swipe of his

fingers, a holographic image appeared above his desk. "This is her," he said. "The Radcliffe girl."

"She looks nice enough," Todd said. "Too bad she's being sent into a meat grinder." Todd was a member of the Special Forces and shared the colonel's skepticism about this mission. "I still can't believe we're sending a civilian in to gather intel. If three of the general's intelligence goons got wasted up there, how's she supposed to succeed? She has to get past the background screening, somehow convince the colony's paranoid security types that she's on Team Chrysalis, get them to cough up the list of names of people who hate the UN's guts, which might actually be most of the colony, and come back in one piece. It's madness."

The colonel frowned. "Duhrer seems to think that her being a Radcliffe will help her up there. I sure hope that's true. I promised her parents I'd watch over her, and I'm pretty sure this isn't what they had in mind." He looked up from Priya's image and focused on Todd. "Sergeant, I'm sure you've guessed why I read you into this."

"Because I have some friends who know people who might know people on the colony."

"That's right. And I'd take it as a personal favor if you pull whatever strings you have. I want a twenty-four/seven overwatch on our girl when she's up there."

"Colonel, I think you're overestimating what kind of strings I may or may not have to pull. Besides, you know it's illegal to have secure-channel communication with the colony."

"That's why I'm not ordering you to do it. This is on the QT.

The girl basically got railroaded by the UN types into taking this on, and it's eating me up inside."

"Let me guess: the general was vague enough that he'd never be brought up on charges, but specific enough that his meaning was clear?"

Jenkins nodded.

"I hate when that shit happens." Todd gave Jenkins a lopsided smile. "Well, I'll see what I can do about those strings—but no promises." The soldier pulled a handheld from a pocket in his fatigues and studied its screen.

Jenkins looked once more at Priya's holographic likeness. She looked so much like the Neeta Radcliffe of history. He hadn't seen it when she was younger, all arms and legs and immature. But now that she was grown, both physically and in personality, the resemblance was uncanny.

Nowadays, at least on Earth, history was often muddled and buried; the emphasis was on looking forward, not back. But Jenkins had grown up with the stories of the Great Exodus. He'd learned all about the exploits of the greats from that era. Dr. Holmes, certainly, but also Burt and Neeta Radcliffe. What they'd accomplished was amazing. They'd saved humanity, and yet they were barely footnotes nowadays. Relics of the past.

As Priya's image hovered above his desk, he felt like he was staring at one of those relics now. And he had sent her into danger. Not willingly, but he was responsible for her all the same.

Todd cleared his throat to get the colonel's attention. "Colonel? I've received orders to ship out to the Midwest tomorrow. Evidently there's some militia group fronting for a bunch of farmers that don't want to sell their produce to the collective, as required by the UN mandates for centralizing food production."

Jenkins grimaced. "We must all follow legal orders…" He pictured Priya boarding a transport to the colony. "No matter how distasteful they may be."

It was late in the afternoon, and Terry sat in his office scrolling through the emails that had been flagged by their security system. Ranger had parked himself next to his chair, facing the entrance to the office and snoring lightly. Terry looked down at the pup, and as if sensing the change in Terry's focus, Ranger looked up at him and gave a huff before lowering his head back onto his paws and going back to sleep.

A new e-mail arrived, and Terry opened it. The text hovering over his desk glowed yellow, indicating it was an official communique from a UN government official.

To: Chrysalis Education Center

Date: 153.122 AE

Subject: Budget approval for the upcoming semester

To whom it may concern:

. . .

Under the UN-Chrysalis Education Charter dated 77.201, the UN Education Review Board has approved the budgets for twenty-three new mining-related internships in the upcoming semester. Attached is the anticipated per diem associated with each student. If there are any concerns, please respond before the anticipated launch date of 153.150.

Carla Smith
UN Education Council

Terry tapped the phone icon on his desk and selected a number on his speed dial. The call was immediately answered.

"Bursar's office."

"Hey, Tony, it's Terry Chapper."

"Chap! What can I do you for?"

"I got a favor to ask. Looks like we're getting a fresh set of interns, twenty-three of them. Can you tell me how many we got during the last round and what we got for their upkeep?"

"Sure, hold on a second..." There was a brief pause. *"Here it is. This past semester we had twenty-one interns, and we're getting two hundred and fifty credits per week per intern. Why do you ask?"*

Terry scrolled through the hovering spreadsheet attached to the e-mail he'd just received "Well, I'm not sure if it's a mistake or not, but it looks like the UN's education folks are doubling their spend to five hundred credits with the next batch."

"Whoa, that's a lot of bank."

"So you weren't aware of this?"

"No. I mean, sometimes they make a cost-of-living adjustment, but that's like a three percent increase, not a hundred percent."

"Okay, thanks, Tony."

The moment he hung up, his phone rang with another call. "Chapper."

"Terry, it's almost time for the staff meeting. Where are you?"

Terry looked at the clock. "Damn, sorry, Jean. Tell them I'll be right there."

The last thing Terry needed right now was to get chewed out by the governor in front of her entire staff.

~

All eight of the governor's staff were present when Terry arrived, but the governor was not. Terry breathed a sigh of relief as he took his spot at the table.

Governor Jenna Welch was many things to the colony. She was a no-nonsense administrator. She was very charismatic when she needed to be. And she was a brilliant strategist. However, she had absolutely no qualms about flaying someone verbally if they fell short on an obligation without good reason.

And she was *particularly* annoyed when anyone was late to a meeting.

Amanda Cummins, the head of colony agriculture, clacked

her fingernails on the lacquered tabletop. "Did she cancel the meeting?"

"No," said Andy Gras, in a thick Hungarian accent. As the governor's chief of staff, he was on top of her comings and goings.

"Well, she's never late, so—"

Ranger whined and sat up in his spot an instant before the door opened and Governor Welch walked in. She was a fit, statuesque woman in her fifties, and despite her near-constant seriousness, for just a moment she flashed a smile at Ranger and scratched under his chin. He responded with a vigorous wag of his tail.

Her seriousness returned as she straightened up. "I've brought a guest with me," she said. As if she'd been outside waiting to be announced, a dark-skinned woman walked in and smiled. In her hands was a round metal object about eighteen inches in diameter. It looked like a picture frame, but without a picture. "This is Nwaynna Stewart, our head of advanced research and Earth-based intelligence. She was briefing me on our latest… actually, Nwaynna, why don't you tell them."

"Does everyone have Deadman clearance?" Nwaynna asked.

Deadman clearance was a classification level that had been established soon after the colony was founded. It was required for any information on the existence of non-human intelligence. Very, *very* few people had Deadman clearance, and only those who did were aware that there had once been alien life forms on Epsilon, the planet their colony was orbiting.

"They're all read in," the governor said as she took a seat. "You can speak freely."

Nwaynna placed the frame on a stand at the end of the table and gave everyone a nervous smile. "Well, as you're aware, some of the alien artifacts that were discovered on Epsilon have been useful in intelligence-gathering operations. Recently we've managed to get some of this tech into the office of a staff-level member of the UN intelligence wing, and it captured some video that I felt needed the governor's attention."

Carl Gustav, head of mining operations, raised his hand. "Excuse me. Are we to believe we got a signal out of such a secure site? The Earth-based government may be fools, but they're not stupid. Are we sure this, whatever it is, isn't something they wanted us to see? You know, an orchestrated attempt to mislead us?"

Nwaynna shook her head. "I doubt it very seriously. We're using alien transceivers that they're entirely unaware of and that even we cannot duplicate. The signals are operating at over one exahertz and—"

"Miss Stewart?" Terry raised a finger. "For us meatheads who didn't get a PhD in alien tech… exahertz?"

She laughed. "Sorry, exahertz is a frequency. Like kilohertz and megahertz. It's basically a billion billion waves per second. Which means these transceivers can chirp messages at over one hundred million gigabytes per second. One second of video surveillance takes all of about a nanosecond to transmit." She turned back to Carl. "On top of which, it's all scrambled. Given all that, it's virtually inconceivable that anyone who doesn't already possess this alien technology could even detect it, much less hack into it."

Governor Welch made a rolling motion with her hand. "Maybe you should just show us the video."

"Yes, ma'am." The scientist placed her fingers on two spots on the frame, and a high-definition holographic image appeared above the conference room table. It showed an office with a large desk, and sitting at the desk was a gray-haired and well-decorated general. Terry noted the small ribbon indicating this man was part of the UNIB, the UN Intelligence Bureau. The UNIB had the same mysterious reputation as organizations like the CIA, MI6, and the KGB did in centuries past—but unlike those organizations, the UNIB was attached to official military units that could control troop movements.

The general was reading a sheet of paper. That was surprising. Did they really still use paper? The general flipped the paper over, and it sounded to Terry like it was happening right in front of him. In fact, everything in the room, audio and visual, was reproduced with remarkable fidelity.

A knock sounded at the door.

"Come in."

A soldier in fatigues walked in and took a seat in front of the general's desk. Terry felt the hairs on his neck stand up; his swagger, his stooped posture, the white streak down the middle of his otherwise dark hair. He knew the guy.

"Sir," said the soldier, *"I've got the info you were looking for."*

"Go ahead, Sergeant."

"Bradshaw was ID'd by their security team last week and has been disposed of."

The governor shot Terry a look, her eyes flashing a warning that he'd seen many times over the years.

"Crap." The general leaned back in his chair. *"Is this one hundred percent confirmed?"*

"Yes, sir. Our guy confirmed it through DNA evidence."

"Have we gotten any more on their tech?"

"Yes and no. Our guy managed to track Bradshaw's path through the mines. He got as far as level twelve before whatever's down there blocked Bradshaw's signal."

"Hold on. You assholes assured me that the signal couldn't be blocked."

The soldier shrugged. *"I don't have an answer for you, General. All I know is that his signal disappeared, then reappeared when his body was carried out of level twelve and brought back up to the surface. By then, his vitals had flatlined. General, I know we've got intel about something being down there, maybe even alien tech. And we got real close this time. But since they caught Bradshaw, it's safe to assume they'll be on alert. We may have to hold off on things for a while."*

Terry felt a chill creep up his spine. He knew what was down there at level twelve of the mines. And now, apparently, so did someone in the UN Intelligence Bureau.

"Negative," said the general. *"I've got plans for an infiltration they won't expect. I'll send you the details to pass on when I finalize the arrangements. Did you have anything else?"*

"No, sir."

"Dismissed."

The hologram vanished.

"What in the world would they want down in level twelve?"

said Carl. "There's just interconnecting passages between the mine shafts and some storage down there."

Nwaynna was about to respond, but the governor held up her hand and cut in. "I'm sorry, Carl, you don't have clearance."

Carl sputtered. "Clearance? To know what's in the mines? I'm in charge of mining operations!"

"And to do your job you don't need to be aware of everything that's down there," the governor said firmly. "It's from way before your time."

Carl's face turned red, and he looked like he was about to explode, so Terry quickly cut in.

"Governor, I know the man who was reporting to the general. His name is Mark Dixon. He and I were in phase one of the Q-Course together."

"Q-Course?" asked Amanda Cummins, head of colony agriculture.

"It's a qualifying course for the UN's Special Forces down on Earth," Terry explained. "I trained down there for about a decade." He addressed the full staff as he continued. "Dixon washed out during phase one, and I have to say not a single soldier was sorry to see him go. He's a real ass, and honestly I'm surprised he's still in the service. No sane person wanted him on their squad. It worries me that someone like that, in the UNIB no less, is even close to knowing anything about what's on level twelve. Even here on Chrysalis there's only a handful of people who know, and only one person who can even explain what it does."

The governor's eyes flashed a warning. Terry was toeing a

line he didn't dare cross, not with her. Carl noted the exchange but uncharacteristically held his tongue.

"Madam Governor," said Nwaynna. "Is there anything else you need from me?"

The governor shook her head. "You can return to what you were doing. Thank you."

Nwaynna left the conference room, and the door closed behind her.

The governor turned to Carl. "Carl, I want security at the entrance to the mines doubled, and nobody gets below level ten without direct authorization from me. Are we understood?"

Carl's face was still red, but he nodded. "Yes, ma'am."

The governor shifted her attention to Terry. Even though he was forty, when she looked at him like that, he felt like a kid being scrutinized by the school principal. "I want security to go through the personnel records of each and every person that has access to the mines. We caught one guy, but now we know there's someone else. Someone out there who knows something they shouldn't."

"Understood." Terry grimaced. There was a confirmed spy in their midst, and it was on him his people to find them.

The governor panned her gaze across the attendees and said, "You all know that Earth's government wants to rip up the treaties which give this colony its sovereignty. They'll go to any lengths to justify it, and as you know, they've been sending spies to further that cause. And now, their target seems to have gained a focus." She stood. "I can't answer the question that you're all thinking about. What's on level twelve. Suffice it to say it's a secret that has guaranteed the colony's safety since before any of you were born—and we can't let those UN bastards get ahold of it. I'll be sitting down with each of you later to go over some contingency plans if things go to hell, but in the meantime, make sure you keep your eyes peeled for anything that looks out of the ordinary. Make sure any concerns go to our head of security." She hitched her thumb toward Terry. "We now know for certain there's a concerted effort by the UN to penetrate our defenses. People, this is as serious as it gets. Stay alert. Dismissed."

CHAPTER FIVE

Priya sat in her apartment's kitchenette with her Aunt Jen, who was sniffling with a cold.

"Herbal tea," said Aunt Jen to the food processor, and not for the first time. "I want *herbal tea.*"

"Myrtle tea is not in this unit's database. Do you want me to connect to the manufacturer's website and check for updates?"

"Bloody hell!" Priya snapped. "*Herbal* tea, you pile of rusted-out bolts. Herbal bloody tea!"

"You're asking for herbal tea, please confirm."

"Yes!" they yelled at the same time.

The machine began making a brewing noise. Seconds later a stream of steaming tea dribbled into Aunt Jen's oversized mug.

Priya shook her head. "You'd think that bloody thing would have a voice recognition that could deal with head colds, for God's sake."

Her aunt retrieved her tea and sipped at it. "It's an old unit. I got it back home at the West End. A solid British brand, but it does take a little fussing with." She sat down across from Priya. "So, what's with this internship mail we got today? You're not seriously thinking about changing your major after all this time, are you?"

Her aunt's concern gave Priya an ache in her stomach. She didn't want to lie to her auntie, but she sure as hell couldn't tell her the truth. "Yeah, I meant to say something about that, but I'm not really supposed to talk about the details. It's sort of hush-hush and all. Anyway, I got an offer for future employment that's really fantastic, but they wanted me to get some experience at the colony."

"Really?" Aunt Jen said, frowning. "Isn't it all hooligans and roughnecks? Is it even safe?"

Priya laughed, even though inside she wanted to cry. "It's fine, Aunt Jen. Trust me." She sipped at her own tea. "Did you realize there are places we can't go on the tube network?"

"Where is it that you need to go?"

"It's not that I want to go there, it's just… I mean, I started looking into it, and for me to visit friends far away, like, let's say, Idaho, I'd need to file a request with the transit authorities and wait until they give me permission to go. And I've heard some people actually get denied travel, like they're common criminals."

"Oh, pish posh." Aunt Jen blew her nose in a napkin. "You can't just expect to use resources like the tube willy-nilly. These things need planning. Arrangement for proper usage of a limited thing. There's only so many tubes, and we can't all be going everywhere at once. Someone needs to coordinate the use of resources so that those with a real need are prioritized. It's not so big of a deal. I took a tube to Los Angeles once; it only took a day or two to get cleared for that trip."

Priya sighed. "It just seems odd to me. I've read stories about people driving wherever they want, whenever they want."

"Driving?" Her aunt frowned. "My Gran told me about that. You have no idea how unsafe those vehicles were."

"The tubes aren't exactly safe either," Priya said quietly.

Her aunt realized her mistake. "I'm sorry, I didn't mean—"

"No, I'm sorry. That was a long time ago."

Aunt Jen took another sip of her tea. "Generally speaking, the tubes *are* quite safe, despite the tragedy with your parents. Those vehicles people used to go in… they were suicide. And this is much better for the environment."

Priya quickly shifted the conversation before her aunt could begin one of her rants about the environment. "Aunt Jen, have you ever read *On the Road* by Jack Kerouac?"

"I can't say that I have."

"It's from before the Exodus. I've read a lot of that stuff. There was another one called *Blue Highways*. They talked about all these places that aren't serviced by the tubes, and… I just wonder what happened to those places. What those places are like."

"Well, if they don't have a tube station, they can't be very nice," her aunt said. "What made you read those old books anyway?"

"It was a while ago. After Mum and Dad died, you remember I buried myself in my books."

"Ah, yes. I was glad you found an escape in them."

"I guess I did. But partly because the people in those books, the authors of those books, they found *real* escapes. Like Neil Peart, the author of *Ghost Rider*. His wife and daughter died, and he dealt with his grief by riding a motorcycle all across North America, down to Mexico, and even further south before coming back. He visited friends, cried, and just… rode. It's hard to imagine such a thing nowadays… being alone with my thoughts. It seems like an impossible thing to do."

"And *dangerous*." Aunt Jen set her mug on the table. "Priya, are you okay? Do you need something?"

"No, I'm fine," Priya lied, draining the rest of her tea.

She did need something, but the world she lived in couldn't provide it.

~

As Priya walked into her bedroom, Harold tapped a message on her scalp. *"A signal activated as we entered your room."*

She turned around and returned to Aunt Jen, who was working a crossword puzzle she'd activated on the holo-device.

"Has anyone been in my bedroom?"

Her aunt nodded absently. "As a matter of fact, a maintenance person came earlier today to do a deep clean of the air vents. Why, is there something wrong?"

"No, it's nothing."

Priya tried to act calm as she left the apartment, but her heart was racing. She was being watched. In her own home.

Adrenaline dumped into her bloodstream, and panic bloomed in her chest. She felt like there were eyes everywhere, and she had to get away. When a neighbor looked at her and smiled, she could barely stop herself from sprinting in the opposite direction. Somehow she mustered a small wave and strode quickly out of the apartment complex.

But when she was down the street, she began running.

She ran all the way through North Coral Springs, not slowing until she reached the woods at the edge of the neighborhood. The sign there warned her away from the woods, labeling it a restricted area, but for once she didn't care. She had to get away. She had to be alone. The last six weeks had been hell on her. Ever since that first meeting with the colonel, her life had been ripped away from her. Ever since then, she'd been on edge.

She ignored the sign and entered the woods.

But after a hundred feet, she collapsed to her knees. She wasn't used to running like that, and she felt an iron band around her chest as she gasped for breath. Her physical exhaustion, combined with her suddenly out-of-control fear and paranoia and her fading adrenaline rush… it was all too much.

She covered her face and began to cry. Deep, shuddering sobs.

She felt Harold move from her head, sliding himself down and into her lap. She needed his comfort, and she reached out to pet him. But instead of a kitten in her lap, she felt something hard and smooth.

She looked down. Harold had turned himself into a tray.

"Harold?"

The middle of the tray shimmered, and a video clip appeared. Two figures that Priya recognized: Neeta and Burt Radcliffe. Her many-times-great-grandmother and grandfather.

They were holding each other, and they were crying.

Priya's emotions drained away as she watched the scene. She'd never seen this video in any archival footage. When was this?

Neeta pulled her husband's face to her shoulder and rubbed the back of his head. As she did so, she turned to face Priya directly, her cheeks still wet with tears, and spoke.

"If you're seeing this message, it's because the alien device has recognized the time is almost right. The time when you, my dearest child, need to be strong for us all."

Burt raised his head and faced Priya as well. His face was rugged and wrinkled—he was probably deep into his seventies. But despite his age and bloodshot eyes, there was a fire burning there, and when he smiled, his face lit up.

"With your grandmother's blood in you, I have complete faith in your ability to do what's needed." He gave his wife a kiss. *"It's time you know what really happened during our flight from where humanity came from. I wish we could tell you all this in person, but with the way things are, I'm sure that we'll be long gone before you get this. If things are as we fear, you have probably been told a bunch of lies."*

Neeta picked up from there. *"First, you must know that David Holmes did* not *die of a heart attack like the government has probably told you. They've already started that lie in our time. Hell, it's possible they'll have washed him out of the history books altogether by the time you receive this. But David Holmes... he was the man who truly saved all of humanity during what they're now calling the Great Exodus. Don't believe anyone who says otherwise. And they killed him."*

Burt nodded. *"It's true. They killed him, and now they're silencing everyone who knows better. Which is why we need to record this message."* He sighed. *"Since there's no way of knowing what history is teaching you, I suppose we need to start from the beginning: with the discovery that there had been alien life on Epsilon…"*

Priya watched attentively as her two ancestors took turns telling her about what had *really* happened well over a century ago.

~

Priya sat for a long time after watching the video. So many things were now rattling around in her head. Some of it chilled her to the bone with its prophetic nature, while other parts made no sense. So many secrets. So many lies. And so much of it was confusing. Neeta and Burt hadn't known when their message would be heard—and probably didn't expect it would lie dormant for a hundred and fifty years—and so didn't really know what precisely would need to be explained.

And Neeta looked so much like her. Or maybe it was more accurate to say that *she* looked so much like Neeta.

Harold had changed back into a kitten, and she rubbed his belly. "I always knew you were something different. Alien technology? I guess I'm not surprised. And thank you." She scooped him up and kissed his nose. "Thank you for carrying that message for so long. I'm forever grateful."

The last golden rays of sunshine were piercing the woods

when a twig snapped nearby. Priya quickly hopped up onto her feet to find a soldier approaching, a rifle held at the ready.

"These woods are restricted, ma'am. Didn't you see the signs?"

Panicking, Priya blurted out a slightly modified scene from a twentieth-century movie she'd watched some years ago. "I'm sorry! My best friend's sister's boyfriend's brother's girlfriend heard from this guy who knows this kid who's going with a girl who heard that there's a ghost in these woods."

The soldier paused as if trying to absorb all that.

"Sir, is there a ghost in the woods? Because my best friend's sister's boyfriend's—"

"Stop!" The soldier shook his head, his expression pained. He pointed his gun back in the direction of the neighborhood. "Go tell your stupid friend she's wrong. And if I catch any of you kids in these woods again, you'll regret it."

Priya nodded. "Yes, sir."

As she ran back to her apartment, she couldn't help but feel amazed that something useful had come from the ancient classic *Ferris Bueller's Day Off*.

~

It was pitch black outside as Sergeant Todd Winslow, who wasn't in uniform for this mission, climbed through the break in the chain-link fence. He was in unmonitored territory—a place where the standard video surveillance and security services were unavailable. As he was in charge of perimeter security for Cape Canaveral, he knew where the gaps in surveillance were. Strictly speaking, it was illegal for citizens to enter such places. Strictly speaking, he didn't plan to get caught.

He jogged about two klicks north to a dilapidated bomb shelter that was left over from the twentieth century. A building that was in service long before the UN took over the US's military operations and things went to hell. Todd neared the dark shadow of the concrete bunker and heard the call of a seagull.

It wasn't really a seagull. Not at this time of the night.

He reached into his pocket and pressed three times on a button that did nothing but make a distinct *click click*.

Three shadows materialized out of the darkness. One whispered, "One second and it'll be here."

There was no moon in the night sky, and Todd could barely make out the three men—his contacts for the local faction of the Rebels. The Rebels were a militia group that lived outside normal society; they'd been on the UN's hit list for ages. Todd's father was the leader of one of the larger Rebel groups somewhere in the wilds of Montana.

From above came the buzzing sound of an approaching drone. It came down and stopped on the ground inches from his feet.

"It's already autodialed and connected to Chrysalis," one of the men whispered. "Do it quick, because it's programmed to go back in one minute."

Todd knelt down and watched with fascination as the drone morphed into a rectangular box with a long antenna. A high-powered transmitter.

He put the box to his ear and heard a voice. *"Remember, there's a four-minute delay between our locations. I won't be able to respond to anything you say before the transmitter deactivates. Just send me what you need to be done. I'll do what I can."*

Todd plugged a secure storage chip into the alien device. "I'm sending an image of a new intern. She's a Radcliffe. She'll be leaving here in a few days. You know what to do."

The transmitter vibrated briefly. He removed the storage chip, which immediately crumbled to dust. He set the transmitter back on the ground. The metal moved as if it were alive, transforming itself back into a drone that launched itself into the sky and vanished in the night.

The men that had met him had also disappeared.

Todd said a little prayer as his message streaked at the speed of light to the colony. "I hope I haven't done something that will bite me in the ass."

~

"For those of you who have never been off the grid, let me fill you in on a few facts..."

Priya stared out the window of the bus as it drove along the ancient highway called US 119 North. They were passing through a farming area, and the neat rows of vegetation were unlike anything she'd ever seen. Out here, you could see for miles and miles. The only time she'd ever seen such a vast expanse was when she was at the beach, and even then, the erosion prevention facilities rose up about a half mile offshore, blocking her view of anything more distant.

"We'll be covering just over three hundred miles on our journey to tour the decommissioned Marshall County Mine. With

tube travel, this would be a pleasant ten-minute journey; by bus, this is a three-hour trek. So sit back and enjoy the view. What you're seeing are the remnants of a time long past when people worked the land and commuted using fossil fuels."

The woman talking was standing at the front of the bus, speaking into a microphone. If it weren't for the microphone and various speakers throughout the vehicle, the road noise would have drowned her out. It was quite a contrast to the quiet of travel in the tube network.

"You can thank the UN Education Council and Virginia's Department of Mines, Minerals, and Energy for giving the Virginia Mining School permission to take this unusual trip. If you have questions at any point during the ride or the tour, please don't hesitate to ask."

One of the interns raised his hand. He had to shout to be heard. "This highway is hundreds of years old—pre-Exodus according to the literature you gave us. How has it stayed in such good condition?"

"Good question. As you can see, most of these lands were converted for farming use. Millions of acres are being processed by machinery to grow the food we eat. The highway system is still used to transport those harvests—using much larger vehicles than this one—and is maintained for that purpose."

Priya raised her hand. "Does anyone live out here, in the unmonitored areas?"

"Sure. There are people whose only job is to maintain the equipment that automates our harvest. There are also a few of those who prefer a more remote life. But they're all wearing these." The woman raised her hand and pointed at her bracelet.

Priya was wearing an ID band too. They all were. They'd been snapped on as they boarded the bus. Priya hated being tracked, but she wasn't going to be allowed to board without it.

The guy sitting next to her leaned over and whispered. "There are supposed to be some outlaws out here, too, people who aren't monitored at all. No ID, no access to civilization. It's like the Wild West from the 1800s. Or at least that's what my uncle used to say."

"What happens if you get into trouble out here, and you don't have a bracelet?" Priya asked.

"Then you're out of luck, I guess. But some people don't care. My uncle's family was from New Hampshire, and they were all about the old motto of 'Live Free or Die.' Myself, I can't imagine living out here with wild animals and dirt and outlaws looking to rob me."

"Okay, folks, if that's all the questions for now, I'm going to play you an audiotape that we recovered from the mine we're about to visit. It's over two hundred years old. I think you'll find it interesting."

Some music began playing and then a man's voice broadcast through the speakers.

"We are the largest privately owned coal company in the United States and the largest underground coal mining company in the world. We are Murray Energy Corporation, and we produce over seventy-six million tons of coal annually. This is high-quality bituminous coal produced through the efforts of nearly seven thousand people..."

Priya tuned the voice out and watched the land race past. Everything was so different out here. No stores, no libraries, no schools. No jobs, for that matter. It really would be like living in the early Americas, doing whatever you had to do to scratch out an existence. The idea both intrigued and frightened her.

At least her trip out here was just for one day, she thought. Chrysalis would probably be just as strange, just as foreign, and she would have to stay there for six months.

That is, if she could survive that long.

She knew that others had been sent to spy on Chrysalis and never came back, and that thought loomed like a sword of Damocles over her head. How could anyone expect her trip to have a different outcome? Odds were, she was going to die up there.

She pulled in a deep breath and wished things were different, that she had never ended up in this impossible situation.

And suddenly, she smiled. "There *is* something I can do."

"Huh?" said the guy next to her.

"Nothing." She waved dismissively.

Priya turned to the window. She couldn't wait for this day to be over. Because tomorrow she'd break all the rules.

~

"One passenger for the Bizarre Bazaar at Times Square. Please be aware that this is a premium location and will require the Transit Service to debit three credits from your account each way. Please confirm."

Priya rolled her eyes. "Confirmed."

The sound of rushing air grew louder behind the metal doors to the tube. *"Establishing vacuum. Queuing request for trans-*

portation link between Coral Springs-North Junction and the main terminal at the Bizarre Bazaar-Times Square."

Priya paced back and forth excitedly. Today was her last day on Earth, for now at least, and for all she knew, forever. Which meant she was going to blow an obscene amount of credits. After all, credits wouldn't do her any good when she was dead.

"Link complete. The car is arriving in three… two… one…"

The doors slid open, and Priya entered the single-seat capsule, preparing herself for the twenty-minute ride to the only place she knew of where she'd be able to get what she wanted.

"We are about to depart."

Priya smiled and gripped the armrests as the capsule accelerated.

~

The heavenly scent was hard for Priya to describe. It reminded her of a campfire, but somehow it seemed more pungent, more primal.

She'd read about real meat, but she'd never before found a place that actually served it—and now that a fresh-grilled patty of ground beef sat before her, she knew that the books had failed to do it justice. The smell alone was exquisite, and her mouth was watering.

The waitress hovered. "Do you have any questions?"

Priya wasn't used to having an actual person take her order, deliver it, and be there to respond to questions. "Well… I guess… what's the best way to eat this?"

Priya had spent more on this two-ounce "slider" than she'd

normally spend for a week's worth of groceries. The last thing she wanted was to screw this experience up.

The waitress pulled out a laser pointer and aimed a red dot at the meat, the miniature buns, and the vegetables. "Many of our customers enjoy eating the meat alone, to savor what's illegal outside the bazaar. But it's supposed to be a sandwich. The history books are pretty clear about what people used to put on it. The meat of course, tomato, lettuce, sometimes a pickle, and maybe a little bit of ketchup or mayonnaise or both."

Priya decided the waitress was right: she wanted to try the meat alone. She sliced a tiny piece of meat from the patty, feeling silly that she was so excited over something as basic as food, and popped it into her mouth.

It was delicious—so unlike the manufactured and processed ingredients she'd grown up on. The savory juiciness of the meat, combined with a mild taste of char… She let out an embarrassing moan.

The waitress grinned. "Good, yeah? If you need anything else, just wave and I'll be right over."

Priya wanted to duplicate that first bite, but she decided she'd better try it the traditional way. The meat sandwich.

She assembled the ingredients as the waitress had instructed, including the ketchup and mayonnaise, and took a sample bite.

She moaned again. She'd never forget this gustatorial experience. She savored it, chewing each bite slowly, appreciating every moment, but it was gone too soon.

She took another look at the digital menu. She'd blown through most of her credits already today, but she had enough left to order maybe one more thing. There was no point in saving her money—tomorrow before dawn she'd be going to Cape Canaveral for a trip she might never return from.

She waved at the waitress, who came over immediately. "How was the slider?"

Priya made a sound between a moan and a grunt.

The waitress laughed. "That was pretty much my reaction the first time I had one. Is there anything else you'd like?"

"Can you tell me more about the cheesecake? What's that like?"

"Oh, child, where do I start?"

~

"You're sure this signal came from alien tech?" Terry asked. He was standing beside Nwaynna at an alien console that showed several recently received signals. The signal of interest had triggered an alert just fifteen minutes ago.

She swiped through several different complex charts that apparently meant something to her, though they meant nothing to him. "Without a doubt. The frequency is several orders of magnitude beyond anything we could produce, and of course Earth scientists are generations behind us in tech. If not for our alien signal sniffers, we wouldn't have picked it up at all."

"Can you decode the message?"

"Afraid not. It was transmitted using an auto-scrambler. It's not that hard. All anyone would have to do is seed the random frequency hopper with a unique seed and they'd be able to get a private signal through without us knowing what they're saying."

"How about source and destination?"

She smiled. "There I have better news. Our alien receivers have pretty good spread spectrum analyzers. They have their limits, but I manage to get enough captured frequencies to triangulate, and…"

The scientist swiped once more, and an image of their solar system appeared. Tau Ceti was at its center, with Earth as the farthest orbiting planet. Epsilon was closer in, being orbited by Chrysalis. An animated graphic showed a signal originating from Earth and traveling across space to the mining colony.

"The signal was sent from the southeastern part of North America on Earth. I can't get a lot more precise than that. As for its destination…" She spread her fingers, zoomed in on the colony, and pointed at a particular building. "It went there."

"You're sure?"

"One hundred percent. The signal was very tightly focused, probably for security purposes." She smiled proudly. "But we caught it anyway."

Terry patted the scientist on her shoulder. "Good work. Thanks for the information."

As he walked out of the lab, Ranger hopped up from where he'd been waiting and trotted at his side. Terry pressed a button on his collar.

"Yup?" replied the on-duty security officer.

"Jason, I need a lockdown of Dorm Block C. Everyone stays inside until we've had a chance to clear them."

"Oh, damn. Okay, but you realize that's like three hundred miners. What do you want me to say?"

"Don't say anything, just lock it down. I'll be there in a bit. And one more thing. Go through the surveillance tape for the last fifteen minutes. If anyone left the dorms during that time I want them held until they can be interviewed by me."

"Terry, we're going to get a lot of flak for this. You sure?"

"Just do it."

"You got it. I'm locking down the buildings... now."

Terry disconnected and jogged toward his transport. This could be the break he was looking for.

CHAPTER SIX

The sun hadn't risen yet when the mining students lined up on the tarmac at Cape Kennedy. Everyone fidgeted in the cool morning breeze, and the excitement was palpable.

Being so close to the shuttle, Priya couldn't help but admire the design of the transport ship. Its giant engines were a hybrid design that made the transport operate like a plane in the atmosphere, but in the vacuum of space, they could swivel to accelerate in any direction. By orienting the engines so they aimed "downward" in space, one could create the illusion of gravity for everyone aboard while the ship accelerated toward its destination.

The first of the students gave his name to the transport officer, who checked him off his list and sent him toward the escalator that had been stationed next to the ship. Priya felt her heart thudding as the transport officer moved down the line. She was both excited for the new experiences she was going to have, and scared to death of the dangers that would be lurking around every corner. Because she wasn't a miner; she was a spy. Her job was to dig into the loyalties of the miners and find terrorists. Get names.

And evidently some of her mission wouldn't be explained to her until after she got there. She had no idea how that would even happen.

The transport officer stopped in front of her. "Name?"

"Priya Radcliffe."

The woman looked at her tablet and frowned. "Radcliffe, you said?"

Priya felt a trickle of sweat at the base of her neck. "Yes. Radcliffe, with an 'R'."

The woman swiped at her tablet, scrolling through her list of names. "Are you sure you're cleared for this travel session? I don't have you on the list."

"Yes." Priya dug out her pocket PC and showed the woman her student ID and her enrollment certificate for this session's mining internship on Chrysalis.

The officer motioned for Priya to step aside. "Okay, let's get through everyone else first, then we'll figure this out."

As the officer moved on to the next intern, Priya felt a combination of embarrassment and indignation. She pulled out her communicator, swiped for a number, and put the device to her ear.

"Yes?"

"Ted, I'm on the tarmac right now, and the transport officer says I'm not on their list. What are—"

"I'll be right there."

The line disconnected.

Priya stared at her phone. “Okay then… I guess I’ll wait right here.”

The sun had long since crested above the horizon, and still Priya stood on the tarmac. The ship should have already taken off by now, but because of her, it was still on the ground. The other interns were all comfortably aboard—and no doubt impatient to get moving.

Agent Ted had appeared within minutes of her call, but the transport company had to call in the UN immigration service before anything could be done. Now the immigration officer had finally arrived, only to argue with Agent Ted about his request.

“I’m sorry, but what you’re asking is highly unusual. Any changes to the manifest need preapproval from the colony.”

Agent Ted flashed his badge—again. “I don’t care what your manifest says, Miss Radcliffe is approved for travel. This transport isn’t authorized to leave without her. Contact the UN Travel Authority and refresh your manifest.”

Priya had dreaded this trip from the beginning. But after all she’d been through—the training, the shots, the TMS brain machine, and on top of it all, the most godawful dreams—she’d now be disappointed if it fell through. And yet it looked like that was what was going to happen. At the last minute, everything was unraveling.

As the immigration officer talked to someone on a communicator, Agent Ted came over and handed her a billfold. “Here’s a copy of your approved visa just in case the folks on the colony end give you any grief."

"Are they even going to let me on?"

Ted waved dismissively. "You'll get on. We set this up at the last minute for your security. It's why I was on campus—I knew you'd probably get some grief."

"My security?" A fresh wave of anxiety washed over her.

Her discomfort must have been evident, because the creepy agent's expression morphed into something that was almost… warm. He put a hand on her shoulder. "Only a handful of people know about this trip of yours. That's on purpose. Trust me, we've taken every precaution we can. You'll be perfectly safe."

The immigration officer returned his communicator to his belt and said something to the transport officer. The woman nodded then walked over to Priya.

"Miss Radcliffe, you're approved for boarding." She pointed to the escalator. "Go ahead and board. I'll call up to the crew so they're made aware."

Agent Ted shook Priya's hand. "Best of luck."

Priya felt a surreal moment as she walked the fifty yards to the escalator. In her mind's eye, she saw flashes of a spaceport that she knew she'd never been in. A sign on the wall said "Welcome to Chrysalis"—and the smells were similar to those of the Bizarre Bazaar.

As quickly as the vision appeared, it was gone.

A flight attendant greeted her at the top of the escalator. "Welcome Miss Radcliffe. We'll be taking off at any moment. Please take Seat 12B."

As Priya walked to her seat, several of the interns flashed her looks of annoyance. It was her fault they were still here on the tarmac rather than on their way to Chrysalis.

She sat down and buckled her seatbelt.

"Ladies and gentlemen, welcome to ISTS, the Interplanetary Shuttle Transport Service. My name is Diane, and Kevin and I will be attending to your needs today. Today's transport is being piloted by Captain Igor Chernyshevsky and his first officer, Buck Sexton.

"For those of you who have never been off-planet before, this trip will be an exciting experience—but not too *exciting, if you know what I mean."*

Some of the interns chuckled. Priya felt anything but mirthful.

"We'll be taking off on runway 3C, heading east over the Atlantic. Once we're past the twenty-five-mile zone, we'll angle up, and you'll experience a peak G-force of about three times your body weight. It will take about twenty minutes to clear the Earth's gravitational influence, then we'll throttle back and will maintain a one-G acceleration and deceleration through the remainder of our trip.

"Chrysalis and Earth are currently close in their orbits, at a distance of only twenty-three million miles, and we should arrive at Chrysalis Spaceport in about thirty-six hours. For now, on behalf of the ISTS and the flight deck and crew, we ask you to buckle up and enjoy the ride."

Priya relaxed and rested her head against the seat. She could still see the image of the area welcoming her to Chrysalis. Now that she'd seen it once, she could bring it up at will, like a memory. The same thing had happened with other places she'd dreamt about after her session with Agent Ted's machine. Was that how his machine worked? Drilling data into her subconscious that eventually pushed its way forward as a memory?

She wondered how accurate these fake memories actually were. And as the transport began to move, she knew she would soon find out.

Priya blinked the sleep out of her eyes. The voice of a man with a strong Russian accent was being broadcast through the cabin.

"Ladies and gentlemen, this is your captain speaking. We have hit the midway point in our travel to the Chrysalis mining colony, and we're about to shift orientation.

"For the last eighteen hours, we've been accelerating at a constant rate, and we've now hit our peak velocity of about 1.4 million miles per hour. That's just over eighteen hundred times the speed of sound, or approximately point two percent of the speed of light. In that time, we've traveled across nearly thirteen million miles of space.

"Now that we are at the midway point, we will reverse orientation, and our constant rate of acceleration will become a constant rate of deceleration. Once the maneuver is completed, you will notice no difference, but during the shift, you may feel a brief moment of weightlessness. For the comfort and safety of both the passengers and crew, we ask that you all stay seated."

Everyone around Priya tightened their seatbelts. Hers was already tightened, so she merely gripped her armrests.

After a moment, she both heard and felt the change as the engines cut off. The transport ship fell silent, and she felt almost as though her seat cushion was pushing her upward. It was both disturbing and exhilarating. The stars out the window turned as the transport rolled, then the engines came back on and she sank back into her seat.

The mining intern sitting next to her shook his head. "I don't understand why they had to turn the engines off."

"It's pretty simple," Priya said, and immediately bit her tongue.

"Oh? Then explain it."

Priya sighed and held her hand out in front of her, palm down. "Imagine my hand is the ship, going toward Chrysalis. My palm is the floor of the ship. The top of my hand is the ceiling."

The redhead looked a bit annoyed at the way she was explaining this, but he nodded. "Okay."

"The entire time we've been in space, going toward Chrysalis, it's felt like we're on Earth. We walk around to the bathroom and get drinks and everything seems just like normal." She mimicked fingers walking on the top of her hand. "That's because the engines are accelerating us 'upwards,' or at least, upwards relative to the floor our seats are attached to. The floor moves up against us, so it feels like we're pressing down against it." She moved her hand upward slowly. "In space, of course, there's no such thing as 'up,' we're just going toward Chrysalis. We just have to travel there ceiling first, if you will.

"But now we have to slow down, which means the engines have to fire in the opposite direction, pushing away from Chrysalis. But they still need to push 'upwards,' from our perspective, so that we feel gravity against the floor. To do that, the ship has to travel the rest of the way floor first." She turned her hand over, palm up, but kept moving it upwards, her fingers walking along what was now the "bottom" of her hand.

"And if the captain didn't turn off the engines while we turn over…"

The intern interrupted, his eyes widening. "I get it. If he didn't turn the engines off when he flipped the ship over, the ship would have been pushing itself sideways, or in a loop or something. And if he just swiveled the engines instead of the ship, then we'd all be stuck to the roof of the cabin."

"Pretty much." Priya smiled at the visual of everyone being scraped off the ceiling.

"The maneuver is complete," the captain announced. *"You're now once again free to move about the cabin. On behalf of the cockpit and crew, please sit back and enjoy the remainder of your trip to the Chrysalis mining colony."*

~

Kevin, one of the flight attendants, stopped his cart at Priya's row. "Would either of you care for a refreshment?"

The redhead looked up. "What are my choices?"

"Your choices are yes and no," Kevin said gruffly.

Priya had to cover her mouth to suppress a laugh.

"Um, yes, then," the redhead said meekly.

Kevin poured him a glass of water, then turned to Priya. "And you?"

"Yes, please," Priya said, still smiling.

When Kevin moved on, the redhead said, "Glad I can be of some amusement. My name's Mike."

"Hi, Mike. I'm Priya."

"I know. I was behind you when the lady started fussing about not finding your name on her list."

"Yeah, sorry about that."

Mike shrugged. "It's not your fault they screwed up their list. So, after the internship, where are you off to?"

"I'm not sure yet." Priya tried to keep her discomfort from showing. She hated liars, yet for the next handful of months she knew she'd have to get very good at lying. Lying was basically her job now. "I'm keeping my options open at the moment."

"That's cool. My brother's a miner on Asteroid X-55, out on the edge of the solar system. Lots of gold and rare minerals out there. Pretty nice bonuses too. He's working on getting me a gig there as soon I'm finished here."

"X-55? Isn't that more like a planetoid?"

"Yup. Almost nine hundred miles wide. But it doesn't compare to Chrysalis." Mike grinned. "He's already jealous I landed this internship."

"Ladies and gentlemen, this is the first officer speaking. Keep an eye out for your flight attendants, as they'll be coming down the aisle with presents for each of you."

Kevin showed up almost immediately, dropping a shrink-wrapped package onto Mike's lap.

"Ow!" Mike said. "Holy crap, that's heavy!"

Kevin placed Priya's package gently in her lap. Clearly the man played favorites.

"I'm sorry, ma'am," Kevin said, "but due to some kind of

snafu we didn't have one of these prepared for you. I think this will work, but if it doesn't, you call me."

Priya saw that although Mike's package was stenciled with his name and seat number, hers said merely, "Female, 125-150 pounds." Mike was right though: it was really, really heavy.

"I'm sure it's fine," she said.

The first officer's voice returned. *"Great gifts, aren't they? Weight harnesses to wear while stationed on Chrysalis. Just what you've always wanted, am I right?"* He chuckled. *"Since Chrysalis gravity is only forty-five percent of Earth's gravity, you'll need these harnesses to compensate. You'll want to wear them at all times—it'll help prevent the loss of bone density that can result from extended stays in low-gravity environments."*

"Jesus, this thing weighs a ton," Mike said as he stood and wriggled into his harness. Despite its weight, it looked like an ordinary vest.

Priya had a lot more trouble with her harness. As she struggled with it, Kevin appeared and, without saying a word, helped her into it. Mike looked sheepish, like he'd missed an opportunity.

Kevin took a step back and studied Priya with a doubtful expression. "You sure that's the right weight for you?"

Priya nodded. "I think it's okay. I just need to get used to it. Thanks."

She definitely needed to get used to it. As she sat back down, she wasn't one hundred percent confident she'd be able to get back up again.

Mike chuckled. "I wish that guy would have helped me. I think I pulled a muscle putting this thing on."

Sure you did, Mike, Priya thought inwardly. *Next time help out a lady.* But outwardly she just smiled.

~

The captain's voice came over the speaker a few minutes later. *"Passengers, we'll be arriving at the Chrysalis Mining Colony in approximately one hour."*

Priya felt a pang of fear race through her. She was almost there.

"You'll be okay," Harold tapped at her scalp.

The captain continued. *"In compliance with the UN-Chrysalis Immigration Charter, all passengers disembarking at the mining colony need to have been treated with Innoc-64 prior to arrival. This will ensure that all Earth-based pathogens have been eliminated from your systems, protecting the health of both you and the colonists during your stay. The flight attendants will be coming around with injectors. We appreciate your cooperation."*

Priya hoped to get Kevin again, but the flight attendant who stopped at her row with a cart of injectors was the other one, Diane. Priya held out her arm.

"You won't feel a thing," Diane said with a smile.

The woman was a liar.

The injection itself wasn't bad—just the usual cooling effect of the anesthetic and the quick bite of a needle puncturing her skin. But about five seconds later, the effects kicked in. Her skin felt suddenly hot and her face flushed. She was burning up as the drugs went through her system, killing off whatever germs she might or might not have.

It wasn't just her; Mike, too, was red-faced and fanning himself with his hands.

Priya wanted to take off the weight harness, but she feared she'd never get it back on again. She settled for pulling at the front of her blouse to increase the airflow against her sweating skin.

As she waited for the hot flashes to disappear, she hoped this was the worst of what she'd have to go through—yet she knew very well that that wouldn't be the case.

Terry sat with Carl Gustav in the governor's private conference room, facing the scrutiny of the governor. That was never a place Terry wanted to be.

"Three hundred and fifty-three miners were held in isolation in Dorm Block C for two days," the governor said, giving Terry a withering stare. "They were held incommunicado, no family, no visitors, and for what?"

Carl cleared his throat. "Madam Governor… our mining throughput wasn't affected by the work stoppage—"

"Because you shifted resources and delayed needed vacation time for the others!" She stopped herself, took a breath, and waved dismissively at Carl. "It's fine. You did what you needed to. You made the right call."

She turned back to Terry. "But *you*…" She paused. "Tell me about the missing miner."

Terry winced. How could she know about that?

"Of course, Madam Governor. Two minutes after the incoming alien signal was detected, video surveillance captured an unidentified miner leaving the dorm. Through process of elimination, we determined the miner is a man named Gerry Riddle. Three hours ago, we searched his room. We found this."

Terry tossed a slip of paper onto the conference room table.

Governor Welch peered at it. "Radcliffe? Is that what this chicken scratch says?"

Terry nodded. "As far as I can tell, yes. But I checked. We don't have any—"

A buzz sounded, and the governor tapped a flashing light on the conference room table. "This is the governor."

"Governor Welch, this is Denise. We just received a priority call from the tower at the main arrivals gate. There's been a manifest change on an incoming flight. This change was not preapproved, so the flight is being held in orbit right now. And since only you and Mr. Chapper are authorized to approve a manifest change..."

Terry leaned forward. "What's the change?"

"There was a late addition. A new intern."

The hairs on the back of Terry's neck stood on end.

"Do we know anything about this intern?" the governor asked. "Have we received his files?"

"Yes ma'am, we have. They just came in. And it turns out it's not a he, it's a she—a twenty-four-year-old woman. Her profile is pretty bare though. Just her school records. No biographical data."

Terry swiped his finger on the mute icon. "Governor, I'll bet you this is the spy. Twenty-four? And she's three years older than any other intern they've previously sent. Something's not right."

The governor unmuted the call. "What's her name?"

"Priya Radcliffe."

The governor's eyes widened, and Terry gave her a look that said, *Told you so.*

"Send me her records," the governor said. "Do they contain an image of her?"

"Yes, ma'am. Sending the records to your shared drive now."

The governor tapped at the access panel, a green light flashed across her face, and a holographic image of the intern's records appeared above the table. Terry only had an instant to scan the school record—the girl had gotten top marks—before the governor swiped to an image of the girl. She was trim, dark-skinned, pretty. Probably Indian descent.

Terry shook his head. "So she's Indian, and her last name is Radcliffe. I guess we're supposed to believe she's a descendant? I thought they'd all died out."

But when he looked up at the governor, he was shocked to see that not only did she not share his disbelief… she was crying. It was only a single tear running down her cheek, but it was only the second time he'd ever seen this woman cry, and the first was at his father's funeral, almost twenty years ago.

Carl averted his gaze and looked around the room, decidedly uncomfortable.

After a moment, the governor wiped her cheek and shook her head. "Denise, the manifest change is approved."

"Yes, ma'am." Denise disconnected, and the room fell silent.

After a few long seconds, the governor turned to Terry. "I

want you to be on this girl like white on rice. Do you understand me?"

"Yes, but—"

"No buts about it. She is most definitely a Radcliffe—but that doesn't mean she's not a danger to us. Under no circumstance is she allowed in the mines until we sort out what her story is. That guy who's missing… I don't get it, but the last thing I want is for Neeta to come to harm."

"Neeta?" Terry said.

The governor waved her hand dismissively. "Or whatever this girl's name is." She swiped at the image, turning back to the girl's school record. "Priya. I want a security detail on Priya Radcliffe at all times. You got me?"

"Yes, ma'am."

The governor motioned toward the door. "Go. Greet her at arrivals. You and I will talk about the other matter later. Just remember—"

"I know, I know. Keep an eye on the girl."

"Hey, Gene," said Terry, pulling up a chair and plopping down next to the young air traffic controller. "I heard we've got an incoming Earth vessel."

"We do, but hold on a second." Gene tapped on a button and spoke into his microphone. "Mining Shuttle 135, this is Chrysalis tower, for noise abatement turn right forty-five degrees."

"Chrysalis tower, we're at thirty-five thousand feet. How much noise can we be producing? Mining Shuttle 135."

"Mining Shuttle 135, this is Chrysalis tower, have you ever heard the noise a local mining shuttle such as yours makes when it hits an Earth-based transport shuttle breaking out of orbit? I repeat, turn right forty-five degrees."

"Chrysalis tower, roger that, turning right forty-five degrees. Mining Shuttle 135."

Terry chuckled and patted Gene on the back. "I see you've grown a sense of humor on the job. That's good."

Gene collapsed against the back of his chair and shook his head. "Some of these pilots just stress me the hell out. That's all I need on my conscience: some dipwad ignoring me because I sound young, then going and getting himself and his entire crew killed."

"Hey, I get it." Terry pointed upward. "How's our incoming Earth shuttle?"

Gene gestured to a radar image on his left. "They're on final approach. Looks like they're lined up with the runway. I'd say they should be taxiing into the gate in about five minutes."

Terry hopped up to his feet and patted Gene on the shoulder. "I'll wander downstairs to the gate then. Keep up the great work."

As he left the room, Ranger barked at his side.

"Come on, good boy. I've got a whole shuttle full of people for you to sniff."

Terry watched the new arrivals from the security room. It wasn't often that people from Earth disembarked at the colony. Almost all of the traffic between the colony and Earth was for trade goods, so when there was actually a person disembarking, security was on full alert. Especially on a day like today, with a full two dozen visitors.

"Spies come in all shapes and sizes, so I don't care if they're only interns," groused Ian Wexler, one of Terry's security supervisors. "I don't trust anything coming from Earth anymore. Not after the crap they've pulled."

"Agreed. Bring the scanners up. They're about to release the first one."

Ian swiped at the security console, and the window overseeing the arrivals gate glowed with a digital overlay. As the first visitor walked into the arrivals waiting area, the overlay populated with information.

"John Lockhart," Ian said. "He's taken the Innoc-64. Age, height, and weight all match what's on record."

The display also showed a rotating image of Mr. Lockhart, using the dyes in the Innoc-64 cocktail to highlight anything nonorganic. Terry pointed at a glowing spot on the intern's hip. "What do the medical records say about that?"

Ian scrolled through the intern's record. "Accident at his uncle's farm. Ceramic-on-ceramic total hip replacement."

Terry looked over the composition scan once more. "Okay, this guy looks clear. Send the next one in."

For the next forty-five minutes, Terry and Ian scanned twenty-two more interns. The last one to be allowed to disembark, at Terry's direction, was going to be the Radcliffe girl. When her turn came, Terry shrugged his shoulders to loosen the tension.

"Last one is Priya Radcliffe," Ian said. "She's positive for the Innoc-64. Age, height—" He stopped. "Holy shit, Terry. What the hell is on her head?"

The visual image of the woman looked normal, but the biometric scan revealed something entirely different. Draped over her head and spreading down to her shoulders was an unidentified substance.

There was only one substance Terry knew of that could disguise itself like that. And it was alien tech.

"That's not all," Ian said. He zoomed in on the girl's arm and pointed. "See there?"

The Innoc-64 had done what it was designed to do, highlighting a small implant just under Priya Radcliffe's skin. He read the analysis chart aloud. "Silicon-etched circuit with a near-field transponder encased in a silicate glass."

Ian stood. "I'll take care of this."

"No." Terry put his hand on his friend's shoulder. "The governor asked me to keep an eye on her. I've got a plan."

CHAPTER SEVEN

Priya stepped off the transport, breathed in the air of a new world, and smiled. "Amazing," she whispered. She'd never really traveled before—certainly never off-planet. Not even to the moon.

As she walked along the airtube that connected the transport to the arrivals gate, she was greeted by floral scents that spoke of springtime, mixed with warm musky odors that were reminiscent of her visit to the Bizarre Bazaar. It was exhilarating.

A large banner at the arrivals gate read, "Welcome to Chrysalis Mining Colony, Class of 2220!" Priya smiled at the old-fashioned style of date. Beyond the gate, the other interns were already mingling and enjoying refreshments that had been laid out for them. Padded lounge chairs all around the area gave off the distinct aroma of leather—an aroma that didn't exist on Earth anymore. And yet it was a smell she recognized.

Because she'd been here before.

Everything about this place was familiar.

Priya felt her heart thudding in her chest as she looked up, knowing exactly what she would see, and yet at the same time feeling surprised that it was there. She looked up and saw a tile mosaic that covered the entire ceiling. Thousands of colored tiles showed an image of Earth traveling away from their old solar system. There was Saturn with its ring, and Jupiter with its great red spot, and all the other planets that were now footnotes in history.

She knew this mosaic well. It was that damned machine they'd plugged her into. She now had memories that weren't even hers. Whose memories were they? And what other memories were lying dormant in her head, waiting to pop up when she least expected it?

Ahead of her, a door opened, and a man walked through. He was maybe in his late thirties, with very closely cropped hair, a perfect physique, and brilliant blue eyes that were looking right at her.

"Miss Radcliffe?" he said as he approached.

"Y-yes?"

He displayed an ID. "I'm Officer Chapper with colony security. Can you come with me?"

"Is there anything wrong?"

Chapper smiled and shook his head. "No, this is completely routine. Since it seems you were a late add to the class, we're missing some of your paperwork. I just have some standard questions for you so I can finish up your immigration profile."

"Sure." Priya scanned the room. "I have a suitcase—"

"Don't worry about that, Miss Radcliffe, I'll make sure it gets to your dormitory."

"Please, call me Priya."

"Okay, Priya. You can call me Terry." He motioned toward the door, where a German shepherd sat waiting. "After you."

As Priya walked past the officer, she breathed in deeply.

Wow, he smells nice.

"And your parents, they're miners?"

Priya's stomach did a flip. She'd been prepared to lie about herself, but her parents too? What was she supposed to say? And what if this guy double-checked what she said? She knew the UN had covered their tracks when it came to her background—mostly they just had to hide that she'd spent most of her educational career in a grooming school for military service—but her parents? If they came up with a cover story for them, she was never told about it.

Harold tapped his advice on her scalp. *"Relax. Tell the truth."*

She looked down into her lap. "No. They were both scientists."

"And what took you down the path of being a miner?"

Priya looked up. "I've never been anywhere before, and it seemed like a good way out."

"Out? Out of what?"

Unexpectedly, Priya felt her emotions well up inside her. She took a deep, shuddering breath. "Well, my parents died in a terrorist attack, and they never got a chance to see anything outside the four walls of their lab. They were astrophysicists. I just didn't want to have the same fate."

Terry's expression softened, and he paused before his next question.

"Radcliffe," he said. "An unusual name, especially for someone of Indian descent. You're aware of—"

"Yes, I'm well aware of the Radcliffes. They do still teach history on Earth. And before you ask, yes, I'm one of *those* Radcliffes." She pulled out her pocket PC, unlocked it with a swipe of her finger, and showed him a picture. "These are my parents."

Terry nodded. "Interesting."

"Yes, they're both light-skinned," Priya said flatly. "And mine's darker. But I'd rather not be judged by the shade of my skin."

"Whoa." Terry sat back, a crooked smile on his face. "I wasn't judging you. I was just remarking—"

"You were just assuming I'm from India. I'm not. I was born in East London. My family has lived in Britain or the US for as long as I'm aware of. I don't know if customs are different here than on Earth, but we try not to make assumptions about people based on their looks, especially their skin color."

Terry looked amused. "You do realize that I didn't at any time mention anyone's skin color. I'm sorry you took offense, because none was intended."

Priya blinked, replayed the conversation in her head, and realized he was right. She'd just come off as a bloody idiot. Her cheeks grew warm with embarrassment. "I'm sorry. I don't know what made me get on you over that. Of course, yes, I'm of Indian descent. I'm also sometimes a bit bonkers, I guess."

Terry chuckled. "No worries. You've had a long trip. I'd probably be a bit touchy as well." He stood and motioned for her to follow. "I don't have any other questions at this time. Let's go get you situated at the dorms. Your suitcase should already be there."

Terry and his dog, Ranger, led her back through the arrivals area, which was now empty, and through the near-empty building to a pair of glass doors that led outside. They slid open, and the dog, which was leading the way, stopped, turned to face them, and woofed.

"What are you waiting for, goofy boy?" Terry said. He snapped his fingers and pointed outside. "Be careful with cars on the street."

The dog backed through the doorway, and they all stepped outside. The light was different here; Epsilon was rising, partially blocking the rays coming from Tau Ceti, humanity's new sun. And the land was different too—spacious, open. Though they had just exited a huge building, the opposite side of the road contained nothing but open grassland. There were some trees in the distance, maybe some buildings, but they were all very far away.

Once again Priya couldn't shake the surreal sense of familiarity.

"What is it that I'm smelling?" she asked.

Terry sniffed. "I think that's probably a fireplace. The breezes carry scents a long way here. It's supposed to get cool tonight, and some people like the idea of sitting by a fire. Personally, I think it's more trouble than it's worth."

A fireplace? The concept was so… foreign. Exotic. At home, the intentional burning of wood was prohibited by environmental regulations.

"Have you ever been in a car?" Terry asked.

Priya felt a prickle of excitement. "I've been in a bus. Are we actually going to ride in a car?"

Terry smiled. "We actually are."

He led her to a brushed-steel four-door vehicle and lifted one of the gull-wing doors. Ranger hopped in, and Terry motioned toward the back.

"Get in the back, fur face. You know better."

The dog barked once in protest but dutifully clambered to the back.

"The bus that took the interns to the dorms is long gone," Terry said, "so unless you relish a fifteen-mile walk, driving is your only option."

He held the passenger door open for her, and she climbed inside.

It was like a tube capsule, but built for more utility. Two seats in the front, one bench seat in the back that could sit three people —or one very large furry companion—and in the far back was open space, probably for packages. Terry got in the other seat and pressed a button, and the console lit up in front of them, featuring all sorts of indicators and gauges. Music blared through speakers, but Terry immediately muted it, then shifted a gear on the steering wheel.

Priya gasped. "*You're* going to drive it?" A seatbelt automatically wrapped down her shoulder and across her lap.

"Of course."

Priya braced herself as Terry moved the car out of its parking spot and started down the road. Her heart was racing. "What if you lose control?"

"I won't."

"But what if you do?" At that moment another vehicle approached from up ahead, its headlights shining a dire warning. "There's someone coming!" she shouted.

Terry glanced at her with a look of mild curiosity.

"Don't look at me, pay attention to the bloody road!" she shrieked.

Terry laughed. "Priya, I've been driving for probably as long as you've been alive. It'll be okay. Trust me."

They passed the other vehicle without incident. Priya swallowed hard and tried to relax. It wasn't easy—they were going over a hundred miles per hour, and yet the vehicle was entirely under the control of this man next to her.

And then it began raining… hard.

Yet Terry didn't look at all nervous. He even pointed out sights as they drove.

"That's mine shaft number one," he said as they passed a large hill with a lit gate at its base. "The very first one ever opened, over a century ago."

"Is that where I'll be going for my internship?"

"Could be. I'm not sure. There's twenty-three other mines across the colony."

As the sky darkened, dots of lights appeared in the distance. Civilization. Maybe once they got there, Priya would feel more comfortable. Out here, on this open plain, the world was just too *big*. Along the tube network, everything was packed in tight—no view of the horizon, not many open spaces. This place was more like the unmonitored areas back on Earth.

"How big is the colony?" Priya asked.

It was ridiculous that she had to ask, but there was so little public information available on Chrysalis. She hadn't even been able to bring up a proper map.

"Well, the moon's circumference is about thirty-eight hundred miles around its equator. The colony itself is harder to measure, as it's dotted all over the place. In some ways it's more like a bunch of settlements rather than one colony. But all told, we have about the same amount of land on this moon as the United States does. Just with a less gravity. More than on Earth's moon, because Chrysalis is much denser, even though it's smaller. But only about half of what you're used to on Earth."

Priya looked down at her weight harness. She hadn't really thought much about gravity since she'd been here, but the harness was no longer heavy. Moving around in it felt… natural here.

"Do you have a tube network here?" Priya asked. "Or do you drive cars everywhere?"

"No on both. In that sense, we're very much a throwback to the twentieth or twenty-first century. If I'm going somewhere local, I drive, but if I'm going somewhere farther, for instance, Outpost Radcliffe—"

"No!" Priya turned in her seat, for a moment forgetting that she was in a car with no computer controlling it. "There isn't a place named after the Radcliffes, is there?"

Terry smiled. "Why wouldn't there be? Your ancestors were part of what saved humanity. I don't know how it is on Earth, but here on Chrysalis, we haven't forgotten where we came from. It wasn't really all that long ago."

Priya leaned back again. Terry seemed entirely sincere. Maybe the UN intelligence guys were right about this Radcliffe thing. She recalled General Duhrer's words. *"You're here because you're a Radcliffe. You may not appreciate the significance of that, and it may not even* be *that significant here on Earth. But it's significant to the people on Chrysalis."*

"Anyway," Terry continued, "if it's more than a couple-hour drive, most people take a flight. The airports are pretty small, nothing like the spaceport we just left, which is the only place equipped to receive interplanetary visits."

The lights ahead had grown much closer, and Terry pointed through the windshield at a set of well-lit buildings. "We're almost there. These are your dorms."

A bus was parked in front of a giant multi-story concrete building with "Dorm Block E" on the side. It was even bigger than the apartment complex she lived in, which housed over five hundred families. Terry pulled the car up behind the bus, and an awning automatically extended over them. He pressed a button, and the door on Priya's side of the car yawned upward.

A man approached, wearing the same security uniform that Terry wore, and offered Priya his hand. "Miss Radcliffe?"

"Yes, I'm Priya Radcliffe."

"Pleasure to meet you. My name's Tom. I'll help get you get checked in."

Behind Priya, Terry said, "Tom's also with colony security. He'll take care of you."

"Thanks, Terry." She leaned into the car to shake his hand, and when she leaned back again, Ranger barked and climbed into the front seat. Terry chuckled as he closed the door and drove off.

Tom motioned toward the building's entrance. "You've got to be exhausted. Let's get you settled in so you can rest."

Priya took a deep breath and let it out slowly. She knew she'd never be able to truly rest here. She had a mission. A mission to betray any trust these people place with her.

It was for their own good.

~

After signing what seemed like an endless supply of papers, Priya was finally asked to input her biometrics. She pressed her hand on an ID plate, and a light rolled across her palm. The device beeped.

"Thank you, Miss Radcliffe," said the woman at the front desk. "You are now all registered with the system. Your palm scan will open all the external doors into this building, as well as get you into your room. Did you have any questions?"

Priya's stomach grumbled. "Is there anything to eat around here?"

The woman frowned apologetically. "Oh, I'm afraid the cafeteria is closed at this hour. But let me see if we can make some kind of arrangement for you, okay?"

The woman waved to Tom, who'd been patiently waiting in a chair across the room while she got her stuff squared away.

Tom rose to his feet and came over. "Are we all set?"

"We are." The woman handed him a slip of paper. "That's her room, third floor of the east wing. While you show her up, I'm going to make some calls and see about getting the poor dear a late-night snack."

Tom nodded to Priya. "Come on. We'll collect your suitcase on the way. It arrived before you did." As he guided her across the lobby, he added, "I'm sorry about the food situation. Miners tend to be on a pretty set schedule, so the cafeteria only operates at certain times. But if Miss Bridget doesn't figure something out, I'll see what I can do. I don't live far; I could at least bring you back a sandwich or something."

Priya shook her head and smiled. "That's very kind, but there's no need. I won't exactly starve if I miss a meal."

They passed through a huge room with a pool table, several sofas, and a couple of large monitors hanging on the walls. "This is one of the break rooms where the miners relax between shifts," Tom said. "Don't hide out in your own room all day; the break rooms are where all the fun happens."

"Rooms?" Priya asked. "There's more than one break room?"

They arrived at an elevator, and Tom held the door open for her. "One on each floor. The second floor has a Ping-Pong setup, and the third floor has a bunch of game consoles."

They got off on the third floor, and after retrieving Priya's suitcase from a storage locker, Tom led her down a couple more hallways to her room. "Here you are. Just press your hand or any finger on the plate, and you're in. I'd suggest getting some shuteye right away if you can. The interns are served breakfast from six a.m. to seven."

Priya pressed her index finger against the biometric reader. A green light flashed, and the lock disengaged. She pressed lightly on the door's handle, and the door swung open.

"Looks like you're all set," Tom said. "Do you need anything else?"

"No, I'll be fine. You've already gone out of your way. Thank you."

"Remember—get some rest. Goodnight."

As Tom walked back down the hall, Priya stepped into her room. It was *huge*. Three times the size of her bedroom at home. It contained a great big bed, a dresser, a nightstand, a desk, and a closet that was way too large for what she'd brought.

She hadn't expected such luxurious trappings for a mining intern. She hoped they weren't treating her special because of her last name.

On the desk was a handwritten note.

I'm sorry I kept you so long with the interview process. The mess hall is closed, but I did manage to snag you something that I hope will tide you over until morning. See you at six. —Terry Chapper

Beside the note was a basket of fruit and a pitcher of an orange-colored liquid that was still cold, condensation beading on the glass. She poured herself a large cup, took a sip, and sighed contentedly. *Fresh-squeezed orange juice.*

Who'd have guessed that was available on this distant colony?

After drinking some juice and eating what was probably tastiest and juiciest peach she'd ever had, she decided she'd leave unpacking for tomorrow. If breakfast was at six, she needed to get some sleep. So she set her suitcase aside and shrugged out of the weight vest. Only then did she notice just how much less gravity there was here. She felt like she could jump across the room with a mere hop. Instead she merely turned off the lights and collapsed onto the bed.

"Any signals?" she whispered to Harold. "Any anything to worry about?"

"No. Do you want the kitten?"

"Please."

Harold crawled down from his perch on her head and shoulders, and within moments the purring kitten had nestled itself in her arms.

"Can you wake me at five, so I can shower?" she whispered.

His kitten paws pressed rhythmically into her arm, forming the Morse code for "yes." And she fell asleep with Harold purring in her ear.

~

Terry sat across from Priya in the dorm cafeteria, eating his usual bowl of oatmeal with a dollop of fruit compote on top. But she wasn't eating; she was just staring at her meal.

"Is something wrong?" he asked.

She leaned forward, her long hair still wet from the shower. "I don't want to be treated differently because of my last name."

"What are you talking about?"

Priya hesitated, and then the words poured out. "First you leave that basket for me, which was really nice and thanks for that, and then my room was really more than I was expecting, and now this..." She pointed at her breakfast. She'd ordered shakshuka, a stew made from peppers, onions, and tomato sauce, with three poached eggs on top. "I mean, I thought the menu was speaking euphemistically. But this thing has eggs in it."

"Is there something wrong with it?" Terry asked. "You can return it and we can get you something else."

"No, it's exactly what it said it would be. But there's no way..." She craned her neck to look at one of the other interns' breakfasts, and her eyes widened. "Is he eating... an omelet?" she whispered.

Terry finally understood what was wrong, and he tried to keep his amusement from his voice. "You weren't expecting real eggs, were you?"

"Well..."

"I get it. I've heard you guys are all vegans back on Earth. Just tell the chef, he'll prepare it any way you like."

Priya shook her head. "No, we're not all vegans. At least... not by choice."

She plunged her spoon into one of the eggs, breaking the yolk, and watching at the thick golden liquid mixed with the spicy tomatoes making a luscious sauce, which she shoveled into her mouth. She chewed, paused, and smiled.

"Oh my god, this is so good."

Terry chuckled; clearly this ordinary breakfast was a sinful treat to her. "I'm glad you like it. And I'm glad you liked the fruit. But I promise you're not being treated any differently from any other intern. You're just beginning to experience life on the colony. We raise quite a few chickens, cows, pigs, and other animals for food. It might seem barbaric to you…"

"No, it doesn't." Priya wiped her mouth with a napkin. She leaned forward and added in a whisper, "In fact, just before coming here, I had a beef slider at a place that's sort of like a gray market for exotic items."

"The Bizarre Bazaar?"

"Yes!" Priya smiled—a genuine smile that crinkled the corners of her eyes. "How do you know about it?"

"I was stationed on Earth for a few years. I got so sick of the food, I spent almost every credit I had just to get a taste of something that wasn't some central government's idea of what was healthy for me."

Priya laughed. "I spent more at that place in one day than I've ever spent in an entire month."

"Well then, you'll be happy to know they serve hamburgers and sometimes even steaks for dinner. And it's all covered in your tuition, paid for by the UN."

Priya grinned. "Oh my goodness, I'm going to get so fat."

Terry chuckled. "Well, try not to overdo it."

She focused her gaze on him, assessing him. "Don't get me wrong," she said, "I'm glad to have someone to talk to for breakfast, but… is there a reason you're here? I mean, why is a colony security officer sitting with me in the miners' cafeteria?"

Terry drained his orange juice. "Just following orders. I'm supposed to see you safely to and from the mines."

"Why? Is there a problem?"

There was, but he certainly couldn't tell her all he knew. So he shrugged. "Not sure. It may be because you're a Radcliffe. The higher-ups probably just want to keep an eye out for your welfare. If you were to have an unpleasant experience, well… I suppose it would reflect poorly."

Priya waved dismissively. "Trust me, there's nothing special about me. I'm just a regular person who happens to have some historically significant ancestors." She smiled and pushed her plate away. "So, does that mean you're taking me to the mine in that crazy car of yours?"

Terry grinned. "I'm afraid so, Miss Radcliffe. There will be no buses in your immediate future."

CHAPTER EIGHT

"This is from the general's office? Duhrer?" Terry asked.

He was watching over Nwaynna's shoulder as she began replaying the transmission.

"Yes, we received it about thirty minutes ago."

This image was taken from a different angle than the last one. The video feed was still coming from somewhere near the ceiling, but now the camera faced the desk directly, providing a head-on view of General Heinrich Duhrer at work. Terry had done some research on this general. He was a career UN intelligence officer with an exemplary record—which basically meant that he left nothing to chance.

A knock sounded on the door, and the general said, *"Come in."*

Dixon, the Special Forces washout, stepped inside, closing the door behind him, and stood at attention.

The general motioned toward a chair. *"Have a seat, Sergeant. You've got an update on our colony asset?"*

"Yes, sir."

"Out with it."

"She's enrolled in the mining class, as expected—"

"Cut to the chase. Has she gotten down into level twelve yet?"

"Not yet, sir. But they've had her under 24/7 surveillance since the moment she landed. She's even been excluded from the usual transport to and from the mine, where we'd normally be able to reach her. Best I can tell is she's got a private security escort."

Terry frowned and scribbled a note to himself on his handheld PC: *Run a deep background check on all dorm route bus drivers.*

"Then what is your plan, Sergeant?"

"Our guy will arrange contact."

The general set aside his writing stylus and focused on the sergeant. *"We need this girl's intel before we can make our move. This isn't a game we're playing. You understand me, Sergeant?"*

"Perfectly, sir."

The general waved toward his office door. *"We're done, soldier. Dismissed."*

Nwaynna stopped the transmission and turned to meet Terry's gaze. "I ran their voices through stress analyzers. None of that was playacting for our benefit. The intel integrity of what we just witnessed is high."

"Thanks, Nwaynna. Keep me posted on anything else you find."

"Will do."

Ranger hopped up and followed Terry as he left the lab. He tapped on his lapel transceiver, and Tom answered.

"Hey, Terry. What's up?"

"Tom, where's our girl?"

"She's at the dorm. Why?"

"Where are you?"

"At home eating dinner. Is there something going on?"

"Who do we have at the dorms?"

"Well, it's past seven, so that would be Walsh. Terry, you sound agitated. What's going on? Should I go over there?"

Terry paused and took a deep breath. "No, you go ahead and finish dinner. I'll reach out to Walsh."

"You sure? I'm only five minutes away."

"It's fine. I have to go over that way anyway for something else."

"Okay, bro, but don't be a hero. If you need something, just ask."

"Thanks, Tom. It's no big deal."

Terry clicked off and headed for the exit.

He needed to talk with Priya.

~

Priya sat in the break room sipping a seltzer and watching a group of interns play a videogame. She'd rather be in her room reading, like she usually did at home, but she was trying hard to be social.

It was exhausting.

She was only twenty-four, just three years older than these guys, but to her they felt like kids. She tried to follow their game, but it was boring—just a bunch of shooting and fighting and explosions.

As she watched, a holographic arm projected from the screen and bashed one of the interns on the head. He jumped to his feet.

"One-shotted? What a load of crap! That boss totally cheated."

The others laughed. "Derrick, you have to have your shield up just right or you'll get all of your hit points drained."

Priya rolled her eyes. Boys.

At that moment the lights in the room flashed on and off, and an alarm sounded. "Everyone clear out of the building!" shouted a voice in the hallway.

Priya hopped up from her chair and walked with everyone else down the stairs. Along the way they blended with other people coming from other directions, some barely awake and wearing robes.

Outside, in the cool of the night, the alarm blared even louder. Priya looked around, spotted the woman from the front desk, and walked over to her. "What's going on?"

"It's the fire alarm," the woman said. "We didn't have a fire drill scheduled, so it might be the real thing."

Sure enough, just then someone yelled, "I smell smoke! Get away from the building!"

Everyone backed away, moving across the parking lot toward the street. As Priya passed between some vehicles, a man brushed past her and pressed a package in her hand while whispering, "A present from Agent Ted."

Priya turned, looking for the man, but he'd already vanished into the crowd.

Stepping farther away from the crowd and turning her back to them, she reached into the envelope and pulled out a metal disc. She knew she'd never seen the thing before, yet some implanted memory told her that this thing was key to getting her past some door somewhere in the mine. She slipped the disc into her pocket and tossed the envelope.

Her throat tightened. The UN was still watching her. Even here, they managed to reach out…

Someone placed a hand on her shoulder, and she let out a shriek.

"Sorry, I didn't mean to startle you." It was Terry. He'd come up behind her. "Are you okay?"

Priya stared blankly at him. She was anything but okay. "I'm —I'm fine," she said. "What are you doing here?"

Terry shrugged. "I was in the area and noticed the commotion."

The alarm suddenly ceased, dropping a shroud of silence across the crowd. A voice yelled, "All clear! False alarm."

"Are you sure you're okay?" Terry asked. "You look spooked."

"I'm good, I just… thought there was an actual fire. Someone said they smelled smoke."

She started following the crowd back toward the dorm, and Terry followed.

"Well, I'm glad it was a false alarm," he said. "I'll see you in the morning."

"Yeah. See you then." Priya tried to sound casual. But as she re-entered the building, all she could think about was where to hide the device in her pocket.

~

Priya swiped her finger on the biometric reader and walked through the turnstiles.

"Good morning, Miss Radcliffe," said the guard manning the mine entrance. "I hope your day goes well."

"Thanks." She returned his nod.

She'd been coming here every morning for two weeks, and still it felt weird having strangers know who she was. They'd been greeting her in the same way since her first day of orientation.

Evidently, her being a real Radcliffe had spread like wildfire through the folks working at the mine. That and there weren't that many women in the mines, so it was pretty easy for people to put two and two together.

As she walked through the caverns toward the classroom on the first level, she wondered when they'd actually learn something about the actual act of mining. So far, all they'd done was review mining safety—that somehow took the entire first week—and various refinement methods employed at the facility.

"Hey, Priya, how goes it?"

Mike had come up next to her—the same guy she'd met on the flight from Earth. She'd decided he wasn't the shiniest apple in the class, and in fact, she tried to not sit next to him, since she didn't have the patience to deal with his inane questions.

"Not too bad," she said. "You absorbing everything they're covering in the class?"

"Pretty much, though most of it's reviewing old stuff," he said dismissively.

Then why all the questions, Mike?

They arrived at the classroom, and Priya put her hand on the security panel. The door clicked open, and she walked through. Mike started to walk in behind her, but was stopped by a guard. They were stationed everywhere within this mine.

"No tailgating," the man said sternly.

Mike's eyes widened. "Oh, sorry."

As he was scanning himself in, Priya took the opportunity to find a seat between two other interns, so that Mike couldn't sit next to her. Unfortunately, the minute she was in her seat, one of the interns saw a friend and changed seats to sit with them. Which left the seat beside her open for Mike.

And of course, he took it.

"These guys get really pissy about security around here," he muttered.

She shook her head. "There's 'no tailgating' signs everywhere. Everyone's gotta scan in."

"I suppose. I wonder why they call it that. Tailgating."

Priya closed her eyes and wished that he wouldn't verbalize every single thought that came into his pea-brained head.

"Okay, class, let's get started."

A short man with a crazy mop of gray hair was pacing back and forth in front of the class. His accent reminded Priya of Boston.

"Today, you'll be receiving your first assignment."

A murmur rippled through the room, and the professor had to raise his hands for silence.

"Yes, class, we'll finally be moving from theory to practice. It's very exciting, but I'd prefer you keep the murmurs to yourself. Now, in your mining career, it's likely that you'll spend most of your time on larger asteroids and planetoids that will allow you to work with gravity-based separation ore sifters, so that is where we will begin.

"However, for now we'll be working on a small scale. This is a very exacting discipline, and if you can't do it on a small scale, you can't do it on a large scale. One day down the road, you'll be mining by the ton. You'll have no choice, because for many precious metals, you'll be lucky to find five grams of what you're looking for per ton of rock. That means sifting through more than two hundred tons of ore to extract a kilogram of gold.

"Anyway. We'll be heading down to level two to begin the exercise. I'll need you to split up into teams of two. Grab a partner, and let's head for the freight elevators."

A partner? Priya had been as social as she could, but she hadn't formed any close relationships. Yet as she looked around, she realized it probably didn't matter. The rest of the class had almost immediately formed into pairs… leaving only Priya and Mike.

"Hey, teammate," he said with a grin. "This sounds like it'll be pretty cool."

Without saying a word, Priya trudged to the door, taking deep breaths in and out, all the while praying for patience.

~

It was surprisingly warm and humid on the first level underground—easily twenty degrees warmer than the ground level they'd been having classes in. The corridor they passed through was illuminated by lights embedded directly in the rock, and Priya could see cracks in the walls. She wondered if the mine had settled or if the moon was geologically active. Each crack had some type of metal funnel built over it—she couldn't fathom what these might be for. It annoyed her that she knew so little about this place.

As the class snaked through what ended up being about a quarter mile of iron-heavy rock, the professor's voice boomed from speakers in the walls.

"These upper levels are mostly dedicated to the extraction of high-value metals used in industry. On the lower levels we're able to extract special-purpose elements, but that calls for mining techniques that won't apply to your future assignments, so we'll be sticking to the upper levels."

A jet of steam burst from one of the cracks in the wall, but the attached metal funnel shunted it up into the ceiling. Was that what it was for?

"But even these upper levels are going to differ significantly from your future projects, because Chrysalis is built on a thermally active satellite. I'm sure you've noticed the cracks in the walls, which are strategically created to relieve outgassing pressure from the lower levels. By contrast, your future mining locations will likely be geologically inert, with very low temperatures and no atmosphere."

One of the interns ahead of Priya raised his hand and yelled something that was hard for Priya to make out.

"Excellent question. I'll repeat it for the benefit of the others who may not have heard it. The question is, why *is this moon geologically active when others—like Earth's moon, which is larger—aren't?*

"As you students already know, billions of years ago, the Earth was struck a glancing blow by a Mars-sized planet, and the Earth's moon was formed from the jettisoned material. It took well over a billion years for the moon to cool. This moon was formed in a similar way—by an impact on Epsilon—but that impact was far more recent, and thus, unlike the Earth's moon, Epsilon's moon is still in its cooling phase. Hence the activity.

"That brings up another interesting point: this moon has a much different, denser composition than Epsilon itself. Thus we believe that what we're standing on is not the jettisoned material from Epsilon, but the jettisoned material from the planetoid that struck Epsilon. Specifically, we believe this moon is formed primarily of that planetoid's metallic core."

The group exited the corridor and entered a massive cavern with an underground lake at the far end. The professor led the interns to the shore of the lake, where several tables had been set up, each table holding a set of old-fashioned mechanical scales.

"Here is where today's lesson will take place. I'll have you working on a centuries-old technique for retrieving precious metal from otherwise useless dirt. Specifically... we're going to be sifting for gold." He held up his hands. *"And before you say it, I already know what you're thinking. You came here to learn* new *techniques, not an ancient pre-Exodus approach. But trust me, what you'll learn here—including patience—will apply to the commercial-sized rigs that I'll be introducing you to later."*

The professor pointed to the lake behind him. *"Stations have been set up on the shore for each team. You'll find a shovel, a pan, and a hand pump to move water from the lake across your work. Your instructions are simple. Shovel a scoop of the shore composite into your sifting pan. Ensure that the material is nice and wet. Roughly shake and swirl the pan around to help the gold settle to the bottom of the pan—remember, gold is heavier than just about anything else you'll find in this dirt. Then tip your pan at a very shallow angle and have your partner slowly pour water into it, so the current carries only the top layer of silt and sand away. Then pour again, always moving the pan back and forth in the current to help loosen the next layer and make sure you don't let the good stuff get away from you. Eventually you'll get to the bottom and all you'll see is some very fine black sand. Swirl the water in the pan gently and look for the tiny flakes of gold. Some pans of dirt won't have any at all; that's okay. Patience will be rewarded.*

"You'll want to work with your partner, see who is best at which role. And remember, you're a team.

"Your day will be over once you've gathered two grams of gold dust. That may not seem like a lot, but unless you luck into a nugget, which you won't, you'll have to compile those two grams from tiny flakes, so it's going to take time. Now get to work, and good luck."

As Mike and Priya walked to the nearest station, Mike groused. "This is nonsense. We're gathering gold by hand? How does this teach us anything useful at all?"

But Priya was surprised to find herself thrilled at the opportunity. She'd actually done this before. Back when she was a kid, before her parents moved to the US, she and her father would go out for the weekend, camp, and pan for gold on the River Swale and then in the Northern Pennines near Nenthead Village. One time she found a seven-gram nugget, which she still had back in her apartment, hidden in a sock drawer.

"He's just trying to teach us the principles behind larger-scale operations," she said. "It's just a starting point." She gestured toward the objects at their station. "So, do you want to handle the water or the pan?"

Mike let out a dramatic sigh. "I'll man the pan." He grabbed the shovel, dug out some surface gravel and dirt, and dumped it on the pan.

"It's more likely that we'll find stuff just below the surface rather than directly on it," Priya suggested.

Mike waved dismissively. "I got this."

Priya knelt next to the water pump. It had a corkscrew shape, a design first invented in ancient Egypt. As she cranked it, the water slowly crawled up the pipe and then gushed forth. Mike shifted the pan left and right in the resulting stream.

Unfortunately, he sloshed the dirt far too forcefully and hastily. He wasn't being patient and careful. If there were any gold flakes in this dirt, it was getting washed away along with everything else.

"You need to swirl the water less forcefully—"

"I got this," he said again, annoyed.

After a few minutes, another team cheered. Evidently they'd gotten something. This only pissed off Mike, and his panning method became even more rushed and sloppy.

They went through two pans like this, finding nothing of

course, when Priya opened her mouth to make another suggestion. But Mike cut her off.

"You think you can do better?" he snapped. "Fine, let's switch."

Without a word, Priya grabbed the shovel and dug through about a foot of the surface soil. When she got to the thicker sludge that lay below, she put a shovelful in the pan. "See how the deeper dirt has less pebbles and much more dirt, along with a bit of clay?"

Mike's face darkened, and he immediately turned the crank on the pump at breakneck speed, sending water splashing everywhere.

Priya hopped away from the splash zone. "Bloody hell! You're going to drown us. Slow it down."

Mike looked ready to snap at her yet again, but instead he slowed to a more reasonable pace.

Priya swirled the water slowly, and the dirt slowly sloughed away. "Can you slow it even more, just to a trickle?"

Mike did as he was told, and Priya continued moving the pan back and forth, loosening the dirt and then slowly swirling the mess until she needed more water. "You see, sometimes the gold flakes will settle where the soil transitions to clay. That's why I suggested we look deeper than just the surface."

It took a couple of minutes, but it worked.

"There! I see a flake!" she said.

Mike leaned forward to see, inadvertently sending a surge of water into the pan, blasting the flake onto the ground, along with almost everything else in the pan.

"You bloody idiot!" Priya yelled.

The professor's voice came over the speaker system. *"Is there a problem?"*

Priya looked toward the professor and shook her head. Then she took a deep breath and let it out slowly.

Mike at least had the sense to look sheepish. "I'm sorry about that. I guess I just got excited."

"It's fine." It wasn't, of course, but she was stuck with this idiot until they were done, so she had to get along with him.

She grabbed the shovel and started a new pan. This was going to be a long day.

~

Governor Welch laughed as she watched Priya yell at the hapless intern she'd been paired with. She turned away from the projected image and looked back at Terry and the assembled security team. "So that's her?"

Terry nodded. "Surveillance footage from thirty minutes ago. It doesn't seem like she's good working in a team."

"I wouldn't say that. At least not yet." She chuckled and shook her head. If she were in Priya's shoes, she'd probably have decked that partner of hers for being a moron. "Did you get anything else when you dug into the records of this would-be miner?"

"Oh yeah. The UNIB guys did a number on her record. The official report shows her as a diligent mining student, but we have a snapshot of the last semester. She wasn't on any mining college's roster just six months ago. Her history is totally manufactured."

Welch nodded and clacked her fingernails on the lacquered conference room table. "Her parents were astrophysicists?"

"Yup." Terry pushed a paper toward her. "It's all in her record. Lived in the UK, then moved to the US."

"How about this: Let's figure out what this girl is really made of. Pull her from the intern rotation tomorrow. I've got a little test for our mining girl. I'll call Director Timpf and arrange for a class that Miss Radcliffe may be suited to work with."

Terry frowned. "She's going to ask questions—"

"Good, let her. Tell her that the professor questioned her temperament, and she'll need to work with our Director of Education to address her shortcomings. Prove that she's capable of getting along with others."

Terry nodded. She could tell he didn't agree with her decision, but he would commit to it. He was a good soldier, a great head of security, and she was proud to call him her son.

~

"What do you mean I'm not going to the mine?" Priya asked.

"I don't know the details," Terry said with a shrug. He drove past the turnoff to the mine and continued down the road. "Evidently there was some trouble yesterday in your class? And Director Timpf—she heads our Department of Education here on the colony—she wants to meet with you."

Priya's mind replayed the previous day. She and Mike had been the second-to-last to leave that stinking mine, but they had done what they'd been asked to do: they'd found 2.1 grams of gold. And frankly she should get a medal for not killing Mike along the way.

Could that be the "trouble" Terry referred to? Her interactions with Mike? And how much trouble was she in? Was she going to get kicked out of the program? She was here to save lives. She couldn't afford to jeopardize all that just because of some idiot intern that got on her nerves.

Ranger stuck his head between the seats, whined, and gave her left elbow a lick.

"It's okay, big boy." Terry gave the big dog a scratch under his chin. "We're almost there."

It's not *okay*, Priya thought. She concentrated on controlling her breathing. She'd do whatever it took to stay in the program. She had to.

"I have to what?" Priya asked, her eyes growing wide. "I'm not qualified!"

Director Timpf's eyes bored into her. "Which is exactly why we're asking you to do this. It's clear that you need to work on your interpersonal skills. Acting as a substitute teacher for this class will give you the opportunity to do that. To work on your patience."

Priya shrank under the director's withering stare. "Okay… If that's what it takes, I'll do it."

"Good. Follow me."

The petite blonde woman led her out of her office and through the corridors of the building. The place felt deserted—it smelled of antiseptic and old paper—and was eerily silent. There was no noise other than the clicking of Director Timpf's heels on the tile floor and the swish of the automatic doors.

But then they entered a new area that felt more vibrant, more like a university campus. In a long hallway lined with doors, the walls were covered with astronomy charts, math proofs, and other various graphs.

The director opened one of the doors, motioned for Priya to enter, and walked in right after her.

Priya found herself standing in front of approximately twenty kids who were all about ten years old. *I'm not ready for this.*

"Class," said the director, "this is Miss Radcliffe. She'll be taking over for Miss Henderson today." She patted Priya on the shoulder and, with no further instruction, left the room, closing the door behind her.

Priya stared at the class, petrified. Her first instinct was to race out of the classroom and tell the entire colony to sod off.

"Hello, Miss Radcliffe!" said everyone in unison.

Priya took a deep breath and pasted on a smile. "Hi, class." She scanned the room, trying to figure out what lessons they were teaching in here, but there was nothing on the walls, and the whiteboard behind her was entirely blank.

"Can you guys help me out?" she asked. "What subject was Miss Henderson teaching?"

To her surprise, every single kid raised their hand. Priya pointed at a boy in the front row.

The boy stood. "Miss Henderson was covering the history of aviation."

Priya breathed a sigh of relief. At least she had a passing

familiarity with the subject. "And where did she leave off? Are you guys using a textbook, or is there a syllabus?"

The kids all raised their hands again—enthusiastically. *Was I ever this excited to answer a teacher's question?*

She pointed at a red-haired girl in the corner. Like the boy, the girl stood before answering.

"Miss Henderson said she was going to cover supersonic travel next. And Miss Henderson didn't use the textbook. She said it was full of Earth lies."

Priya pressed her lips together to avoid laughing. "Okay. Great."

She turned to the whiteboard, picked up an old-fashioned dry-erase marker, and wrote down the equation for determining the speed of sound. "Can anyone tell me what this equation does?"

She pointed at a boy in the back, who stood. "That's the square root of the gas constant, multiplied by the absolute temperature and specific heat of the gas. It's how you figure out the speed of sound."

"Very good." These kids were smart. Really smart.

Priya motioned for the same boy to stand back up. "Is there anything else you can tell me about the factors involved in the equation?"

"Well, I think the equation means you can estimate what the speed of sound would be depending on the type of gas and the temperature of the gas. My daddy also said that because our atmosphere is made of diatomic nitrogen and oxygen, and the temperature depends on the altitude, to do a proper estimate requires a math model that he said is kind of complex."

Priya nodded. "Your daddy was right. The modeling is a bit much even for older kids—but maybe we'll get to it later."

The student smiled from ear to ear.

"Okay, so it seems like you guys have a good grasp of the basics. Let's see where Miss Henderson left off. Did she tell you about General Chuck Yeager?"

The entire class raised their hands, and with a laugh, Priya motioned for them to put their hands down. "Good, then I won't cover that. After his rocket plane broke the sound barrier in 1947, subsequent engines were developed to push airplanes faster and faster. But it turns out that air-breathing jet engines have a maximum limit of right around Mach 3.5, or about three-and-a-half times the speed of sound. That's about one kilometer per second. There's a reason for that."

She drew an outline of a jet engine on the whiteboard. "A jet engine is composed of four sections. There's the intake, a compressor, a combustion chamber, and a turbine. The turbine is connected to the compressor via a central rotor. With the intake, the air flows into the engine through a giant high-speed fan. That fan, or set of fans, is where the air is compressed and ultimately slowed to subsonic speeds, which increases the pressure, thus raising the temperature of the air. This leads into the combustion chamber where the air and fuel are mixed. The air-fuel mixture is then ignited, causing a rapid expansion, further increasing the pressure, driving the turbines and helping to propel the exhaust out through the back end of the engine. The higher the speed, the higher the pressures and temperatures. But…"

She paced along the front of the room. "Think about the problems that could occur when you build up higher pressure and higher temperatures. No need to raise hands or stand up, just go ahead and say what problems would occur if you try to go too fast."

"The engine blows up?" one student suggested.

"It gets too hot?" said another.

Several other students gave guesses, some of them quite creative. These kids were good thinkers.

"You guys are all mostly right. It comes down to how hot things get due to the friction of the air and the stresses on the blades within the engine."

A girl at the front blurted out, "Miss Radcliffe, if you're going high speed already, do you even need a compressor or a turbine? I mean, you said they're connected, right? And if you didn't need them, then couldn't you go faster just with the other parts of the engine?"

"Exactly right." Priya smiled. "What's your name?"

"Ayanna. Ayanna Stewart."

"Well, Miss Stewart, you kind of guessed where I was going next. Ramjets. They were designed just like you suggested."

Priya drew a modified version of the engine. "In this engine, there's no turbine or compressor. Instead we have an inlet, combustion chamber, and a nozzle to exhaust the fuel. This can take us up to Mach 6 or so… but then we again run into issues with the pressures and temperatures. Which leads us to another concept: the scramjet. This is a modification to the ramjet, but it doesn't require slowing the airflow to a subsonic speed.

"Ultimately, the problem is friction. Even without moving parts, these engines are flowing through the atmosphere, so friction is inevitable—and each engine is limited by the properties of the materials it's made from. If you guys are up for it, we can talk about some mathematical models for calorically imperfect gases."

Another student raised his hand and hopped out of his seat as soon as she nodded to him. "Miss Henderson said you might be related to Burt Radcliffe, one of the colony saviors. Are you? And if so, can you tell us about the Alcubierre engine? Is it really the fastest engine ever made?"

Priya hesitated. Their teacher had clearly gotten some notice about her coming. Was this whole thing some kind of setup because of her last name?

But as she looked at the kids, she was reminded of what she'd been like at their age. She'd had a voracious appetite for knowledge, and would have given anything to learn from someone "famous." To these kids, the name Radcliffe made her famous. It probably meant more to them than it did to her. In fact, it was a name she'd never be able to live up to.

"Yes," she said. "My many-times-over great-grandfather was Burt Radcliffe."

"And he was married to Neeta Patel!" said Ayanna. "She was a savior too!"

Priya smiled. "Yes, Neeta was one of my great-grandmothers." She pulled up a chair and took a seat in front of the class. "Come," she said. "Move your desks into a semicircle and I'll tell you all about it."

As far as she knew none of her ancestors had anything to do with creating the fastest engine ever made—that was David Holmes—but she could still tell them the history as she knew it.

And she wanted to. These kids' enthusiasm touched something inside her.

As soon as they'd settled, Priya began. "I'm going to tell you guys a story about a threat that was approaching Earth—and how that threat not only became what ended up saving us all, it resulted in the creation of the fastest engine we've ever known. It all started when scientists detected a miniature black hole approaching Earth..."

CHAPTER NINE

Governor Welch couldn’t resist smiling as she leaned back in her leather chair and watched the video stream of Priya Radcliffe, of all people, laughing with a bunch of fifth-graders as she told stories that must have been passed down in her family for generations.

She looked across the conference table to Nwaynna, who also had a smile on her face. “Nwaynna, what do you think of our mining intern?”

“May I speak candidly?”

“Of course.”

“She’s no mining intern.” said Nwaynna. “I call BS on that. She maybe has a mining background, I can’t say one way or another, but she’s wicked smart. She has at least graduate-level education in the sciences. I mean, she just walked a bunch of ten-year-olds through a proof that would challenge most graduate students. And her explanation of the Alcubierre/Holmes engine is probably the best I've ever heard." She shook her head. "I don't know who she's trying to fool, but she's got a solid physics background."

The governor turned to a gray-haired man she'd known for years. "Evan, you're a forensic psychiatrist. What's your assessment?"

Evan frowned. "She's interesting. Today's footage is a stark difference from the video of her work yesterday at the mine. Today, she seems quite personable. It's quite obvious she's enjoying her time with those kids, and they're enjoying her, even though some of what she's talking about is well beyond them. She's managed to engage with her audience, even though she's not particularly aware of them in the same way I think you or I would be."

"What do you mean?"

"Well, this is only a guess, but I think that she came into that classroom expecting things to be a disaster, and because things are going relatively well, the kids are checking off all her boxes for satisfaction. She didn't have high expectations of them, and they're very bright. So of course she's pleased. By contrast, had they been older, or like her co-worker in the mine, I suspect she'd have had higher expectations, and then things might have gone very differently today. More like they did yesterday. We saw how impatient this young lady can be with those who don't meet her expectations."

The governor laughed aloud, causing looks of surprise on the faces of her science advisers. She turned back to the image of Priya, who was still captivating the class. "I swear to God, my friend, you've been reborn," she muttered.

"Pardon?" Evan leaned closer.

The governor waved dismissively and tapped on the phone icon embedded into the lacquered table.

"Operator 63, how may I help you, Madam Governor?"

"Get me Kat Timpf."

"Connecting to Director Timpf..."

After a few moments of silence, a woman's voice came through the speakers in the ceiling. *"Governor? What can I do for you?"*

"Hi, Kat. I'm assuming you've been watching the class?"

"I have."

"What do you think? Is there a place we'd be able to use her in one of our facilities?"

"As a teacher? A researcher?"

"Sure, or whatever makes sense."

"Well, probably. But is that what she'd *want?"*

The governor glanced at Evan, who shrugged. "Well, I can't imagine she wants to be a miner. Not that there's anything wrong with that, but she can be so much more. Why don't you give her the choice—see what happens."

"Okay. I'll let you know what she says. But if she chooses to stay with the mining interns, should I—"

"Go ahead and let her. I just would like more for her. Maybe find a place for her here on the colony."

"Understood, I'll see what she has to say."

As Kat clicked off, a flashing light indicated an incoming call, and the governor switched lines.

"Terry, what's up?"

"We've found the miner who went missing from Dorm Block

C just after we intercepted that signal from Earth. He was caught lurking outside the third level of mine shaft number one—right outside the section where the interns were being introduced to some mining equipment. I'm heading over to the holding cell to have a talk with him."

The governor frowned. "Use whatever you need to learn the truth. It's preapproved."

"Got it. I'll figure out what's going on."

"Thanks. Before you go, hold on a second." She put the call on hold and turned to the psychologist. "Evan, you remember what I asked you to do back when we got that spy a few years back?"

The old man's eyes narrowed, but he nodded.

"Are you still up for an extraction?" The governor hitched her thumb toward the image of Priya. "Her safety may be at stake."

Evan stood. "I'll do it."

She took the call off hold. "Terry, I'm sending Evan to help."

There was silence on the line for a full five seconds before Terry said, *"Understood."*

Terry had to wait almost thirty minutes for Doctor Evan Pritchard to set things up. Evan was one of the few people who spooked the hell out of him. It was almost like the man could read minds, and with his medical background, the things he could do to people during an interrogation were the stuff of nightmares.

The miner was a big man, around six and a half feet, two hundred fifty pounds, mostly muscle. He was strapped to a gurney and hooked up to an IV, heart monitor, pulse oximeter, and more. Most notable was the metal band around the miner's head—some kind of magnetic resonance device that Evan had adapted for his own use.

"Are we ready?" Terry asked.

Evan was studying a monitor that displayed a series of squiggly lines. "He's under mild sedation. We'll still need to establish a baseline for him."

The straps didn't look particularly sturdy. "If this guy gets pissed, he looks pretty capable of tearing out all your fine wiring."

"I have that covered." The psychiatrist cleaned the injection port on the IV with an alcohol swab and plunged a syringe into it. "Sometimes the simple stuff is the best answer. That's Quelicin—some potent stuff. It'll completely immobilize him without knocking him out. It'll only be about a minute before it takes effect. I'll attach an infusion pump to the IV so that he gets a constant four milligrams per minute throughout the discussion. You tell me when you want him wiggling again, and I'll make it happen."

"I'm ready when he is," Terry said.

The doctor attached a few more wires to the miner's chest with some adhesive, then rolled his stool back to the monitor. He punched a button, and a bunch of wavy lines projected above the miner where Terry could see them.

"I've got the EEG running for the baseline. Go ahead and wake him up."

They both knew that an Earth spy would be trained to resist any manual extraction methods—and would as soon die before telling him anything. But by monitoring the man's brain waves directly, they'd bypass the guy's training.

Terry grabbed a capsule and broke it under the miner's nose. The smell of ammonia permeated the air.

"He's conscious," announced the doctor.

The miner hadn't moved even an eyelash.

Terry leaned in close. "Mr. Gutfeld, my name is Terry Chapper, head of Chrysalis domestic security, and you're perfectly safe. You're being held in a state of immobility, but don't worry about that, it's temporary. We have a few questions for you, and if you cooperate, this will go a lot easier."

Terry held up one finger, which was the agreed-upon sign for when he was about to say something truthful. Just as with a standard lie detector test, they would need a few control questions to calibrate the responses. "Mr. George Gutfeld, you were born on the Chrysalis colony nearly fifty years ago."

Evan tapped something on the screen and nodded.

Terry held up two fingers. A lie was coming. "Greg, your mother's name is Georgina."

He continued with control questions for the next couple minutes, until Evan gave him a thumbs-up, indicating they were ready to start with the real questions.

"George, I'm going to ask you a series of questions. I want you to think about the answers. Our equipment will pick up your conscious thoughts and translate them for us. We'll take it from there. Are you ready?"

"I'm afraid." A synthesized male voice spoke in his ear. A

transmission from the doctor's gadgets that translated the man's thoughts to a voice.

"There's nothing to be afraid of. Okay, first question. Have you been communicating with people on Earth via non-authorized channels?"

"No."

The doctor gave a thumbs-down. A lie.

"Listen to me, Mr. Gutfeld. That was a lie. This will go on a lot longer and make things much worse for you if you lie to me. How about we start with something simpler. You weren't assigned to mine shaft one—so why were you lurking outside the ore processing station on level three?"

There was a pause, and Terry watched the projected squiggles scrolling by. *"I heard about a Radcliffe coming in as an intern. I wanted to see for myself."*

"Why?"

"Because she's a Radcliffe. A descendant of one of the saviors."

Terry frowned. This guy knew that the Radcliffe was a she. "Is that the only reason?"

"I also wanted to make sure she was safe."

"Any other reasons?"

"No."

The doctor gave a thumbs-up. The miner was telling the truth.

"Roughly three weeks ago, you left the dorms in the middle of the night and didn't come back. Why?"

"I'd been warned before that..."

"Warned about what?"

"We're loyal to the colony and hate what's happened to Earth."

Thumbs-up from the doctor.

"Why'd you leave the dorms in the middle of the night?"

"It's the protocol. We know about what Dr. Holmes discovered on planet Epsilon. If an ally reaches out to one of us, we need to move. We sacrifice for the good of the Rebels, and for the colony."

Thumbs-up.

"Did you mean to harm Radcliffe?"

"No. She's in danger. I'm supposed to protect her."

Thumbs-up.

Terry's blood turned to ice. "Protect her from what?"

"I don't know."

Thumbs-up.

"You don't know." Terry ground his teeth. "What was the message you received from Earth?"

There were no changes in the brain pattern for a full five seconds. *"I don't remember."*

The doctor flashed a thumbs-up and began typing something, the words appeared under the projected squiggles. *Ask him to think about the night he received the call.*

Terry came very close to the man's head and whispered, "I believe you. Now think really hard. Think about the night you received the call. Just keep trying to remember."

Lights on the metal band around the miner's head flashed, and an image popped up next to the brain-wave monitor. It was grainy and dark. A memory yanked from the miner's head and visualized for them via holographic projector.

Something buzzed, and lights flickered on in the miner's memory. He was in a dorm room, scrambling to the desk drawer and pulling out a vibrating metal object. As the miner touched it, it transformed into a communicator.

Terry stared wide-eyed. How had this guy gotten ahold of alien tech?

From the holographic memory, Terry heard the communicator's message.

"I'm sending an image of a new intern. She's a Radcliffe. She'll be leaving here in a few days. You know what to do."

Terry frowned.

The communicator displayed a scanned image of Priya's student ID. But it wasn't from a mining school. The ID indicated she was a student at the David Holmes Education Campus at Cape Canaveral.

Even Terry had heard of the David Holmes Campus. Only the best of the best attended.

And they definitely didn't teach mining tech.

~

The interns had only one free day a week, and today was it. It was beautiful and sunny, and they all took advantage in their own ways. Some slept in, some played cards or videogames in the rec rooms, still others played basketball on the courts below.

Priya sat in the dorm's third-floor rec room, gazing out the window and thinking about everything that had happened so far in her short stay at the colony. Only a few days ago she'd feared she would be kicked out of the intern program and be forced to leave the colony altogether—and then, out of nowhere, the head of the colony education system asked whether she'd be interested in staying on at the colony *permanently*. Director Timpf said they could find a position for her that she would like better than being a mining intern.

It was a dream offer—and one she suspected she was receiving solely because of her famous last name—but it was one she couldn't accept.

After all, she'd already accepted a dream offer with the military back on Earth. She wanted to be a part of the space program, and the colony couldn't help with that. And then there was the looming threat of terrorists at the colony. She'd promised to provide intel from the mines, and she wouldn't be able to do that if she took a position outside the intern program.

In the end, she had no choice but to stick with the internship. Doing so had left her feeling both ungrateful and frustrated.

Because there wasn't a cloud in the sky, she could see clear to the horizon—which was closer here than it was on Earth. In the distance, beyond the parking lot, she spied a body of water. A lake?

She walked out of the rec room, went downstairs, and headed for the front exit.

"Hold up, Miss Radcliffe." It was one of the colony security officers. "Where are you going?"

Priya pointed north. "I saw a lake not too far off. I thought I'd take a look. Am I not allowed?"

"Oh, you can go anywhere you please. But I've got an order to ensure you've got an escort."

"Why?"

The officer shrugged. "Truthfully, I'm not sure. I just do what I'm told. But don't worry, I'll make it quick." He pulled out a communicator, cupped his hand over the receiver, nodded a few times, then turned back to her. "Someone will be here in three minutes to take you wherever you want."

"Thanks."

Priya felt a little guilty that the colony was making such a fuss over her. They weren't doing this for the other interns. Were they really concerned for her safety, as Terry had said, or were they were escorting her around for some other purpose?

A car stopped right in front of the entrance to the dorms, and she was surprised to see Tom hop out and hurry inside.

"Tom! I'm sorry if you got called away in the middle of something."

"Don't even think twice about it." Tom smiled and motioned toward the exit. "Shall we?"

Moments later, they were pulling out of the parking lot.

"Where do you want to go, Miss Radcliffe?"

"I saw a lake to the north. Can we go there?"

"Sure, that's Lake Hager. Anything in particular you wanted to do there?"

Priya shrugged. "To tell you the truth, I just wanted to see something other than the dorm and the other interns. I guess I'm not exactly a social butterfly."

Tom accelerated down the road. "You seem personable enough to me."

"Sometimes. But I can also be a real bitch." Tom opened his mouth to say something, but Priya cut him off. "No arguing about it. It's just who I am. Some people just really get on my nerves."

The security officer chuckled. "You make it sound like you're mean on purpose. I don't see that."

She smiled and shook her head. "Trust me, I have my moments."

In minutes they were pulling into a small parking lot about fifty yards from the lake. "Well, here we are," Tom said.

"It's pretty." Priya looked around. "What do most people do here?"

"A few brave souls attempt to go swimming, but I wouldn't advise it. The water's pretty chilly." Tom pointed at a spot near the shore. "See that ramp? That's a boat ramp. Some people go fishing."

"Fishing? As in… you can go catch fish in the water and eat it?"

Tom laughed. "Of course."

"How long does it take to get a pass to do that?"

"A pass?" Tom looked at her as if she'd grown a second head. "A pass for what? To fish?"

"To fish, to swim, whatever."

"No passes required here," he said with a smile. "This isn't Earth. You can come here whenever you want, and do pretty much whatever you want. You don't need permission. There's no interprecinct commission to control who goes from one colony precinct to another. We live pretty freely out here."

The idea felt bizarre to Priya. People could literally come and go as they pleased? Drive wherever they wanted to? That was just… weird.

"Well," she said, "*you* guys are free. *I* still need an escort."

"The higher-ups want to make sure you don't run into any trouble. I can tell you don't realize the power of your last name, but trust me, it means a lot to us here."

Priya turned back to the shoreline. "Would it be okay if I go over to the shore and just sit there all by myself?"

Tom looked around. The place was deserted. "Sure. But I'll sit here in the car, just in case."

Priya was surprised that she didn't get any resistance. "Really? You sure it's okay?"

"Of course. I'm not trying to get in your way. I want you to enjoy yourself while you're here."

Priya felt a knot forming in her throat. She put her hand on his, gave it a squeeze, and hopped out of the car.

A gravel path led to the lakeshore, and the rocks crunched under her feet as she walked. The smells here were unlike those of the ocean. There was no salt in the air, but there was something—a marine smell that was oddly comforting. That was good, because being out here in this wide-open space, all alone… was a little unnerving. Surreal.

She glanced back to the car. Tom waved.

At the shore, she knelt and dipped her fingers in the water. It was more than "a little chilly." It was freezing.

She walked over to an oak tree, sat down at its base, and leaned her head back against the trunk. "This place is amazing," she said aloud.

She felt Harold climbing off her head and shoulders, and within seconds he had turned himself into a purring ball of fur.

"Harold, could you have ever imagined a place like this?"

The AI didn't respond. His programming was sophisticated enough to discern a rhetorical question from a real one.

Priya's throat tightened once again, and she felt waves of emotion threatening to burst out of her.

There were no curfews here.

You didn't need permission for off-hour transportation.

No visas to visit relatives in other places.

"Freedom like this is unheard of at home, Harold. Freedom's dying or maybe even dead back on Earth. And people don't even realize it."

Harold shifted and stretched. But he wasn't just stretching—he was changing. His fur retracted back into his body, and he morphed into a rectangular picture frame. A video device.

Priya sat up excitedly, then quickly glanced back at the car. Tom was still there, too far away to see. Relieved, she looked back down at the device that Harold had become.

She wondered what had triggered this. This kind of unrequested change from the AI had only happened a dozen or so times in the past, and it usually foreshadowed some kind of message. Would it be another communication from Neeta and Burt?

It was neither. A dark-skinned man looked up at her from the screen and waved.

"Hi there!"

"Hi." She waved back and giggled as she reminded herself it was just a recording.

"I'm Dave Holmes, and though I don't know you in person, I know who you must be. You're one of the Radcliffe descendants. I was hoping this message would never be needed, but if you're

seeing this... clearly the artificial intelligence has deemed it necessary. For that I am sorry.

"I grew up in a time that I knew as the twenty-first century. You probably know it as the pre-Exodus. It was a time when countries were sometimes at odds with each other, but overall, there was more peace than war. Each country held its own sovereignty, and in most of the world, there was freedom.

"Sadly, things are changing in the post-Exodus. I'm seeing the beginnings of a dangerous trend, especially for future generations. Let me share with you a quote from a US president who governed in the twentieth century. His name was Ronald Reagan. I think even now, especially now, in these times, it holds much wisdom.

"'Freedom is never more than one generation away from extinction. We didn't pass it on to our children in the bloodstream. The only way they can inherit the freedom we have known is if we fight for it, protect it, defend it, and then hand it to them with the well-fought lessons of how they in their lifetime must do the same. And if you and I don't do this, then you and I may well spend our sunset years telling our children and children's children what it once was like... when men were free.'"

The words hit Priya harder than she could have imagined.

Holmes looked sad as he continued. *"The flame of freedom burned brightly in many of my generation, but I've lived long enough to see the brightness of that flame begin to fade. I hope to God that what I'm seeing now doesn't come to pass on Earth. Because if it does, it may be freedom's last gasp, especially if there's nobody left to nurture that flame."*

The image faded to black.

Priya began sobbing uncontrollably. She wrapped her arms around herself and worried about her home. Harold's kitten form returned, and she scooped him into her arms and buried her face into his purring body.

David Holmes was viewed as practically a god, even in this century. There wasn't a person alive that didn't know who he was. And this deity of a man had just laid on her a warning that she knew deep down in her heart was a real concern.

Freedom *was* practically gone on Earth.

And she hadn't even realized it.

Only when given a taste of how life could be different, how life *was* different here on the colony, did it become clear to her just how enslaved to the government she'd become.

And that thought brought to mind why she was at the colony in the first place. To spy on them. To take intel to Earth. To save lives.

But now she felt a creeping doubt.

Was she *actually* saving people's lives? Or was she snuffing out the last flickering flame of freedom?

CHAPTER TEN

The smells in the Central Market—really an open-air plaza of farmers' stalls and merchants hawking various wares—were exotic. Priya detected cinnamon, fenugreek, other Indian spices that reminded her of her mother's dishes, fresh citrus, and grilled meat, the last of which made her mouth water. But as she looked around, she saw that some things she was used to were missing.

She turned to Tom, who walked beside her through the market. "Where do they sell protein charging kits?"

"Protein charging kits?"

"You know, the supply packs that go into the food generators."

"Oh, yeah, I've seen those. You're talking about the devices that create prefabricated meals from vegetable proteins. You'll see someone who owns one here and there, but they never really caught on in the colony. Those things might make food you can survive on, but I don't think I'd enjoy my life all that much having to eat that goop. I tried a Salisbury steak from one of those things once." He grimaced. "Never again."

Priya frowned. "Then I don't understand how you get your meals. Normally I buy packs with the right ingredients and databases built into them to create French, Asian, Indian cuisines. Don't get me wrong, the food I've eaten here is shockingly better than what I'm used to, but what do you do? Does everyone just..."

Tom paused in front of a fragrant shop featuring barrels of colorful powders and dried items. He looked amused as he leaned in and whispered, "Yes, we cook, believe it or not. We take whatever ingredients we want, and we make things according to our own personal taste, or recipe, or both. One of these days I'll have to demonstrate to you that it's actually possible."

Priya felt a bit foolish. Of course it was possible, she just had never imagined it would be so widespread a practice on the colony. "Change of subject. You know Terry Chapper, right?"

Tom laughed. "I should hope so. I'm his brother." He held out a hand. "Tom Chapper. Nice to meet you."

"Seriously?" Priya laughed as she shook hands with him. "How is it I didn't know that? You guys don't look a lot alike, but maybe it's your mannerisms or something that kept reminding me of him."

"It's a well-known fact that older brothers take after their younger and more talented siblings." Tom deadpanned. "Anyway, it isn't a secret. That's part of why Terry and I were assigned tag-team responsibility for your safety."

Priya felt a pang of guilt. These people were doing everything in their power to make her safe and at feel home, and she was lying to them about why she was here. Tom was a genuinely nice person. So was Terry.

And she was a total ass.

Tom pointed at a stall. "Do you like mango?"

"I *love* mango."

"Then come with me. I'll bet you've never had a mango smoothie made with real mango ice cream. *And* you can watch them make it right in front of your eyes. No fancy machinery required."

Tom led her to the stand, ordered, and paid. The man behind the counter prepared two drinks, and within a minute she and Tom were both holding large, frosty cups. They clinked cups of the semi-frozen treat, and Priya took a sip.

It was delicious. Not too sweet, with that tropical mango flavor that put a smile on her face.

"Pretty good, eh?" said Tom.

Priya nodded. She had to suck hard on the straw, as the drink had a thick consistency. In fact it wasn't exactly a drink at all, but nor was it like the ice slushies she'd had at home. Was that the ice cream? Whatever it was, she liked it. A lot.

As they continued to wander, Tom took it upon himself to serve as tour guide, talking about the history of the market, where the products came from, and the different kinds of things you could expect to find, or even special order. They passed the fruit stands and moved into an area with leather goods hanging everywhere. Purses, wallets, belts, clothing. The smell was musky, pleasant, and entirely foreign to Priya. Such things weren't bought or sold at home anymore because of animal cruelty legislation.

She didn't like the idea of animals being killed for their hide, but she couldn't help but eye an attractive backpack. She was tempted to ask how much it cost, and had to force herself to look away.

Priya finished her drink and tossed the empty cup into a garbage can. "Thanks for that. It was really delicious."

"You're welcome," Tom said with a smile. "I thought you'd like it." He'd finished off his drink earlier.

Bells chimed from somewhere nearby.

"What's that?" Priya asked.

"Those are the bells of the Saint Thomas Aquinas Church."

"Can anyone go there?"

"Of course. Follow me." He led her through the stalls, and within a few minutes they were approaching a large brick building with a bell hanging from its steeple. "Are you Catholic?"

"No, I'm not really anything. I was just curious. Does it matter that I'm not Catholic?"

Tom shook his head. "No. In fact, I *am* Catholic and it's been a while since I attended services. Actually now I'm feeling a bit guilty."

They walked up the steps to the doors of the church, and from ahead of them came a voice raised in prayer.

"That's the voice of the Pope transmitted from Earth," Tom said. He stopped and bowed his head.

Just above the lintel, the text of the prayer scrolled past in both Latin and English.

. . .

Oremus.

Let us pray.

Gratiam tuam, quæsumus, Domine, mentibus nostris infunde; ut qui, Angelo nuntiante, Christi Filii tui incarnationem cognovimus, per passionem eius et Crucem ad resurrectionis gloriam perducamur. Per eundem Christum Dominum nostrum.

Pour forth, we beseech You, O Lord, your Grace into our hearts; that as we have known the incarnation of Christ, your Son by the message of an angel, so by His passion and cross we may be brought to the glory of His Resurrection. Through the same Christ, our Lord.

Amen.

Amen.

An elderly nun in a flowing black habit walked out of the church, but stopped when she spotted Tom. "Thomas Chapper! Well, look who comes for a visit right after the Angelus prayer." She walked over, clasped one of his hands in both of hers, and smiled. "It's been too long. Are we going to see you this Sunday?"

Priya smiled as she watched Tom squirm under the woman's steely-eyed gaze.

"Yes, Sister Teresa. I'll come."

"I'm counting on you. And Father Patrick will be delighted to see you." She turned to Priya. "Good evening, child. Are you and Thomas—"

"No!" Priya blurted.

The sister smiled and tilted her head questioningly. "Child, I was simply asking if you and Thomas were friends."

Her cheeks burning, Priya worked hard to seem unaffected. "Oh. Yes, we're friends. I'm visiting from Earth, and I was curious when I heard the bells. We don't have many churches where I live."

"From Earth, really?" The sister shook her head. "It's sad how our ancestral home has fallen so far. Were it not for his holiness, the Holy Land itself, and what the scriptures promise, I'd lose hope that it could ever be redeemed. Il Papa holds out against the evil that remains." She reached out and clasped Priya's hand. "I keep you all in my prayers. I really do. What's your name, so I can pray for you specifically?"

"Priya."

The old woman gingerly cupped Priya's face. "A beautiful name for a beautiful girl." She tilted her back toward the church. "Would you like to come in? I can show you what our church looks like inside. Maybe meet Father Patrick?"

Priya glanced at Tom, who shrugged in response. "I'd love to."

"Wonderful." The nun draped her arm over Priya's shoulders, and all three of them walked inside.

But just as they crossed the threshold, a loud chirping sounded. The nun paused, her eyes widening with concern, and slowly backed them all out of the entrance.

"I'm sorry, my dears, it's our security system. It detected

something."

She pulled from within her habit a small metal rod with a loop at its end, and waved the rod across Tom's chest, arms, legs, and head. Then she did the same to Priya—or started to. The moment the rod passed over Priya's right arm, it began vibrating.

"Oh dear." The nun pressed a button on the device and moved the loop down Priya's arm once more. This time it revealed images within—veins, arteries, and…

"What's that?" Priya asked, panicked.

The loop had revealed a red object, almost like a spider, pulsing within her forearm.

The nun backed away and made the sign of the cross. "Child, I'm so sorry. Revelation 13:16 and 13:17 say, 'It also forced all people, great and small, rich and poor, free and slave, to receive a mark on their right hands or on their foreheads, so that they could not buy or sell unless they had the mark, which is the name of the beast or the number of its name.'"

"What does that mean?" Priya looked from the nun to Tom, her heart racing.

"It's the mark of the Beast," said the nun. "I'm sorry, child. Nobody with such a mark is allowed in God's home."

She turned abruptly, entered the church, and closed the door behind her with an echoing thud.

Priya stared at the closed door, mouth agape.

"I'm sorry," said Tom. "That was harsh."

She felt his arm on her shoulders and pulled away. Sudden fury coursed through her. "What the *hell* is in my arm?" she shouted.

Those UN bastards! They put something in me!

Her head pounded and she struggled to breathe. She felt like a band was tightening around her chest, and though she heard Tom saying something, his voice was distant, weak.

Then the world tilted and she felt Tom's arms catch her as everything went black.

"I don't know. She was upset, and the next thing I know, she's faceplanting right in front of me." Tom's voice.

"Lucky you were there to catch her," replied a woman. Priya didn't recognize that voice.

"Is she okay?" Tom asked, sounding concerned.

"She's fine. Her bloodwork came back normal. She's just a bit dehydrated and her blood pressure is a tad low. I have fluids going into her, and that seems to be doing the trick."

Priya opened her eyes.

Tom was beside her bed, looking concerned and then relieved. "Hey, Sleeping Beauty. You're in the market clinic. You gave me a bit of a scare."

"Sorry about that."

Priya sat up, feeling the tug of an IV attached to her arm. She was in a tiny room, not really a hospital room, furnished with just a bed and a bit of portable equipment. In addition to Tom, a nurse was there, studying a machine that tracked her vitals.

"I think I fainted."

Tom chuckled. "Yeah, I think you did."

At that moment Terry walked in. For some reason he looked

not concerned, but amused. He patted Tom on the shoulder. "I've got this."

Tom shot Priya a smile. "Feel better, Priya."

Before she could even think to thank him, he'd left.

"Nurse," said Terry, "when can she get up?"

The woman smiled. "I don't think we need to keep her. She's got some fluids in her, and her vitals are all back to near normal." She turned to Priya. "How are you feeling?"

"Good, I guess. Just a bit embarrassed and confused."

"Pfah!" the nurse waved her words away. "It's a warm day, these things happen to the best of us. Here, let me unhook you and we'll get you on your way. But be sure you drink plenty of fluids and take it easy. And if you start to feel lightheaded, you come back here, or to another medical center, okay?"

"Okay. I will."

As the nurse unhooked the IV, Terry said, "I heard what happened." He caught Priya's eye. "Why don't we talk more back at my place? I'll make you a homemade meal." He tilted his head slightly toward the nurse, and shook his head.

His message was clear. *Let's not talk about it here.*

Priya nodded. "Okay."

Moments later, Terry had signed her out and they were walking toward his car. Priya opened her mouth to say something, but Terry put his fingers to his lips and shook his head again. He pulled out a handheld PC, wrote something on it, and then showed it to her:

I'm taking you somewhere where we can talk without them listening. Until then, just talk about anything other than what happened today.

Priya glanced back and forth between the message and Terry, whose expression told her nothing. Suddenly she wanted to do nothing *but* talk about what had happened. *They're listening? Who is they? Did Terry know about the implant already? He must have. But then he knows I'm a spy. Or does he?*

She nodded and kept her mouth shut.

They reached Terry's car, and he opened the passenger's side door. Ranger was sitting in Priya's seat, and barked a greeting.

Terry snapped his fingers. "Get in the back, you silly boy."

The large dog clambered into the rear, his tail thumping back and forth, and Priya took his place in the front passenger seat.

Terry drove the car out onto the road. "I hope you like things cooked on the grill, because that's what my wife—Steph—is firing up tonight. I figure it would be good for you to experience how we live in the real world. Outside the dorm."

Priya took in a deep breath and let it out slowly. She was tense as hell and felt the tightened muscles through her neck and shoulders. She leaned against the passenger's side door and studied Terry's profile as he drove. He looked calm, and why wouldn't he be calm? *He* wasn't the one who'd just realized there was some strange spider-like device embedded under his skin. Priya, by contrast, was freaking out inside.

They soon approached a neighborhood—and the homes were unlike anything Priya had ever seen. No, that wasn't right. She'd seen them, but only in old movies, from the twentieth and twenty-first centuries. The buildings weren't even connected to one another, and each home was surrounded by lush greenery—lawns of grass, sculptured bushes, and flower beds.

"How many people live in each of these?"

Terry shrugged. "It depends on the family. It could be one, maybe two, upwards of four or five I suppose, at least in this neighborhood."

"One to five families?"

He laughed. "No, people."

Only five people? For all that space?

Terry pulled into a driveway and turned off the car. He turned to Priya. "Home sweet home. It's cozy, but it's enough room for the wife and me—and our furry friend."

Ranger barked.

Terry opened both passenger doors, and Priya and Ranger got out. "This place is huge," Priya said. It was about the size of four or five apartments back home. And the land the house sat on was even bigger; it could host an entire apartment complex.

Terry smiled. "I keep forgetting you're from Earth. Let me ask you, do you know how many square feet your apartment is?"

Priya walked with him to the front door. "Around four hundred square feet. It's two bedrooms and two baths. Pretty big for just the two of us… or at least that's what I thought."

Terry put his hand on the doorknob, and the door beeped. Terry opened it and motioned for Priya to enter ahead of him. "This place is twenty-two hundred square feet, three bedrooms and two baths. It's nice as colony homes go, certainly not the biggest, but not the smallest either. We have a different sensibility when it comes to living space here in the colony. We like things more spread out."

Priya looked around in amazement. The entryway alone was

almost as big as her entire apartment, and the ceiling went up a whole extra floor—a decadent waste of living space.

A blonde woman walked in from another room. "Hey, honey." She gave Terry a kiss, then turned to Priya with an extended hand. "You must be Priya. I'm Stephanie, Terry's wife. I'm really glad to meet you."

Priya shook the woman's proffered hand. "Thank you for having me."

Terry cleared his throat. "If you don't mind, I'm going to go take a shower before dinner." He smiled boyishly. "You girls okay on your own?"

Steph waved him away. "We're fine, you goof. Go." She turned back to Priya. "Want to help me with dinner?"

"Can I?"

"Of course. I figure you probably haven't had much chance of cooking anything from raw ingredients, so this might be fun for you."

"What are we cooking?"

"Have you ever had a hamburger?"

Priya flashed back to the beef slider at the Bizarre Bazaar, and she let out a moan.

Steph laughed. "That's the same sound Terry makes when he eats them."

She led Priya into a huge kitchen with stone countertops and steel appliances. Everything looked new and beautiful.

"You have a beautiful home," Priya said.

"Thank you." As Steph took a package of meat out of the refrigerator, she pointed at the far end of the counter. "Now, if you can get me some of those onions, I'll show you how to make a proper hamburger."

Priya found the onions right where Steph pointed, nestled in a basket between various jars and containers. But what she wasn't expecting was the handwritten note lying right on top of them.

Priya—

Three steps. Step one, relax, and let's all enjoy our dinner. Step two, we'll go somewhere where we can talk about our secrets. And step three, let's take care of your little problem.

CHAPTER ELEVEN

Priya sat back against her chair, her stomach full, and smiled. "Thank you. Dinner was amazing."

Steph smiled back. "Thank you for helping. It was fun having some company in the kitchen."

As Steph gathered up the plates, Terry pulled out his pocket PC, typed something, then slid it toward Priya. She read the message.

I have a room in the back of the house where it's safe to talk. Until we're in there, just go along with whatever I say. I'll explain when we're in the room.

Priya looked up at Terry and nodded.

When Steph had cleared the table and returned, Terry stood. Ranger yawned loudly and got up from his spot under Terry's chair, apparently recognizing no more treats were going to be snuck to him, and settled down on a doggie bed in the corner.

"Priya," said Terry, "have you ever had a microwave chocolate cake before?"

Priya stood as well. "I don't think so. Is it different from a regular cake?"

"Oh, it's so much better." Terry motioned for Priya and Steph to follow, then continued talking as they walked out of the dining room and down a hall. "Steph, you need to show her your recipe and how easy it is. It might be something she could use when she goes home." Terry stopped in front of a closed door and grabbed the doorknob. A green LED flashed, and he pushed the door open and entered.

"Here," said Steph, gesturing for Priya to enter ahead of her. "I have a few cups already set up. Go ahead and put the first one in, set it for ninety seconds, and hit start."

Priya stepped through the door. It looked like an ordinary office—a desk, two additional chairs—with no windows.

As soon as Steph followed and closed the door behind her, Terry smiled at Priya apologetically. "I'm sorry about the weird act. We can now talk candidly." He motioned for her to take a seat.

Priya sat. "What was with the chocolate cake thing?"

"That was my idea," Steph responded. She was rummaging through a duffel bag in the corner. It was filled with gauze, alcohol wipes, and other medical supplies. "Microwaving a cake is a bit complicated for my meat-headed husband—"

"Hey!" Terry exclaimed with obviously feigned outrage.

She blew him a kiss.

"Let me guess," said Priya. "This office is shielded so no signals can come in or leave?"

Steph nodded. "That's exactly right. A special wire mesh is built into the walls and door, encapsulating this space. No signals can leak out. In effect, we're sitting in a Faraday cage."

"Why would your house have a room set up as a Faraday cage?"

"It's coming in handy now, isn't it?" said Terry with a grin. "And we've done this before."

Priya's heart raced as she thought of the other spies who had been sent to the colony—never to be heard from again.

Steph pointed at Priya's arm. "This isn't the first time we've had someone arrive here with a tracking device. Well, more than a tracking device—a spying device. It'll have a geolocator, I'm sure, but if it's like the others, it's also recording what it observes and chirping it back to a local receiver that relays the signal back to Earth."

"What it observes? You mean audio picked up from beneath the skin?"

"Surprisingly, not only audio. We've intercepted a few chirps and have found that the data packets contain some bits of encrypted and compressed video as well. It's still a mystery how a subcutaneous implant is getting video."

Priya thought back to that afternoon with Agent Ted. Could that memory injection have included some way for their tracking device to interact with her brain signals? Maybe…

"Before we get started," Terry said, "do you have any idea how that got in you?"

Priya quickly manufactured a lie. "It must have been when we got inoculations. I was absent the day the rest of the interns got theirs, so the school had me go to an offsite clinic where they gave me a bunch of shots in my right arm. That's the only time I can think of where they'd have been able to insert that thing." She mentally patted herself on the back for her quick thinking.

Terry nodded, looking satisfied with the response. "Well, you almost certainly got set up by the UNIB."

"UNIB?" Priya asked, feigning ignorance.

"The UN Intelligence Bureau. They've been spying on the colony for decades. There's a lot of mistrust between the colony and Earth."

Steph had pulled out a device that looked similar to the wand-and-loop the nun had used. "Well," she said, "regardless of how it got there, let's see what we can do about it."

She moved the loop down Priya's forearm, and just like the nun's device, it showed a 3D representation of what was under her skin in full-color simulation.

Terry rose from his seat to watch. "There's that ugly little bugger."

And there it was—the spider. Its long tendrils connected to various striations under her skin, and it pulsed with her heartbeat, making it look like it was alive.

Steph frowned. "It's tapped into your median and ulnar nerves. It looks more advanced than the others."

"Does that mean you can't take it out?" Priya asked, worried.

"Oh, I had no intention of taking it out. I'm going to destroy it. Hon, can you…?"

"Of course." Terry rolled his chair beside Priya's and took hold of the wand.

Steph dug through her duffel and pulled out a tool that looked sort of like a hammer. "This is an ultrasound wand—it's used in something we call extracorporeal shockwave lithotripsy. It emits high-frequency sounds that destroy hardened objects—like stones in the kidney or bladder. But it also works for creepy implants, if used properly."

"Will it hurt?"

Steph shook her head. "No. At most you'll feel some heating, which you'll have to tell me about if it happens. What I'll do is tune the device to a frequency that resonates with the implant. Roughly speaking, it amounts to sending in shock waves that weaken the device and break it apart. But if it has a thermal reaction—if you start feeling hot—we'll pause and begin again when it cools down."

"How long will it take?"

"Shouldn't be more than half an hour."

"And once it's broken apart… then what? Does it just gets reabsorbed by my body?"

Steph shook her head. "No. Unfortunately, although it'll be broken, it'll still be there—and it'll probably still possess all the data that it's recorded. The previous implants we studied had a block storage device with heavily encrypted data. Our guess is that it's a backup system—some of the chirps the device sends out might get garbled or missed by the receiver, so the block storage keeps everything. And then when you go back to Earth, those intelligence bureau guys will find an excuse to interview you and download everything off the implant. And that's where the chocolate cake comes in."

Priya frowned, confused. She understood everything up until the chocolate cake part.

Steph laughed at Priya's expression. "When I'm done with

the procedure, it'll look like the implant got fried. And since the last possible thing you'll have recorded, and perhaps already transmitted, was about using the microwave, it creates a plausible explanation for the damage—that the microwave itself somehow caused the damage." She gave Priya a wry grin. "Those UN types think we're all morons here at the colony. They probably think we can't safely modify thermal tuners or microwaves without them emitting all sorts of EM signals."

"But the important question," Terry said, grinning boyishly, "is: do we actually have any chocolate cake?"

Priya laughed, and Steph rolled her eyes.

"I'll see what I can whip up when I'm done here." Steph turned back to Priya. "Are you ready to begin?"

"I'm ready."

"Okay. No sudden movements, please. Here we go…"

~

Priya pressed lightly on her forearm. Though it looked absolutely fine after the procedure, it felt terribly bruised, like it had been hit with a sledgehammer.

As Steph left the room to whip up some chocolate cake—apparently she was serious about that—Ranger appeared in the open doorway, wagging his tail.

"Is he allowed in here?" Priya asked.

"Sure. Come on, boy." Terry snapped his fingers.

Ranger's wagging tail accelerated to a furry blur, and he turned around and walked backwards into the room.

Priya laughed. "Goofy boy! Why'd you walk backward?"

She bent down, and he rushed over to her to get his cheeks and head rubbed.

"You never noticed him doing that before?" Terry asked.

"I think I would remember if I did."

"Yeah, I'm sure you would." Terry chuckled. "When I got this big boy, he was a stray with a smashed in nose. Apparently he ran full-tilt into a glass door that he must not have seen. A friend of the vet told me about him, and I couldn't let him get put down, so I paid to have him all fixed up, and I adopted him. But he doesn't trust doorways very much anymore."

"Oh, you poor baby!" Priya rubbed Ranger some more. "That's the most precious thing I've ever heard."

She looked up to see Terry smiling from ear to ear. "What?"

"You aren't as mean-spirited or standoffish as you want people to think you are."

"Oh, be quiet." Priya felt her cheeks getting warm. In a way, she was glad Terry was happily married—that should help her stop thinking about how good-looking he was. Her feelings could safely remain buried.

"Well," said Terry, leaning back in his chair, "now that we're not being spied on anymore, it's time to talk. I'm going to be perfectly honest with you. In fact, I'm probably going to go totally off the reservation as a member of colony security. This is just me and you, two friends, off the record. Okay?"

Priya nodded. "Of course. I owe you big-time for what you guys did." She rubbed at the hidden bruise on her forearm. "I can't even begin to tell you how pissed and shocked I was when I learned about that implant."

Terry nodded. "I know, Tom told me all about it." He took a

deep breath and let it out slowly. "There are some folks who might be mad at me for bringing this up, but… You probably know that the colony doesn't take immigrants unless they already have a relative who's a citizen of the colony."

Priya shook her head. "I didn't know you took immigrants at all."

"Well, it's rare. Anyway, there are folks within the government, people I can't name, who would be willing to waive that requirement if you were interested in staying here."

"This is about me being a Radcliffe, isn't it?"

Terry shrugged. "Honestly, I don't know. I just know that the offer is there. And as I've never heard of such an exception ever being made before, I'd suggest you take it seriously. No pressure—and you don't need to make a decision now. You have another four months or so with your internship anyway. But I just wanted to let you know. And if you want to talk more about this, I'm here."

Priya frowned. It was a generous offer. Generous to a fault, since they didn't really know much about her, and what they did know was a lie. But she couldn't take that offer. She remembered the general's words about what would happen if her mission didn't succeed: *We'll have very few options other than wiping out the entire colony.* Millions of lives were at stake. These were good people, they didn't deserve to be killed because of some terrorist plot from just a few.

She smiled at Terry. "I'll think about it."

But the truth was, her mind was already made up. She had to see this mission through. And she had no clue what her mission really even was. All she knew was that she was supposed to get to someplace in the mine—and that hidden disc in her dorm room was the key to doing it.

~

"We've got intel coming in from the top commanding general of the UNIB as well as several high-ranking officials at UNSOC. No attack is imminent. But Operation Freedom is ready to be deployed on the first sign of trouble."

It was the weekly meeting of the colony's security council, and as always, Governor Welch had started off with status reports. As she listened to Terry, she felt a wave of relief.

"Speaking of Operation Freedom," said Carl, "is anyone ever going to clue us in on the big picture? I have the working directions with regard to the mining operations, but it would help if I knew what this was actually all about."

Terry opened his mouth to answer, but the governor held up her hand. "Let me respond to that."

She met the eye of every person at the conference table. Like Carl, they'd all been read in on their particular domain's responsibilities in support of Operation Freedom, but none of them knew what the full extent of the operation really was. It was better that way. And despite Carl's grumblings, she wasn't about to show her hand now. Not yet.

"We still have unidentified spies in our midst, and the UN is constantly sending more. In fact, just a week or so ago, Terry's team managed to uncover someone who's been communicating with members of the Earth-based Rebels."

The chief of staff raised his hand. “I thought the Rebels were ostensibly on our side. Aren’t they an alliance of anti-UN types?”

“An alliance?” the governor said. “You might even say, the Rebel Alliance?” She smiled, though she knew nobody in the room would understand the reference. “Yes, Andy, you’re right. But I trust nobody.”

She turned to Terry. “Terry, tell the group about the message we intercepted from these Rebels and received by the man we have now have in custody.”

Terry swiped on his handheld PC, then read aloud. “‘I’m sending an image of a new intern. She’s a Radcliffe. She’ll be leaving here in a few days. You know what to do.’”

The chief of staff grimaced. “*That* sounds ominous.”

“Exactly,” said Welch. “And the man in custody was apprehended just outside the location where Miss Radcliffe was supposed to be. To make matters worse, he’s a citizen of the colony going back to its founding. Like I said, it’s hard to know who to trust.”

She looked around the room once more. “Which is why I hope you’ll all understand why I must keep some information close to the vest. Including the big-picture details of Operation Freedom. But I promise you this: when we activate it, it’ll be like nothing you’ve ever seen before.”

~

Priya, in heavy coveralls, walked with the other interns as a new instructor led them deeper into the mines. This instructor was huge with a capital H. Not tall—he was about five and a half feet tall, roughly her height—but with a chest easily twice the width of anyone else's, and his arms and legs were like tree trunks, everything about him reminded her of a concrete block. The man could probably lift a building off its foundation if he tried.

"Okay, folks, we're at level eight of the mine," he said. He was surprisingly soft-spoken. "Which means we're at the last chapter of your introduction to mining equipment." He patted a contraption that looked like a cross between a spider and an eight-foot crane. "This is Bessie. She's a roof bolter, and you'll get to know her well. High or low gravity, it won't matter. Bessie is for underground mining, and I'm sure you're well aware of the difficulties of underground digs. The last thing a miner wants to encounter is instability in the tunnels."

He looked over the class. "Okay, does anybody want to try and impress me with what you know about what a roof bolter's job entails?"

Several interns raised their hands. The instructor pointed at the nearest one.

"Clearing out loose rock in the ceiling?"

The instructor nodded. "Absolutely. The whole point of a roof bolter is to add stability to our work environment. If you notice some cracked or otherwise unstable rock that can't be secured, it needs to be removed, or eventually it'll end up braining one of you guys."

He pointed at another student who'd raised his hand. The student winced. Apparently his comment had already been taken.

Rolling his eyes, the instructor pointed at a third intern.

"Make sure the equipment is safe and in working order?" the young man said hesitantly.

The instructor shrugged, looking unimpressed. “Sure, but that’s a bit obvious. Anyone who doesn’t do that down here is going to get their ass kicked. Anyone have another key element of the job… a safety item?”

He looked over the interns once more, scanning faces, and stopped at Priya. “You. Young lady, tell these would-be miners what it is they need to be thinking about when in a mine.”

Priya felt the entire class turning to her. “Well, don’t they always have to do gas checks, you know… for methane? To prevent explosions.”

The walking block of a man smiled. His teeth were like perfectly chiseled pieces of marble. “Exactly right. Tell me what you know about gas checks.”

Priya was nervous, because she didn’t know much. It was just something she’d read about way before any of this mining business had even started for her. “Well, isn’t that where the term ‘canary in the coal mine’ originated? The canary would die if there was gas, and people would know to clear out… at least, that’s what I read.”

“Very good. What’s your name, young lady?”

“Priya.”

“Well, Priya, that canary story is true. If you can believe it, before they figured out the whole canary thing, the earliest miners would send some poor sap into a tunnel with a wet cloth draped over him, carrying a lit torch. If there were only minor flare-ups, the cloth would protect the miner and he’d know they’d be able to air the tunnel out and be okay. But if there was a major pocket of methane, you’d light the whole place on fire and you’re almost certainly down one miner. Nowadays, of course, we have electronic gas sensors that do the job of the canary or the poor sap holding the torch."

The instructor walked up to the intern who earlier couldn't come up with a response. He patted him on the shoulder and pointed at Priya. "It'll be someone like that girl that's going to save your life, because she's got a good head on her shoulders."

The intern looked down, embarrassed.

The instructor turned to the rest of the class. "You people might think this mining business is like any other mindless job where you dig ditches or fix a leak in a pipe, but it isn't. You need to *think*. Always. This is a dangerous business, a business where people get killed. Always have your wits about you."

Priya liked this instructor. He was smart, blunt, and didn't mind telling people the way it was. Of course, it helped that he'd complimented her. That was a sure sign of good taste.

The instructor motioned for everyone to approach Bessie. "Okay miners, let's go over every square inch of this bolter."

As Priya moved closer, she noticed a freight elevator on the far wall, and suddenly a new memory arose in her mind. She'd been on that elevator before. Or at least, she had the memory of having done it. She'd taken it down to level ten, the deepest it went, then walked to a door that required a special access key. She reached out—or a man's arm did—a disc in hand, and the door opened.

"Priya?"

Priya was startled back to the here and now. "Yes?"

"Would you like to be the first to take the controls of good ol' Bessie?" He smiled, patting the side of the roof bolter.

"Uh, sure."

Priya wiped the sweat from her brow as she removed the drill bit from the chuck, inserted a bolt, and pulled the lever that made the roof bolter's hydraulics press the bolt deep into the ceiling.

"I think you've got this, young lady." The instructor gave her an approving nod and tossed her a dry cloth. "It's sweaty work, but critical for the operation." He pointed to another intern. "Your turn. Let's see if you can operate Bessie without pissing her off."

As Priya wiped her face with the cloth, the instructor approached and said in a low voice, "There no need for you to watch the rest if you don't want to. You've clearly got the hang of this. You might want to get a good night's rest, because tomorrow the work assignments are going to start."

Priya nodded. "Thank you. I'll stay for a bit."

As the other interns took turns with the equipment, many of them struggling, she did pick up another tip or two—mostly learning what *not* to do when one of them made a mistake. But eventually she grew bored. That's when she spotted Terry passing through with Ranger at his side.

What was Terry doing on level eight? Was there a security issue way down here?

Curious, she slipped away from the class and followed in the direction he had gone. She didn't feel like she was trespassing, or at any risk of being lost—she *knew* this place. She knew that over to her right was the freight elevator to the fifth level, and up ahead, where Terry had gone, were the offices. She could even see in her mind's eye the break room at the back of the offices, complete with refrigerator and soda machine.

But when she arrived at the closed door that led into the office area, she found Terry gone and Ranger waiting. The dog spotted her, wagged his tail, and barked several times.

The door opened. "Ranger!" said Terry, stepping through. "What's gotten into you?" Then he spotted Priya. "Oh! Hey, stranger. Are you done with your class?"

"I was given permission to leave early. So when I saw you walk by…"

"You were wondering what I was doing down here on level eight." He looked amused.

Priya felt her cheeks redden. "I guess I'm nosy like that."

"Well come on in and be nosy then. You like games?"

"Games? What kind of games?"

"You'll see."

He led her through the offices to the break room, which was just as she remembered it. Five miners sitting at the table, where various dice and sheets of paper were scattered.

"Want to join?" Terry said. "We could always use a cleric."

A large-bellied miner with a giant red beard groaned. "Hey! I said I'm healing this time."

Terry rolled his eyes. "Okay… well, we can find another role for Priya."

Priya took a seat. "I'm game to play if you guys are okay with a beginner. What are we playing?"

"Dungeons and Dragons," said several of the miners in unison.

She shook her head. "That doesn't help. How do you play?"

"It's a game from the twentieth," Terry said. He sat down and stood a series of cardboard folders in front of him, partially blocking him from view. "It's an adventure game that's played with our imagination. I'm the dungeon master, so I'll sort of be the referee, and the rest of you are going to be a team of different types of players." He pointed to the other miners one by one. "Fred's a fighter, which is pretty self-explanatory. Walter is insistent on being a cleric, the healer for the group. Tony is a bard, who sings songs—"

"And is basically useless," Walter interjected.

"Oh, stuff it," Tony responded.

"Is there magic in this?" Priya asked.

Terry nodded. "There is! Would you want to be a wizard?"

Priya looked at the others. "Would that fit with the team?"

"Oh, hell ya. We can always use a finger-wiggler," said Walter. The others nodded in agreement.

Priya chuckled as she took in the scene. A group of adults, mostly rough-and-tumble types, gleefully engaging in a game based on made-up fantasy characters. It was awesome.

She grabbed a blank sheet of paper. "How do I start?"

Terry slid three six-sided dice toward her. "You'll need to begin by rolling up your character."

"Intelligence is key for a wizard," Tony said.

"Ya, but she'll want decent constitution otherwise she'll be a glass cannon—"

"And don't forget her race. We need someone with infravision, so maybe an elf…"

As everyone got her up to speed, Priya relaxed and had fun—

and for just a moment, she forgot that she was there on false pretenses.

~

"Aw, crap." Priya had just rolled a one on her twenty-sided die.

Her teammates groaned and looked to Terry—who rolled three eight-sided dice and winced.

"Well, the ever-valiant Brianna the elf wizard just took a critical hit from the cyclops. Twenty-three hit points of damage. Since you only had twenty hit points to start, it looks like Brianna… is dead."

Terry pointed at Walter. "And she's *dead*-dead. You're not yet high enough level to resurrect her, so don't even try."

He turned back to Priya. "Sorry, Priya. If you want to keep playing, the merchant NPC that's accompanying the party is a level six thief. You can take over that character while the party drags your body along. Who knows, later they might find a way to bring Brianna back to life."

She shook her head. "I think this is a good place for me to stop. I've got an early day tomorrow." She glanced at the clock. "Holy crap, it's been four hours. Yeah, I really have to go."

"Did you have fun?" Walter asked.

"I did, but don't you dare let anyone know. It'll ruin my reputation for being a total bitch."

They all laughed.

Terry got up and picked up a receiver hanging from the wall. "Tom, she's going to be heading up. Five minutes? Okay." He turned back to Priya. "He'll meet you at the topside entrance."

"Sounds good. Thanks, Terry. It was fun. I'd never heard of this game, but I like it."

"Well, if you want to play again, this is a regular Friday night thing."

Walter piped up. "I'll see about bringing Brianna back to life. I just have to get enough experience points. She was fun having on the team."

Priya smiled. "Thanks. But you don't have to drag my body around. You can just come back for it." She waved. "It was nice meeting all you guys."

She left the break room and the offices, and as she headed down the tunnel toward the elevator going up, she felt guilt weighing heavily on her. She liked these people. Maybe even more than the folks she knew on Earth. And yet she was lying to them all.

She felt Harold shift from his regular position. She was about to whisper that this wasn't the place, when something smashed into her back, launching her forward.

She landed face-down on the ground. She felt no pain, but she tasted blood.

She tried to get up—only to realize she couldn't move.

Her heart raced. *What happened? Did something fall on me?*

There were footsteps nearby.

Someone yelled.

More footsteps, farther away. Running?

A wet thud.

And then everything went dark.

CHAPTER TWELVE

Moments after Priya left, Terry glanced at the clock and realized that the shift was about to change in the mine. There would be dozens of people moving about and Priya walking the tunnels by herself.

Terry grimaced and hopped up from his chair. "Hey guys, I'll be right back. And you better not look at any of my maps, you damn cheaters."

As he walked out of the office area, Ranger hopped up, barked, and walked at his side. They were fast-walking down the tunnel together when the dog suddenly growled and shot ahead.

"Ranger?"

Terry heard a popping sound just as he turned a corner and saw Ranger sprinting toward a collapsing body. Was that… Priya? A man walked toward her, his arm extended, and Terry was about to shout at him to leave her alone. But he stopped short when he saw what happened next. Or what he *thought* he saw.

Did that really just happen?

The man's body slumped forward as his head rolled several feet away.

Terry raced forward, activating his collar transceiver as he went. "Emergency Alert! This is Chapper two three eight. We have two men down. I repeat, we have two men down. I need medic support, level eight, tunnel three alpha. Over."

"Chapper two three eight, copy. Chapper one niner five responding. I'm bringing the cavalry. Be there in three. Over."

Terry reached the two bodies, the decapitated man now lying on top of the other. To his horror, the person on the bottom was exactly who he'd feared it was.

Priya.

And she wasn't moving.

He yanked the man's body off of her. Ranger growled. "I know, boy. He got what he deserved."

He turned his attention to Priya. "Priya?"

No response.

He felt for a pulse. It was there, erratic and weak, but it was there.

There was also a wet spot on her coveralls, right in the middle of her back. Blood? Or worse?

He gritted his teeth as he dug the emergency kit from his utility belt. "Shit, guys, hurry the hell up."

"We're in the freight elevator. Be there in twenty seconds."

He ripped open her coveralls. There was a puncture along her spine, and it was weeping clear fluid.

The spinal column had been ruptured.

With his teeth, he ripped open an emergency packet and dribbled its contents into the wound.

Tom finally came running down the tunnel, accompanied by two medics. "Terry? What happened?"

"She's got a spinal injury with loss of cerebrospinal fluid. I've applied a packet of nanites to the wound."

One of the medics wrapped an instrument around Priya's wrist, looked at the reading, then looked at his partner. "John, set up a gurney. Tom, can you help me get her immobilized and ready for transport?"

"Sure," said Tom. He glanced at the decapitated body and looked at Terry questioningly.

"I'll take care of this guy," said Terry. "You focus on Priya. I need to go look at the security tape. But..." He leaned in and whispered. "Be careful. The thing that chopped this bastard's head off... it wasn't Priya. Just... be careful."

Tom looked at him strangely, but didn't ask questions. "Don't worry, Terry. We'll have her heading to Saint Anthony's in a few minutes. You want me to call Steph and have her meet us there?"

"When you get a chance, that would be great. And I'll meet you there too."

"Really, Terry. It's going to be okay."

"I know."

But as Terry jogged toward the security elevator with Ranger on his heels, he wasn't sure that was true. If the security footage showed what he thought it would, this was something that everyone with Deadman's clearance needed to know about.

The colony's security was on high alert, especially around Priya Radcliffe. Tom was in her hospital room with her, while Terry stood just outside. The entire hospital was on lockdown.

Terry heard a ding from the elevator, and looked down the hall to see the governor's security detail step out, all of them wearing sidearms. The governor followed, and walked briskly over to Terry.

"Are you okay?" she asked.

"I'm fine. But we've got a Deadman clearance situation."

The governor motioned to her security. "Guys, give us some space."

The security detail backed away.

"Tell me," she whispered.

"Let me show you." Terry pulled out his PC, and his mother draped her arm over him so they could both look at the tiny display. With a swipe of his finger he found the surveillance footage and hit play. The video began with the man's attack on Priya.

Terry spoke softly. "We found a CO2-powered weapon that discharged a steel projectile into Radcliffe's back, shattering her spine."

The governor frowned. "Gas-charged to avoid a loud noise."

The video continued, showing the attacker leaning over his victim and bringing his weapon to bear for a second shot. But before he could act, something burst forth from Priya's collapsed form, and the man fell… in two pieces.

The governor leaned back. "What the hell was that?"

"We don't know. When she arrived at the colony, we detected a signature that read alien tech. We figured it was probably an heirloom she'd inherited from her family, likely from the time of the Exodus. But I'm not aware of any alien weaponry among the tech we've discovered."

"I'm not aware of any either. And from what we've gathered, they were a peaceful species." The governor shook her head. "Do you have a slow-mo of that sequence?"

"Unfortunately, the mine's security cameras are at sixty frames per second, and most of this happened within the span of a single frame. But we do know that whatever shot forth from the girl, it sliced her attacker cleanly between the C4 and C5 vertebrae."

"Was there any residue on the attacker? Any hint of a projectile from the tech?"

"Nothing. The best we can figure is that the blur was some whip-like slash that did its job and got reabsorbed in the blink of an eye."

"Who else knows about this?"

"I told Steph, of course. Tom and the two medics saw the body, but I've sworn them to secrecy. Tom has a lot of questions; I merely told him Radcliffe has some kind of protective device. I think he suspects more."

A slight commotion erupted at the end of the hallway. Steph had arrived, initiating a "discussion" with the security detail about whether she was allowed through. Apparently that was a discussion Steph won, because she soon walked over, wearing scrubs and looking particularly radiant.

"Stephanie, it's good to see you," said Governor Welch. "Is it okay for me to go into the girl's room and take a look?"

Steph nodded. "Sure. But I'm just about to give her another exam, so—"

"I won't get in your way."

"I'll wait out here," said Terry. "The room is small enough as it is."

"Good thinking." She leaned down and gave him a quick peck on the lips. "Tom's already in there, and I'd prefer to have only one meathead in there at a time."

~

Priya's world was dark and cold. She was lying on her stomach, and someone had put warming blankets across her back and shoulders, but it did little good. She also felt someone holding her left hand. But that was it. Beyond that, she felt nothing.

She heard a beep, and sensed people moving somewhere around her.

"My God. If I didn't know better, I'd swear that was Neeta Patel in the flesh." A woman's voice. One Priya didn't recognize.

"Well, they *are* related." That was either Terry or Tom. Priya thought about it, and decided it was Tom. He sounded worried, just as he had at the church.

The woman spoke again. "What's her condition?"

A new voice. Steph. "She's stable, but it's a miracle she's alive. If Terry hadn't applied the nanites to the wound when he did, and Tom hadn't gotten her here in record time, I don't think she'd have made it. But even so, I can't explain how she's healed as quickly as she has."

"You mean she's getting better?" Tom asked. "How can you tell?"

Steph let out an exasperated breath. "You meatheads have to meathead, don't you? I know because I've done nerve conduction tests on her extremities. When she got here, there was no signal propagation from her core to her hands or her feet. Now, her core is talking to the rest of her upper body—though the legs are still nonresponsive. Also, by the look of her EEG, she seems to be semi-conscious. I'm still not sure if she's better off sedated or not, but it wouldn't surprise me if she wakes up soon."

"Oh, thank God," said Tom. "You'll be back to giving us all that deadly glare of yours soon enough."

Priya felt someone move the blankets off of her. The fabric moved down her back, but the sensation stopped at her waist. Then fingers gently touched the middle of her back—the place she'd been hit.

"What happened to the wound?" Tom said. "It doesn't even look bruised."

"The nanites?" Tom's mother asked.

"No. They're working on the nerve damage and repairing the membrane that helps keep the cerebrospinal fluid in place. This rapid healing… like I said, I don't understand it."

"Um, Steph?" said Tom. "Maybe you should avoid touching that area. I mean, the guy who attacked her got his head lopped off by something Priya's got on her. I don't want something to happen to you by accident."

Priya felt Harold's taps on her right shoulder. *"Don't worry. These people have evidenced no harmful intent. We're repairing your damage. You're safe."*

Priya's mind raced as the pieces fell into place. It wasn't a falling rock that had slammed into her. She'd been attacked!

And Harold had defended her.

And now Harold was probably covering her wound. Maybe even helping with the healing.

Feeling was coming back to her, and noises were becoming more pronounced. She felt the weave of the cloth under her right hand, and the warmth of Tom's hand in her left.

"She just squeezed my hand!" Tom practically shouted.

"Priya." Steph's voice, only inches from her ear. "You're in the hospital. Everything's fine."

Priya tried to say something, but managed only a croak.

"What'd you say?" Tom asked.

Priya opened her eyes. Tom was in front of her, his eyes bloodshot, a worried expression on his face.

"Tom…" The word barely escaped her dry throat.

"I'm here, Priya. I can hear you."

The room began spinning, and Priya closed her eyes. She felt Tom's breath on her face, it smelled of mint. She licked her lips and managed two more words before the darkness closed in once again.

"I'm sorry."

~

"I was never told why I was *really* here other than some trumped-up story about finding out who some terrorists might be," Priya said.

She was sitting in her hospital room with Terry, and she was telling him everything. All of it.

These people had saved her life. She was done with the lies.

She even had Harold in her lap, in kitten form, comforting her.

She continued. "Years ago there were some terrorist attacks on Earth, and one of the attacks killed my parents. I was told that clues indicated the attackers came from the colony. But at this stage…" She shook her head. "I don't think I can believe anything they told me."

Terry frowned. "I totally get how they got their hooks into you. You do this thing for us, and we'll let you have the career you've been training for since you were a child. But what does that have to do with level twelve? Do they seriously believe there's some secret cabal of terrorists hiding in the lower levels of the mines?"

"I don't know." Priya's chest tightened. "From what I can tell, the memories they shoved in my head are the memories of past people they sent here. Like their implants transmitted info back to Earth, and they took those visuals and whatever else and fed them into me. I'm such a bloody idiot."

"No." Terry put his hand on her shoulder and gave it a light squeeze. "Stop beating yourself up over this. You're the victim here. I'm just sorry this happened to you. We all are."

Priya said nothing. She was a victim, but she was more than that, too. She had come here willingly, fully intending to spy on these people.

Terry withdrew a metal disc from his shirt pocket. "I found this in your dorm. Exactly where you said it would be. What do you know about it?"

She had already told him about the fire alarm and the guy who pressed that disc into her hand before disappearing into the crowd.

"I don't know anything, really, but I think it's a key, based on my flashes of memories." She tapped the side of her head. "In one of them, someone used it to get past a locked door down in the mines."

Steph walked into the room. "How's my patient doing?"

Priya gave her a weak smile. "I'm better."

"Well, let's see about that."

Steph stood at the foot of her bed and ran something along the sole of Priya's foot.

"Stop! That tickles!"

Steph chuckled. "Good, it's supposed to. Now let's check your nerve timing." She pulled out a device that looked like a miniature cattle prod, and pressed it against a nerve in her leg.

Priya's leg spasmed. "Bloody hell, that's worse!"

"Sorry." Steph looked at a readout. "Okay, now wiggle your toes for me."

Priya did. "Thank you for doing all of this," she said. "I'll never forget what you guys have done for me."

"No need to thank any of us." Steph pointed at the purring furball on Priya's chest. "From what I can tell, it's Harold you should thank. He seems to have had at least as much to do with your healing as we did."

She then turned to Terry. "I'm going to have to ask you to leave for a bit. I'm pretty sure neither my patient nor I wants a meathead around for the rest of her exam."

Terry hopped up from his chair. "Okay, I'll leave you two to do your thing. Tom should be here in half an hour. And we still have security posted outside." He gave Steph a quick peck and left the room.

As the door closed, Priya asked, "How long have you guys been married?"

"Five years." Steph removed some of Priya's blankets and prepared to start more nerve conduction tests. "Though it took me two years before that to get that doofus to propose. The Chapper men are stubborn types."

"What about Tom? Is he married?"

"Ha. Seven years later, and Tommy's *still* single. He's even more stubborn than Terry." She wielded her two-pronged electrode once again. "Okay, relax and think of happy times …"

Despite the discomfort of the exam, Priya's mind drifted to what it would be like to be married. She'd always imagined herself ending up with someone in the sciences. But perhaps that was only because those were the only people she ever encountered. She'd never had time to meet anyone outside of school or work.

"How did you and Terry meet?" she asked. "I wouldn't have guessed you two would have crossed paths."

Steph's cheeks turned pink. "I'm kind of embarrassed to say. I saw him at an airport, thought he was cute, and… I kind of just walked up to him and introduced myself."

"Really?" Priya laughed. "Who'd have thought it could be that easy?"

"Well, like I said, it wasn't that easy. It took me two years to land him. But he's the best. I'd have waited for however long it took."

Priya rested her head against the pillow and closed her eyes. "It gives a girl hope."

As Steph continued with her exam, Priya thought to herself, *What the hell is wrong with me? I'm lying in a hospital bed, not even able to walk, and while I'm getting zapped and prodded, here I am thinking about what it would be like to kiss my doctor's brother-in-law.*

~

Terry looked at the disc in his hands. "This little thing contains a quantum computer that can crack every security algorithm in the colony? How is that possible?"

Nwaynna shrugged. "Honestly, I didn't think it *was* possible. I mean, sure using just about any quantum computer using Shor's algorithm for integer factorization, you'd be able to crack any of the standard security algorithms we've used for the last two hundred years. But with the synchronous stream ciphers we now use, we've long believed they couldn't be cracked even by a quantum computer. It seems we were wrong."

Governor Welch shook her head. "Nwaynna, let's pretend for a moment I know nothing about quantum computers or Shor's algorithm. Let's pretend I'm just a politician. What did you just say?"

"Sorry." Nwaynna looked a bit embarrassed. "What it boils down to is that our colony's encryption methods for internal security can be broken by this disc. Luckily, our external-facing comms use alien tech that's beyond that key's capabilities."

Terry set the disc on the table in front of him. "Is this alien tech? Or is it just an Earth-based technology advancement we didn't anticipate?"

"We don't know, but we have a theory. To crack a password using a computer, you really just need to be able to guess enough times until you get the right answer—which is why we use large-key symmetric ciphers, because then even the best of computers would be guessing for thousands of years until they stumbled upon the right answer. However, back at the end of the twentieth, a man named Lov Grover came up with an algorithm that improved things sufficiently that the standard response was to use double the number of bits, basically making it computationally impractical to crack. We think that this disc may employ a new algorithm, coupled with a much stronger quantum computer than we have at our disposal."

"But that's just speculation," Terry said.

"Well, yes," She gave him an uncharacteristic frown. "You only gave that thing to me yesterday. I'd like to put it through our scanners, figure out what makes it tick, but that'll take at least a week or two."

"Nwaynna," said the governor, "how sure are you that our comms are secure?"

"As I said, all official colony communication is done using alien tech. Even if our signals are intercepted, the alien tech uses a hive database that contains randomly generated one-time pads that rotate per use. I don't care what type of computers or algorithms they have, we're hack-proof on the comms. I'm confident."

"And what do you suggest we do about internal security? Are

there any defensive measures we can take to keep this disc from working?"

Nwaynna nodded. "I can strengthen our current algorithm by making the bit length obnoxiously long. That might be enough. We can test that on this thing, and if it works, my team can recompile and start the upgrade process as early as tomorrow morning. We can update biometric keys while we're at it. But Madam Governor, it's probably only a stopgap. If they have tech like this, they'll adapt."

"Do it." The governor pointed at the metal frame Nwaynna had brought. "Let's move on. You've got Earth-based intel?"

"Yes, ma'am. Something interesting from General Duhrer's office."

Nwaynna set up the frame so it was facing the governor, and Terry shifted his seat so he could get a better viewing angle. The center of the frame turned black, then Duhrer's office filled the frame from edge to edge.

A man wearing fatigues walked into the office and closed the door behind him. The general motioned him toward a chair.

"Sergeant Dixon, I hope to heaven and hell that you have good news for me, because I'm up to my eyeballs in crap today. What's the story on our colony asset?"

"I'm sorry, sir, but I don't think—"

"The UN doesn't pay you to think, soldier, just spit it out."

"Sir, we lost the signal on our asset and—"

"Shit." The general made a time-out sign. *"Is she dead? Just tell me and don't pussyfoot."*

"No, sir, she's alive." Dixon sounded almost upbeat. *"The colony reported to us that she was injured in an attack, but that*

she's okay. She's being treated at one of their main hospitals. I don't know specifics of her condition, though. The entire floor is locked down, and nobody can get there, not even our security assets."

Terry and the governor exchanged a look. Someone in colony security was dealing for the other side.

The general fell back against his chair. *"She's alive. That's good. Do we know who attacked her?"*

Dixon shook his head. *"No, sir. They weren't forthcoming with details. But I don't think it's them—the girl's a Radcliffe, after all."*

"Don't be an idiot, of course it's not them. If they wanted to kill her, they wouldn't be telling us she's alive. But if it isn't one of the colonials..." He frowned. *"Did our girl get down to level twelve before she went dark?"*

"The last transmission we received, she'd gotten only as far as level eight."

"Soldier, I'm not sure if it's possible to have a mission go more sideways than this one has. This is totally fubar'd."

"Yes, sir." Dixon sat still in his chair, but his fidgeting feet gave away his nerves.

The general sighed. *"Let's bring her back. If they give you any crap about medical transport, tell them we'll send a space ambulance, if there even is such a thing. We'll take responsibility for her welfare, they just need to present her. I'll call some folks and get a shuttle ready to roll. You just get me a confirmation from those bastards that she'll be at the departure when our shuttle arrives."*

"Yes, sir."

The general motioned toward the door. *"Dismissed, soldier."*

The scene faded to black.

"That's it?" asked the governor.

"Yes, ma'am."

"Thank you, Nwaynna. I need to talk to Terry in private, but if you get anything new, please let us know right away."

"Absolutely." Nwaynna packed up and left the room.

The governor turned to Terry. "What's the story with the guy who attacked her?"

Terry cracked his knuckles. "A miner. He wasn't born here, but he had relatives here, so he was allowed to immigrate. His parents are farmers who sell exclusively to UN Agribusiness for distribution. From his immigration interview, it seemed like his family was sympathetic with the Rebels; they resented the way farmers were being treated, that kind of thing.

"But here's the interesting part. Our attacker's academic resume showed a gap of three years between secondary education and mining university. So I'm thinking this guy got hooked up with the UN opposition.

"Also, we interviewed several people who said he'd been asking questions about Priya. They figured he was just starstruck, so they didn't think anything of it, but apparently it was much more than that."

Governor Welch frowned. "I'm getting sick of these troubles with the Rebels. Have you talked with that prisoner who said he wanted to keep Priya safe?"

"I did, and I may have screwed up on that one. The message he got from Earth was ominous, but it could be read to support his claims."

"Suggestions?" the governor asked.

"Actually… I was going to ask you for permission to set up an infiltration. Hunt down the various leads on Earth and figure out what's really going on with the Rebels."

The governor pursed her lips, then nodded. "I think it's a good idea."

Terry was surprised. She hated sending people on missions.

"But," she added, "you're not going. Find someone else."

"But, I have all the background—"

"And you have other things to do. You've got rats in your organization. Son, that's your job one." The governor leaned forward and grabbed his hand. "Besides, as a leader, you need to learn when to delegate. You aren't the only one who can lead a mission. Send Tommy. He's part of the hacker community down there, he's got contacts that you don't, and he's a better shot."

Terry sat back in his chair, feeling deflated. But his mother was right.

"What about Priya?" the governor asked. "I suppose she's not willing to stay?"

Terry took a deep breath and let it out slowly. "She's stubborn. She thinks that by going back and letting them read the destroyed chip, it'll delay any aggressive actions toward us. She thinks she's helping, but—"

"Don't dismiss that as a possibility." The governor put her chin on the heel of her hand in a thinking pose. "In fact… maybe we can get the UN folks precisely the information they want."

"What do you mean?"

The governor smiled. "I have an idea."

CHAPTER THIRTEEN

Though she wasn't back to one hundred percent, Priya was up and walking, and it felt good to be on her own two feet. It had been six weeks since the attack, five of those in the hospital, one in the dorm. And now she was going back to Earth.

But first, it was time for her to give the UNIB what they'd been asking for. From what Terry had told her, there was nothing to hide on level twelve, and he wanted her to see that firsthand before she left. And it made sense, because if it was true, then she actually could deliver to Agent Ted and his cohorts what they'd asked for. It may not be what they wanted, but it *was* what they asked for.

As they passed through level eight, switching between elevators, she said, "I barely even remember what happened down here."

"Good." Terry grimaced. "I remember it perfectly well, and I'd frankly rather not. I thought you were going to die."

She chuckled. "It's not a big deal. Just have Walter resurrect me once he gets enough experience points."

Terry didn't smile.

She nudged him. "Hey, *I'm* supposed to be the grumpy one." She jabbed him a few times more times, and finally he cracked a smile. "See? That's better."

"I hate to admit it, but I'll miss having you around."

They reached the lower elevator. Terry swiped his finger across the biometric reader and they began descending. When they reached level ten, as far as this particular elevator went—and deeper than Priya had ever been—the doors slid open.

It was loud down here, and dust was thick in the air. Heavy equipment crossed their path, and from down the adjoining tunnels came the scraping of a continuous mining rig. And yet, as foreign as her surroundings were to her, she'd been here. Or at least, one of her memories had been.

She pointed to the left. "Elevator is that way. Right?" She had to yell to be heard over the noise.

Terry raised an eyebrow and nodded.

As they walked in that direction, farther from the active excavation site, the dust cleared. Soon they were at the next elevator. The one that would take them all the way down to level twelve. It was smaller than the others, more of a passenger elevator, only large enough to fit a dozen people.

"You should be able to scan in," Terry said.

Priya pressed her palm against the security pad and hit the button for level twelve. Sure enough, they immediately began their descent.

And it was quite a descent. They moved rapidly, and Priya

could tell they were going a long way. When they passed level eleven, she felt a rise in temperature.

"How far down is this, anyway?"

"About two thousand meters. A bit over a mile."

"Good lord!" Priya's ears popped with the change in pressure. "And how much hotter is it going to get?"

Terry smiled and wiped sweat from his brow. "It's going to get pretty hot. Sorry. Even though we pump iced water down to cool things off, the rock walls are about one hundred sixty degrees, so I wouldn't suggest touching them. That's also why I made you wear your mining gear."

Priya pulled at the front of her overalls, trying to get some air circulating against her sweaty skin. "It's got to be too hot to mine down here, right?"

"Oh, we don't really have this level setup for active mining."

Priya was confused. "Then what is it for?"

The elevator finally slowed to a stop, and the doors slid open. Bright lights in the chamber flickered to life from high up on the ceiling, chasing the shadows from the chamber that stretched in either direction as far as the eye could see.

Priya stepped off the elevator and noticed the chamber was only about fifty feet deep. On the far end, there was a large stack of boxes, and closer to the elevator shaft there were evenly-spaced pillars running the width of the chamber. Directly in front of her was a large central support structure that rose ten stories to the ceiling. The rest of the pillars emerged from the ground at an angle and met with the central structure at the ceiling nearly one hundred feet above.

She stared at what looked like an inverted fan and said, "That's a bizarre design."

"This place is mostly for emergency use," Terry said as they stepped further into the chamber. "This level connects to all the other mines in the colony. If there's some kind of catastrophic issue in any one location, we can have our security team escort equipment and miners down to this level, over to another mine, and bring them up from there.

"Also, I'm told we're able to tap the heat down here, and use it to run a lot of our operations. You know, geothermal energy and whatnot. That's not really my area; you'd understand it better than I would. Speaking of heat…" He unclipped a water bottle from his belt and handed it to her. "The last thing I need is for you to get dehydrated and pass out."

As Priya unscrewed the cap and downed the water, she walked past the support pillars and over to a stack of crates with numbers printed on them. "What's in these?"

"I have no idea." Terry shrugged. "We can find out." He donned a pair of mining gloves, grabbed a pry bar that was resting by the boxes, and began working on the top of one of the crates.

Priya heard a buzzing in her ear. Almost like the sound of electricity arcing somewhere. Or… maybe she didn't hear it, maybe she just felt a vibration in the air. It was almost like someone was rolling something heavy nearby. And then the hairs on the back of her neck stood on end, and she couldn't for the life of her figure out why.

Terry pried off the top of the crate. "Looks like we've got… tools."

Priya picked up a wrench, and immediately dropped it. "Ouch." It was hot.

Terry smiled. "Yeah. That's why I put on gloves before using the pry bar."

Priya looked over the tools. "So that's it? Level twelve is just… storage?"

Terry panned his gaze across the chamber. "Now you understand why we're perplexed that anyone would want access to this place. Beyond boxes and heat, you won't find much down here."

Priya pointed at a small cart. "Is that a golf cart?"

"Actually, we're in a mine, so it's a mining cart," Terry deadpanned.

Priya rolled her eyes. "Can it take us to one of the other shafts? If I'm going to try to convince the muppets at the UN that there's nothing down here, I at least want to explore a bit."

"Of course." He walked over to a refrigerator that had been partially hidden behind the crates, pulled out four plastic water bottles, and held them up. "Miners think of everything. Come on. Let's go for a ride."

Priya stared out the window at the departures gate, her throat tight with emotion as the supply ship taxied toward her. Just a few months ago, she would never have imagined feeling upset about leaving. She also would never have imagined that the colony's higher-ups wanted her to stay, even after learning why she was here and what she'd done. But it didn't matter how she felt or what they wanted; it was time for her to go.

"Leaving without saying goodbye?"

She turned to find Terry standing behind her. She practically squealed as she gave him a hug. "I didn't think you'd be here."

He held her at arm's length and smiled. "I wouldn't miss it for the world." He must have noticed her looking over his shoulder, because he added, "Tom couldn't make it. Unfortunately he's elsewhere on a critical assignment, otherwise I know he'd be here too."

"I understand," Priya said, but inside she was hurting. She'd wanted to see him one last time.

She tilted her head toward the shuttle. "I can't believe I'm the only passenger on that huge thing."

"Well, you and fifty tons of payload."

The doors swung open, and a man stepped through, staring at a handheld PC. "Priya Radcliffe?"

Priya waved a hand. "That's me."

The man came over and grabbed her bag. Then he looked her over and hesitantly offered his arm. "Ma'am, I wasn't told the extent of your injuries. Do you need a wheelchair?"

Priya shook her head. "No, thank you. I can walk."

She turned back to Terry, and was surprised to see how sad he looked. She jabbed him in the shoulder. "Don't you dare make me cry again."

He pulled her in for a hug. "Take care of yourself, Priya Radcliffe, and know that you'll always have a place here."

She stepped back and wiped her eyes. "Thanks, Terry. Don't rip up Brianna's character sheet just yet. This might not be the last you see of me."

Priya felt the strength of Earth's gravity as she stepped from the shuttle. She hadn't been wearing her weight vest since the attack, and she was worse off for it. Luckily, she didn't have to walk; all she had to do was hold on to the rail as the escalator lowered her down to the tarmac.

Agent Ted was waiting at the base of the escalator, his eerie eyes reflecting the sun so that it looked like a fire was burning in his eye sockets. He offered his hand and lowered her into a wheelchair. One of the pilots handed the agent her duffel bag, and Ted rolled her toward a boxy vehicle with a flashing blue light.

"I've arranged to check you into Walter Reed for a complete workup."

She looked back at him. "That's really not necessary. I'm much better now than I was. I'd rather just go home, if that's okay."

He rolled her chair up a ramp into the back of the waiting vehicle. "It's important that we get you checked out. I'm sure the colony's doctors are adequate for simple maladies, but we want you to see a real physician. Besides, I was given a direct order. You're to be in top-flight condition before you head home. It's the least we can do."

Agent Ted buckled into a seat next to her, and clamps came down automatically to hold her wheelchair in place while a seat-belt snaked across her waist. Once they were locked in, the vehicle began moving.

It felt strange to be riding in a vehicle on Earth. She'd gotten used to it on the colony, but on Earth all her travel had been by tube, other than a couple of trips she'd taken on buses.

"I guess you've never been in an ambulance before," said Agent Ted.

She shook her head.

He smiled. "That's a good thing. Generally, you'd rather not need one."

Ahead of them, the yawning mouth of a tunnel appeared. The ambulance raced into its darkness, and LEDs lit the interior of the cabin.

"Guided tunnel system," Ted explained. "Most people don't know about it—it's limited to use by emergency vehicles and for other official purposes. It's nowhere near as quick as the tube, though, so settle in—we'll be at Walter Reed in about two hours."

~

As she was wheeled to radiology, Priya felt Harold shift from her shoulder to her waist. She looked down and saw that she was now wearing a belt that hadn't been there moments ago.

"What are you doing?" she muttered under her breath.

Harold tapped back. *"X-rays. Avoid detection by being in plain sight."*

Of course. They'd scan her, and this way she could just remove her "belt" and keep Harold from being noticed.

She was approached by a woman with a blue smock and pleasant smile. "Priya Radcliffe?"

"That's me."

The woman extended her clipboard. “Can I get a thumbprint for verification?”

Priya pressed her thumb on the pad.

“Okay, great. Looks like I’ve got an order for an MRI cervical, thoracic, and lumbar spine without contrast.” She pulled a flowered hospital gown from a cabinet. “I’ll need you to change into this for the scan. Can you stand, or do you need help?”

“I can manage.”

“And are you claustrophobic at all?”

“I don’t think so.”

The nurse smiled. “Well, if you are, we’ll find out soon enough.”

~

The governor watched with interest as the general received the latest news.

“General Duhrer, I just got the report from Walter Reed,” said Sergeant Dixon.

“Out with it.”

“Yes, sir. I’ll read it as it’s written. ‘Twenty-four-year-old female with no history of spinal injuries presented with weakness and a tingling sensation in the lower extremities. Magnetic resonance image of the lumbar, thoracic, and cervical spine without contrast. Five-millimeter axial images from the—’”

“Get to the point, Sergeant. Is there evidence of an injury, yes or no?”

“Yes, sir.”

“Spinal?”

"Yes."

The general raked his hand through his graying hair. *"The bitch didn't lie about that."*

"Yes, sir."

"How much did the implant capture?"

"Nothing, sir. The implant had some type of catastrophic short circuit. From the data that was relayed live before the short circuit, we believe the damage was caused by exposure to EM radiation, possibly microwave, but we're not certain."

The general's face turned red. *"Nothing? What about the storage? You told me that no matter what happened, there'd always be a backup."*

Dixon's face paled.

"Let me guess," growled the general. *"It's gone too."*

"Irretrievable loss of—"

"Shut up, you imbecile!" The general stood and began pacing.

"But sir—"

The general wheeled around. *"That was an order!"*

Dixon looked like he was about to explode. He typed two words on his handheld and showed it to the general.

The general glanced at the message. *"What good news?"*

"Sir, she was debriefed by Agent Ted Oyama. She managed to get to level twelve."

The general stiffened. *"I assume she was fully debriefed... do we know if she's telling us the truth?"*

"Yes, sir. Agent Oyama had her monitored as he debriefed her. He worked with Agent Stone, a brain wave analyst, to certify the truth of her information."

The general seemed to calm. He sat on his desk, facing the sergeant. *"What did we learn?"*

The governor leaned forward as she watched the scene play out. She'd never talked with Terry about Priya's trip down to twelve, but she knew there was nothing to see down there—not yet, anyway. That would almost certainly be changing in a couple of days.

"Sir, she stated that level twelve connected the multiple mines on Chrysalis. She found some crates filled with tools, a refrigerator with bottled water, and excessive heat."

The general leaned forward. *"And...?"*

"That's it, sir."

"That's it?*"* The general's voice sounded like sandpaper.

Dixon nodded. *"Yes, sir. The agent asked all of the other debrief questions, and they came back as truthful negatives. No noticed sparks. No sudden fluctuations of power anywhere on the site. No spools of any substance."*

The general leapt to his feet, and with a cry of frustration, he swiped everything off his desk. Then he plopped down in his chair. *"Get out, Sergeant! I'm done with you."*

"Sir, yes, sir." Dixon raced out of the office.

For a long time, the general just stared up at the ceiling, not moving.

Beside Governor Welch, Nwaynna said, "Man, is he upset."

"That's an understatement."

Suddenly, the general leaned down, grabbed his overturned phone, and pressed a couple of buttons.

"Operator 17, what can I do for you, General Duhrer?"

"Get me General Carl Maddox at the Pentagon."

"Yes sir, please hold."

The governor and Nwaynna watched and waited.

"Sir, this is Operator 17. I'm connecting General Maddox now."

A gruff voice erupted through the connection. *"Henry, long time no talk. What is it?"*

"I've got an answer to the Chrysalis issue."

"Oh? I'm all ears."

"I recommend going forward with Operation Clean Sweep."

"Shit. You're sure?"

"I don't think we're left with any choice. I'll send the paperwork right away."

"Understood. May God have mercy on our souls."

General Duhrer hung up, kicked the phone into the wall, and walked out of the office.

"That can't be good," Nwaynna said.

"No. It can't." The governor tapped the phone icon on the table and called Terry. *"What's up?"*

"Terry, this one's critical. Reach out to our people on Earth. We need to know every detail there is to know about Operation Clean Sweep."

"Is that something happening now?"

"Now, or it's imminent."

"Well, this might help affirm some of the timelines involved. I literally just now received a recall notice from the UN Education Council. They're pulling back their interns."

The governor scowled. "It's happening. Terry, this is the moment we talked about. Go do what you need to."

"Already underway. I've screened forty-three, found one."

"There'll be more. Make sure your brother gets the message about Operation Clean Sweep. I love you."

"Love you too. Bye."

The governor turned to Nwaynna. "Talk to our friends down below. I figure we have at least four days, but let's be ready in three. Go, and let me know by the end of the day what's happening."

"Yes, ma'am."

As Nwaynna left the office, the governor leaned back in her chair.

This is either going to start a revolution... or finish one.

CHAPTER FOURTEEN

The lid to Tom's coffin-like container cracked open, and a familiar face appeared above him.

"It's about damned time, Richard. I hate these cryo-containers."

Richard Fox was in his fifties, heavily muscled, wearing the uniform of a colonel in the UN's quartermaster corps. He was also the leader of the southeastern US's rebel alliance. He took Tom's hand and pulled him upright.

"I thought you guys were supposed to be in some kind of dreamless suspended animation or something when in these things."

"Just because these things slow our metabolism to like one percent doesn't mean something isn't cooking upstairs." He tapped the side of his head.

Around them, other containers in the UN supply warehouse

—all of them labeled "for recycle"—hissed as their seals were breached. The other members of Tom's team climbed out, also shaking off the cobwebs of medically induced hibernation.

"Did you have any trouble with the customs folks?" Tom asked.

"Nah, you guys were all listed as colony garbage. They ran a bio scanner and released twelve boxes of junk for me to take to the processor."

"Are we in monitored territory?"

"Yes. But…" Richard smiled. "Follow me."

He led Tom and his team through a staggeringly tall maze of shelves and crates. He pressed a hidden button on a shelf, and a section of the floor lowered, revealing a ramp going down.

"That'll lead you to the Underground. Bikes are about fifty feet down tunnel, along with three supply crates. One of those has a really nice sniper rifle. I'm sure you'll do good things with that. You have the map, right?"

"I do."

"Good. It's marked with breather holes where you can pop up in unmonitored territory. Do you know where you're going yet?"

"First place is the hacking station. I need some info from the Oracle."

"The Oracle, eh?" Richard chuckled. "Well, I guess she can handle some stuff I can't. So, any questions?"

"No questions. Thanks, Richard."

Richard clasped his hand. "Godspeed, my friend."

Twisting the throttle to its maximum, Tom ducked low, very conscious of the concrete ceiling just an arm's length above him. The electric motorcycle had no speedometer, but the rushing air threatened to tear his clothes from him, which told him that he had to be going at least two hundred miles per hour.

His goggles featured alien tech that projected images directly onto his retina. Without looking back he could not only see that the rest of his team was close behind, he could see that their target was only minutes away.

A voice with a Russian accent came over his earpiece. *"Rebel team approaching at breakneck speed, who the hell are you?"*

Tom smiled. "Hey, Tina. How's it going?"

Tina Polyudov was a Russian hacker known as the Oracle. She was the eyes and ears of many of the rebels in this part of the country, and Tom knew her well. Her voice sounded like it belonged to a barrel-chested brute of a man, but apart from that, she was all woman.

"Blyat! No fucking way. Tommy-boy, is that really you?"

"It's me in the flesh. I'm going to need your help, girlfriend."

A string of curse words in Russian, English, and probably Demon erupted through the connection. *"Don't you dare try to sweet talk me. I haven't forgotten what you said to me, you asshole. Tell me why I shouldn't blow all of you into scraps that even the rats won't find."*

Tom winced. When they last parted ways, they didn't leave on the best of terms.

"Come on, Tina. We're on the same team. I need help, and I know you're the first person I can count on to help us stick it to those UN bastards. Can we at least sit together like civilized human beings and talk about this? It's a conversation that's kind of tough to have while I'm speeding through a low tunnel on a motorcycle. I promise you, you'll want to help us."

There was silence on the line for a full ten seconds before Tina responded. *"Fine. As long as you agree to leave your weapons in the cooler, my guys will let you in."*

"Thanks. You're the best."

"Fuck off, pretty boy."

The connection ended, but Conrad, one of his men, came over the line. They'd all heard the conversation.

"Man, Tom, you seriously pissed in his corn flakes. And is that guy really named Tina?"

Tom laughed. "Word of warning, guys: that's a girl, and she's pretty touchy about what she sounds like."

"No way. So what did you do to piss her off?"

"Well, I worked with her five years ago, when I was down on a training mission. And I'll be blunt: she's hot. Body, curves, the whole deal. She's also smart as hell. And she's Russian, and maybe they make their women a bit aggressive, I don't know, but whatever it is, she's a big-time flirt. I ended up putting an end to that."

"How?"

"Well, and this is totally petty on my part, I own that, but I couldn't get past her voice. So one of the times she was suggesting we should… you know… I told her I wasn't interested because she sounded like a three-hundred-pound Russian bodybuilder. She didn't like that too much."

There was a chorus of laughter from the team.

"You really are a sweet talker, aren't you?"

Lights appeared up ahead. Tom flashed his high beams and said, "Okay guys, we're here."

Two big beefy guys were waiting for them at the bottom of a ramp leading up to a blast-proof door. Tom hopped off his motorcycle removed the sniper rifle that had been strapped across his back, and handed it to the first guy he came to. He held his arms out and the other guy patted him down. The process was repeated with the rest of his team before they were escorted through the door and into an old bomb shelter from the twentieth. Just a small room, poured concrete, empty but for the frames of a few bunk beds.

A door on the opposite side of the room opened and Tina stepped through, curvy but fit. Her gaze immediately locked onto his, and she walked purposefully toward him, her smile growing larger, and as she came within arm's reach, slugged him in the gut.

"Now we're even!"

She turned to the rest of the team and, with a smile, motioned for them to follow.

Tom groaned and ignored their chuckles as he brought up the rear. *I hope she got that out of her system.*

~

Tom was with Tina in a small room filled with old-style flat screens and humming fans. A mainframe tapped into one of the trunks of what had once been called the information super-highway.

"I don't believe it," Tina said.

"It's true. We think there are factions in the anti-UN types who tried to take out an actual Radcliffe."

Tina shook her head. "Well, there aren't that many comms between here and the colony, so let's just tackle that one first." Her fingers were a blur on the keyboard.

Tom leaned closer to see what she was doing, and got a death stare in return. "Sorry," he said, backing away. "You really do hate people hovering over you."

"Not at all… in the bedroom. But you lost that privilege when you blew me off."

Tom took a deep breath and stared at the back of her head. "What are you doing?"

"All of the alien tech on Earth is monitored, and I've got root access to the comms database. I'm scanning the traffic streams from Earth to Chrysalis looking for keywords and—got it."

Tom scooted closer—but not *too* close. "Got what?"

"Hold on, there's a long list of crap in here. Your Radcliffe chick is evidently a conversation piece with our UNIB folks. Let me extract data references associated with access requests." She tapped at the keys. "Okay, does this sound familiar?"

A man's voice broadcast through a speaker somewhere in the room. *"I'm sending an image of a new intern. She's a Radcliffe. She'll be leaving here in a few days. You know what to do."*

Tom smiled. "That's it. Damn, you're good. The guy who received that message is in a cell up on the colony, but we don't know who the sender is. Can you run an ID on the voice?"

Tina looked back at him. "You're barking up the wrong tree on that one. I know that voice—Todd Winslow. His father is a leader of a rebel group out of Montana. He's a rebel through and through, but he's also active duty with the military. I don't know how he got on your radar, but he's not a bad egg."

"I'd still like to talk to him."

"What, and get your group of assassins on him?" Tina's eyes darted to the door. On the other side of that door were their two teams—probably sharing war stories. "No. *I'll* call him and see what's up."

She turned to a wall of electronics and flipped a particular switch on a panel of a hundred other unmarked switches. A ringing came over the hidden speaker, then a voice.

"Hello?" The same voice as before. Todd Winslow.

Tina leaned back in her chair and adjusted her cleavage. "Boy toy. Can you talk now?"

"No. Twenty minutes."

"Call me."

"Will do."

Tom's pocket PC vibrated with a message from the colony. He took it out and read. *If possible, find out what Operation Clean Sweep is.*

"What is it?" Tina asked.

"A message from the colony. They want to know about something called Operation Clean Sweep."

Tina turned back to the laptop. "What keywords do you want me to use? Operation Clean Sweep, anything else?"

"Let's add Priya, P-r-i-y-a Radcliffe." Tom frowned. "Well, the premise the UNIB guys used to get the Radcliffe girl under their thumb was to figure out who was responsible for some terrorist attacks. So maybe add terrorist, bomb… I don't know, Chrysalis. Start with that and see what we get."

"What *I* get, you presumptuous ass." A smile grew on Tina's face as she typed. One by one, monitors in the room lit up with SQL queries, binary search attempts, and a series of predictive search functions. Tom felt the room get warmer by a few degrees as the processing power of the machinery was put to the test.

"What databases are you searching?" he asked.

"All of them. We long ago managed to find a backdoor in the UNIB's Raven firewall. If it's out there, I'll find it."

A moment later, the first hit popped up. Tom scooted closer to get a better look. "A newspaper article about the tube attack outside Cape Canaveral. That's the one the Radcliffe girl's parents died in. Stuff we already know."

Over the next twenty minutes, more results trickled in, but none of them were particularly revelatory.

And then Todd Winslow called back.

"Ya?" answered Tina.

"You wanted to talk?"

"Absolutely. I'm following up on something and your name popped up. I was hoping you could help fill in the blanks."

"I'll try."

"This is from a couple months ago. I see here that you arranged for a comm with the colony, and it had to do with—"

"I remember it. I don't exactly talk to the colony folks often. What do you want to know?"

"What was the point of that call?"

"I was informed that a girl heading over to the colony might

have been set up for something. You know the UNIB guys, those assholes don't give a damn about anyone, and this girl was a total dupe. She had no idea what she was getting into. So I was trying to get one of our guys to act as overwatch for her."

Tom nodded. That seemed a reasonable explanation, and it fit with what he knew of the case.

"Thanks, *zaichik*," said Tina. "I'll see you soon?"

"I've got leave next week, so I was hoping to get together."

Tina grinned and shifted her gaze to Tom. "Oh, we'll get together all right. Over and over again."

Tom just shook his head. She hadn't changed a bit.

"I have to get going. Love you."

"You too." As Tina disconnected, there was a slight pink on her cheeks.

"*Zaichik*?" said Tom with a smile. "Doesn't that mean bunny?"

"Shut up." Tina pointed at the screen. "Another hit, and I bet this one will be more interesting. Video taken by an alien probe embedded in the UNIB complex."

She pressed a key, and a video began to play. It showed a very up-close image of a file cabinet, the camera angle was almost as if it was captured by a snake oozing into the cracks of the cabinet and then slowly scanning each individual paper.

"What in the world captured that video?

"That's an alien probe. I'm sure you've seen the shapeshifter types. Anyway, we've got them crawling through everything those guys are doing." Tina reached over and twisted a knob on the nearby desk.

"Looks like I have to manually advance to the identified time stamp." The video fast-forwarded rapidly what seemed to be thousands of pages. "Okay, here we go." She highlighted the paper on the screen and zoomed in so they could read it.

Date: 126.12 AE

Subject: Classified Briefing – Terrorist Problem

SGNP: Let's be very clear, gentlemen. This conversation is not to be part of any official record or database. We're getting reports of terrorist activities that are disrupting government services. We know they're illegals coming out of the unmonitored territories, yet the public sentiment is not with us on a crackdown. You promised a solution—that's why we funded the UNIB. What have you got?

CHD: Ma'am, the research on KBP is complete. We have five projectiles at the ready. Each is capable of bringing down the explosive energy equivalent of nearly 500 tons of TNT. That will wipe out anything in a thousand-foot radius.

SGNP: And we're sure that it can't be traced back to us?

CHD/GMB: Yes, ma'am.

. . .

GMB: Madam Secretary, what Henry's developed is silent. No radar cross-section whatsoever. No radiation. We can plant certain things on site to satisfy the forensics team, then leak it to the media. We'll have the media with us, which should create a popular shift to our way of thinking.

SGNP: I'm counting on that. This utopia our forefathers envisioned is only hanging on by a thread, and it needs patriots to care for it.

CHD: Ma'am, I may not be able to guarantee zero casualties from the operation.

SGNP: The same thing that makes the grass grow feeds the heart of what we're doing here, gentlemen. There are sacrifices to be made, and I'm sure any patriot would make that sacrifice, right?

CHD/GMB: Yes, ma'am.

"What makes the grass grow?" Tina asked, confused.

"Blood," explained Tom, shaking his head. "Blood makes the grass grow. This is sick."

"Well, judging by the date on this, twenty-seven years ago,

I'm guessing they were discussing the terrorist attack in The Hague against the UN's First Council. Plenty of blood, that's for sure."

"Is that it? Is there more?" Tom asked.

"Oh, we've got more hits. Hang on." Tina referenced another monitor, then fast-forwarded and zoomed in on another sheet of paper.

Date: 146.205 AE

Subject: Classified Briefing – The Radcliffe Problem

SGNP: How is it that we have two scientists in charge of one of our most important construction projects, and you're telling me that they're in communication with rebel elements?

GHD: They passed their polygraph exams, ma'am. If it weren't for one of the UNIB's men recording a conversation, we wouldn't have thought to put tracers on them. It happens, I'm afraid. And being descendants of a historical figure gives them status with the illegals out there in the unmonitored territories.

SGNP: Well, we can't have them having unmonitored excursions. Who knows what they're divulging to the enemy? But there would also be problems with just letting them go. They'd have the ear of the media.

. . .

GHD: I didn't think that was a problem anymore.

SGNP: Don't be naïve, Henry. Data gets around, even today. We need them pastured, permanently.

GHD: KBP has been dormant for seven years. There's four unused projectiles. It worked well the last time... how about another try?

SGNP: KBP? Oh yes, I remember. Good... there's a reason I recommended you to be elevated to general. But we can't make it look like an assassination. Just killing them would lead the conspiracy theorists to sniff around.

GHD: How about we send two shots this time? One lands in an open field outside Canaveral, no harm done. The other takes out the tube as the Radcliffes approach the area. Takes care of the issue and makes the terrorists look like bumbling idiots.

SGNP: Perfect.

. . .

Tina shook her head. "I can't believe these morons have all this written down, even if it is in some shithole filing cabinet deep in a UNIB vault."

"It's the military way: paperwork then, paperwork now, paperwork forever. They probably figured if there wasn't an electronic record, there was no risk."

Tina grinned. "They were wrong."

Tom leaned back in his chair. "I'm guessing CHD and GHD were Colonel and then General Heinrich Duhrer."

"And SGNP has to be that hag Natalya Poroshenko, the secretary-general. She's a traitor to humanity and needed to find a grave years ago."

"This is getting deep and dark—quickly." Tom shook his head. "The Radcliffes were killed when a missile struck their transport. So clearly, KBP is some kind of missile system."

"I can confirm that. Hang on a second." Tina switched to another computer, tapped away, and then sent an image to one of the larger screens. It was some kind of schematic and system diagram. "Found it right there in the UNIB goody drawer. Everything you want to know about KBP."

Tom looked over the specs. "*Kinetic Bombardment Project.* A satellite-based system. Fifty-thousand-pound rods of tungsten, a guidance system, and a primary boost rocket good for a sixty-second burn. They have these things up in low Earth orbit, just waiting to be dropped. You don't need a massive bomb when something like that is falling out of the sky."

He shook his head. "It's brilliant. Nobody would suspect a thing, because anyone who's looking for a missile attack would be looking for a launch to track—whereas this was launched years ago, each rod probably hidden in the cargo bay during a series of otherwise innocuous shuttle launches. With this, you wouldn't see anything other than maybe a blip up in geosynchronous orbit. It would just fall using Earth's gravity—then slam into its target at thirty thousand miles per hour."

Tom was going to have quite the report to type up. The colony needed to know about this.

~

Tom rubbed his eyes. They'd been looking through incriminating records for nearly half a day, and he'd been writing his report as they went. His fingers were almost as tired as his eyes.

Tina kicked him. "Holy cow. Tom… you need to look at this." She transferred the document image to the main monitor.

Tom scanned the text and felt the blood drain from his face. "Am I reading that right?"

"I got a hit on Operation Clean Sweep. It looks like it's a plan to attack the colony with nukes." She scrolled down. "Holy shit. These bastards are onlining thirteen-megaton warheads. Sixty of them!"

Tom turned back to his computer. "I need to get this information back to the colony *now*."

"What can they do?"

"I don't know. I really don't."

"The doc says four shuttles will be used for the nukes, and four more are carrying forty soldiers apiece in full battle rattle. I'll see if I can get more details about what's going on. Where the shuttles are, where the warheads are, when they're getting deployed…"

"And if they're in orbit already," Tom added.

"Yes. This may take me some time."

"Don't take too much time," Tom said, balling his fists. "Someone out there may be uncrating a nuke right now—and it's headed for my home."

CHAPTER FIFTEEN

Priya was in the kitchen of her aunt's apartment, reading an e-mail she'd just received from the David Holmes Academy.

Due to your performance during the fall semester, you have been placed on academic probation. Your privileges for attending campus-related activities and events are suspended for one calendar year, after which you can reapply with the Admissions Department. Any questions regarding these findings can be forwarded to the Council for Academic Progress.

"What!" she shrieked at her handheld, fury surging through her.

Aunt Jen rushed into the kitchen. "What's wrong?"

"These idiots at the Academy evidently didn't freeze my

records while I was at the colony, so now they're claiming I failed my last semester."

"Oh, dear. I… I did get calls about your lack of attendance. I'm sorry, Priya. I tried to explain to them…"

Priya's entire body shook with anger as she dialed the number for the campus. After all she'd been through…

"David Holmes Education Campus, how may I help you?"

"Please connect me to Colonel Jenkins at the UN Special Operations Command."

"I'm sorry, but we don't have the ability to transfer calls to that part of the campus. You'll need to reach out to them directly. Is there anything else I can do for you?"

"Do you have their phone number?"

"I'm sorry, I do not. Is there anything else I can do for you?"

With a death-grip on her handheld, Priya growled, "No, thank you."

She quickly typed out an email to Colonel Jenkins and hit send.

"Honey," said Aunt Jen hesitantly. "I hate to ask this, but… are you sure you were at the colony?"

"What's *that* supposed to mean?" Priya asked hotly.

"Well, like I said, I got some calls about how you weren't attending classes, and when I tried to explain about the internship, they had no record of it. They even said that such internships aren't given to juniors."

"Well, they're wrong," Priya snapped. "I'm going to campus to fix this."

She left the apartment and ran to the tube station. There was so much adrenaline rushing through her she couldn't even feel the tingling in her legs anymore. When she arrived at the station, she took the stairs two at a time.

The familiar hologram blinked into existence ahead of her. *"Welcome, neighbor! It's people like me who keep the tubes running efficiently and safely. Type *92-8374 on your SMS device to learn more about joining the team."*

"Shut up," she growled as she fast-walked to a control panel on the arrivals and departures platform. She pressed her palm to the touch screen so the display would switch to her normal settings. But instead of transitioning to her preferred aqua blue, the screen turned red, and a woman's voice spoke.

"Good afternoon, Priya. I'm Lexie, your tube assistant. You currently have authorization for zero different destinations on your account. Thank you."

The screen went dark.

Priya stared at it in shock.

Then she pressed her hand against the touch screen again.

"Good afternoon, Priya. I'm Lexie, your tube assistant. You currently have authorization for zero different destinations on your account. Thank you."

An older woman with an empty shopping bag was walking by, and stopped. "Oh dear, there must be some kind of glitch in the system. I'm going to the market—did you need to go there?"

"No… thank you." Priya backed away from the panel.

Her head ached as the crushing reality of what was going on hit her. She was trapped.

Her throat tightened as she hurried back down the stairs, and veered away from her apartment complex and headed toward the edge of the neighborhood where she'd gone once before.

She felt as though the entire world was watching her. The people on the sidewalks gave her sidelong glances, and the curtains in the tiny bungalows along Haverhill Drive swished with the evidence of people peeking through windows. Did everyone know that she'd been marked as a pariah, an outcast?

With more and more eyes seeming to focus on her, panic set in as she ran.

This is a mistake. It has to be.

She'd done everything she was ever asked to do.

It was unfair…

At the edge of her neighborhood, her lungs aching from the exertion, she ignored the warning signs and sprinted into the woods before collapsing at the base of an oak tree and sobbing.

Harold shifted forms and settled across her lap, purring.

"I can't believe they did this to me. The school could have just been a mistake, but access to the tube—that has to be Jenkins, or those assholes in the intelligence building. Agent Ted. Maybe even the general. But *why*?"

She threw her head back against the tree trunk. "I should have never come back. I should have stayed at the colony. I could have started my life over." Tears streamed down her face. She hated Earth and everyone on it. "I just wish I could talk to Terry. Or Tom, or Steph. Anyone from the colony, really."

Immediately, Harold began transforming again—this time changing from a cat into a communicator.

"Harold? What are you doing?"

She put the communicator to her ear. It was ringing!

Priya held her breath and prayed. Praying for what, she didn't know.

"Hello?"

Priya almost started crying again. It was Tom.

"Hello."

"Priya? Is that you?"

"Y-yes." She took a deep breath and let it out slowly, trying to compose herself.

"How in the world are you calling? What's wrong?"

Priya forced a smile. "I used Harold to call you. And… I'm fine," she lied.

"Come on, you're obviously upset. Tell me what happened."

And she did. She explained everything that had happened since she got back home—and how she was now stuck, trapped, like a prisoner.

Tom was silent for a few seconds before answering. *"I'm sorry, Priya. I really am."*

"I know what these people think of me now—pulling my access to the tube tells me that. They're vengeful. They lied to me. And they hold all the cards. Even though I did everything they asked, it must not have been what they wanted, or not enough, I don't know. But I'm screwed here. I should have stayed at the colony. I just hope whatever I gave them is enough for you guys to… you know what I mean."

"I do." Tom's voice was warm, like a hug from afar.

"I'm done with the UN, Tom. I'm done with Earth. I'm done with everything."

Tom hesitated. *"What would you say about going off-grid?"*

"What do you mean?"

"You know what I mean. Listen, I'm currently only a few hundred miles from you—"

"What?" Priya's throat tightened with emotion.

"Sorry I couldn't tell you before. Just... hang on a bit longer. I have something I need to do first, but keep Harold close by. Now that you've reached me through him, I can probably do the same to contact you."

Priya wiped her face on her sleeve. "Prince Charming coming to rescue me?"

"I'll do what I can. Just don't say anything to anyone."

"Are you kidding me? I don't trust any of these people anymore."

~

Tom felt conflicting emotions. Priya was upset, and he wanted desperately to do something to fix that… yet at the same time, she wanted to go back to the colony—which made him irrationally happy.

"Who was that?" Tina asked, not even looking up from her laptop.

"Nobody important," he lied.

"Whatever."

Tom's handheld buzzed with a text.

Scrub the mission. Return right away using whatever means necessary.

"Oh, damn."

"What now?" Tina asked.

"We've been recalled." Tom winced as he thought about what it would take to get back to the colony.

Tina pumped her fist in the air. "Aha!"

"What?"

"I broke in." Tina swiped her screen onto the main monitor. "Lookie there! Two of five shots remaining. Our toys are sitting in geosynchronous orbit fifteen hundred miles above us, with a roughly two-hour orbital period."

"You're kidding."

Tina opened a desk drawer and retrieved a communicator—a colony communicator. He could tell by its markings.

"Who are you calling?" Tom asked.

She waved him away and held the communicator to her ear. After a moment, she said, "It's Tina." She seemed stiff, almost nervous. "I sent you data reports earlier about this. … Okay, sorry. I was able to hack in. … Yes ma'am, two rounds in the chamber, that's correct." Tina turned to look at Tom. "Yes, he's here, and he got the order. … I'll help with the IDs, no problem. Did you have a target—okay, I'll wait." Tina typed something on her laptop. "It looks like six minutes from release to impact. … Yes, ma'am, just tell me where and when and I'll release."

When she put the communicator back in the drawer, Tom said, "The governor?"

"Yes."

"How the hell did you two have a conversation when she's twenty-something million miles away? The light speed lag would be almost five minutes for a round trip."

Tina grinned. "That communicator is an entangled communication device. At least, that's what your brother said when he gave it to me. It enables real-time comms with the colony—if it's critical." She motioned toward the door. "Anyway, I'll keep working here. You and your team need to get going."

"Hold up," said Tom. "What about those shuttles? We don't even know where they're launching from."

Tina grabbed his arm, pulled him close, and pressed herself against him. "I know you're devastated because you're not going to be able to shoot anyone, but you need to leave."

"Wait, I need help reaching someone. Do you—"

"It's not in this room." Tina shoved him toward the door. "Get your perfect ass out of here. I've got real work to do."

~

Back on the tube station platform, Priya waited. She'd been waiting for half an hour, and so far, there'd been no sign of him.

Back at the apartment, she'd left a simple note for her aunt: *Thank you, and all the best.* She said nothing more—that would only risk getting her aunt in trouble.

The sound of rushing air came from the doors to the tube. Could this be him?

The doors slid open, and Priya couldn't keep the smile from her face as Tom stepped out, wearing Army fatigues.

She walked up to him, snaked her arm around his neck, and pulled him in for a brief but firm kiss on the lips. "Thank you for coming."

Tom smiled at her. "And hello to you too."

She frowned. "What happened to your eyes? They're brown now."

He winked. "I know blue suits me better, but I had to make a change. I'll show you why." He walked with her over to a control panel and placed his hand on the touch screen.

"Good morning, General. I'm Lexie, your tube assistant. You have authorization for one-thousand four hundred and fifty-three destinations on your account. Which would you like to go to?"

Priya laughed.

Tom said, "Two passengers for DHEC Cape Canaveral. Priority override omega."

"Two passengers for the David Holmes Education Campus at Cape Canaveral. Please confirm."

"Confirmed."

Air rushed behind the tube doors. *"Establishing vacuum. Queuing priority request for direct transportation link between Coral Springs-North Junction and the main terminal at the DHEC-Cape Canaveral."*

Tom turned to Priya. "You still want to go back to the colony?"

She linked her arm through his. "Yes."

"Good. Because our transport is on the tarmac getting fueled." Tom handed her a badge with her picture on it. "You're now Margaret Huber, product inspector."

Priya clipped the badge onto her lapel and looked up at him. "I miss your blue eyes."

"Honestly? Me too. And my hands feel funny." He pulled at a thin layer of rubberized skin on his palm. "It's a good thing the general and I have roughly the same size hands."

"Link complete. The car is arriving in three... two... one..."

A minute later Priya and Tom were rushing down the tube in a two-passenger capsule. Priya's heart was racing—not because she was scared, but because she was excited.

Tom reached out and took her hand.

Priya smiled. No matter what was happening between them, she knew now that in Tom she had someone she could count on.

~

Terry stood at the viewing window in the air traffic control tower. Beside him, Gene, the on-duty orbital traffic controller, was rotating through floating screens of radar and orbital images.

Terry felt a tension in the air. Word had filtered through the population that the governor would be making a colony-wide announcement—which usually happened only for the yearly State of the Colony report. So everyone knew something was up.

In his ear, he was listening to Ian Wexler's sandpaper voice reporting on the security management channel. Ian was in charge of the early offloading of the mining interns, and anyone else from Earth.

"Scanned the last of them—it looks like we've got a clean crew in Departures, no detected contraband. Sam, what are we seeing in Dorm Block E?"

"It's taking a bit longer than I expected to do the scans. These guys left behind a ton of crap."

"Ya, well, that's what you get when you roust a bunch of kids and tell them they have to pack four months of crap in ten minutes."

Terry whispered into his lapel. "Make sure you're thorough, guys. Remember, seven of our own ended up being traitors to the colony. People you and I broke bread with and trusted. I don't trust any of these assholes, so dot your i's and cross your t's. If you find anything that doesn't look right, make sure my ass hears about it, you got me?"

Several voices gave affirmation.

Terry switched his comms to address only Ian. "Ian, you hear me?"

"Yes, sir."

"Good. When you're done there, I need you to take a team and clear out the trash from the stockade. Take the seven traitors to Departures and make sure they're on that damned shuttle. We don't need their overhead in the colony. Let the Earth officials sort them out."

"Amen, brother. But you know the shuttle captain is going to take a dump on that plan. He'll give me some crap like he doesn't have the seating configuration to accommodate another seven passengers."

"Let them roll around in the aisles for all I care. And tell the captain we don't give a crap what he does once he's out of orbit and on his way to Earth, but if he pulls anything like dumping passengers on the tarmac or any other bullshit, we'll shoot him out of the sky."

Ian chuckled. *"I'm sure I can get that message across. Anything else?"*

"Just keep your eyes peeled. Once these guys are out of our hair, we'll still have a few sleepless nights ahead of us. There's going to be a lot of movement, so spread the word among the team that we'll all be pulling some massive overtime."

"Copy that."

Just as Terry cut off the comm, Gene spoke into his microphone. "Earth shuttle *Vancouver*, this is Chrysalis tower. You're coming in too hot for safe entry. Slow to 14,000 mph and an entry angle of forty-five degrees."

"Chrysalis tower, our normal entry is at 17,500 mph with an entry angle of forty degrees. Earth shuttle Vancouver.*"*

Gene rolled his eyes. "Earth shuttle *Vancouver*, this is Chrysalis tower, you go with that vector and speed and you'll scorch your thermal tiles. You won't survive Earth reentry. If you want a round trip, then I would suggest a 14,000 mph approach at forty-five degrees."

"Roger, Chrysalis tower. Adjusting speed to 14,000 mph and entry attitude of forty-five degrees. Earth shuttle Vancouver.*"*

Terry nodded with appreciation at Gene's patience. "I think you've gotten a good handle on your job."

Gene shrugged as he studied the satellite imagery showing the shuttle making adjustments. "These pilots, I swear, sometimes they just want to argue." He leaned into his mic once more. "Earth shuttle *Vancouver*, this is Chrysalis tower. You're cleared for entry into Chrysalis air space. Lock onto beacon signal kilo x-ray tango."

"Roger, Chrysalis tower. Breaking orbital trajectory. Lock onto beacon signal kilo x-ray tango. Earth shuttle Vancouver.*"*

"Gene, just a heads-up, in short order we're going to be closing all air traffic on the colony except what goes through this airport."

"Really? What's happening?"

"The governor will make an announcement to explain. I'm just letting you know so you can be prepared. As soon as this last shuttle is off to Earth. There'll be a flurry of local shuttles coming and going, but once those are squared away, one of my guys will let you know what to do. Okay?"

"This sounds ominous."

"It'll be fine, just wait for the announcement, one of my guys will give you guidance."

"Okay." Gene leaned into the microphone. "Earth shuttle *Vancouver*, turn right heading one-eight-zero to intercept the localizer, cleared ILS runway Charlie into Chrysalis, maintain two thousand five hundred feet until established."

"Roger, Chrysalis tower. Turn right heading one-eight-zero, cleared ILS runway Charlie into Chrysalis, maintain two thousand five hundred feet until established. Earth shuttle Vancouver.*"*

Terry waved to Gene as he left. Things were under control here, but he wasn't so certain about the rest of the colony. Once the governor told the over three million residents of the colony that they'd all have to go into the mines for their own safety… well, if things were ever going to go sideways, that would be the time.

CHAPTER SIXTEEN

Nwaynna motioned toward the forklift operator as he unloaded one of the 4,000-pound spools of graphene and yelled across the hangar, "Be careful with that! We need one in each of the shuttle's cargo bays. Make sure they're strapped in tight; those shuttles will be taking off as soon as you get these loaded."

Two dozen of Carl's most trusted roughnecks were gathered around her, suited up for a mission they'd been secretly practicing for since the governor had set the roles for Operation Freedom almost two years ago.

"Okay guys, this is all about establishing some geosynchronous space anchors and dropping the landers on their mark. The pilots have the signal beacon for each of the connection points. Are there any questions about what you need to do?"

Everybody shook their head.

"Okay then, fists in the center..." Nwaynna stuck her fist in the middle of the team of miners and as soon as everyone had their hand in, she raised her voice and said, "Freedom!"

"Freedom!" the others echoed and almost immediately, the crowd dispersed, each of them rushing to their respective shuttles.

Nwaynna turned to Carlos. "Make sure you get this done, get back down safely, and tell our girls I'll be there as soon as I'm able."

Carlos leaned down, gave her a kiss and smiled. "I'll be sure to tell them not to worry because Mommy is saving us all." He glanced at the forklift lifting another spool of graphene and winced. "I have to go, I love you." He gave her one last peck on the lips and jogged out of the hangar.

Nwaynna looked at the clock. Just a little more than a handful of hours left. She fast-walked toward the nearest gate as she activated her lapel mic. "Folks, it's almost go time."

Carlos felt a bit queasy as the shuttle's vertical thrusters ceased their acceleration, leaving him in a weightless environment.

"Mister Stewart, we're approaching the requested 7,000-mile altitude from the colony surface. I'll be opening the cargo bay doors in approximately five minutes."

"Roger that," Carlos replied, easing himself to his feet and latching his safety harness to one of the metal loops on the cargo bay's floor.

With the magnetic soles of his spacesuit now activated, he

plodded very much like Frankenstein's monster, struggling to lift his foot and place it ahead of him as he marched toward the giant spool of graphene ribbon. This ten-foot spool was three-feet wide and weighed nearly two tons on the colony, but thanks to the lack of gravity, Carlos was able to easily turn the spool on its spindle and grab the metal rod that had been melded to the end of the ribbon.

He slowly pulled on the rod, and watched as the dull semi-transparent ribbon unfurled behind it. Dragging the end of the ribbon toward the lander, he fed the metal rod and about two feet of the attached ribbon into a slit on the top of the four-wheeled vehicle and slammed his gloved fist onto a button next to the opening. The opening immediately clamped shut, securing the end of the sheet of graphene to the lander.

Running his fingers along the seemingly fragile ribbon, it was hard to imagine that even though the ribbon was less than the thickness of a hair, it could easily hold many tons scrambling up and down it. After all, that was the purpose of a space elevator.

But he knew better than that. His wife may be one of the best scientific minds in the colony, but he wasn't an idiot. This wasn't going to be used for a space elevator. There's no way. Why suddenly, during the evacuation of the entire colony does the governor suddenly need twenty-four space elevators installed *right now*. Even if he didn't really know… he knew this project was more than just installing a space elevator, he wasn't an idiot and neither were the rest of the miners. There was more to it, and they didn't need to know, that was fine. Hopefully, after this was all done, Nwaynna would tell him what he'd helped put together.

The pilot's voice spoke through the speaker in his helmet, *"Evacuating the air from the cargo bay in three ... two ... one...."*

Suddenly, a horn blared in Carlos's helmet. The graphene fluttered with the whoosh of air escaping from the cargo hold. He leaned over the lander and checked its settings. "Hey, Pilot, have you detected the infrared designator on the surface for the rover to home in on?"

"Of course. It's broadcasting at the designated 1,033 nanometers."

Carlos grabbed the lander by one of its handholds and wheeled the weightless vehicle over the still-closed lower hatch of the cargo hold.

Staring at the wide ribbon of graphene attached to the lander, his gaze followed the transparent film up to the giant spool and nodded with approval. "The lander is aligned with the spool. I'm ready here." He took a few steps back, away from the cargo doors, as the yellow warning lights flashed through the cargo bay.

"Roger that. Opening the lower cargo hatch in three..."

Through the soles of his boots, Carlos felt the vibration of the heavy latches unlocking, then he watched as the cargo bay doors yawned open. The lander floated above the opened doors; its programming automatically activated. With its vertical thrusters, the rover slowly lowered itself below the deck, following the beacon that had been planted on the colony's surface.

The ribbon unspooled faster and faster while the rover thrust itself toward the colony's surface.

Just as he began to wonder about his transport, Carlos felt another vibration in the shuttle and smiled.

"Mister Stewart, your transport down to the surface has docked."

Walking to the airlock, Carlos imagined the lander in a controlled descent, speeding ever faster with the long ribbon that would form the basis of the space elevator's scaffolding trailing behind it. He knew there had to be something huge at stake for everyone in the colony. These things they were putting in place would be so much more than a simple way of transporting stuff off the surface; Carlos suspected that this would maybe be a part in saving all of their lives.

There were two dozen thermal pipes sticking out of the ground along the colony's equator, and Nwaynna stood at one end of one of them. It felt weird to be wearing the comms headgear, but they'd all need the eye protection as well as the visual assistance. There was almost no breeze, which was good; it would make things easier.

She turned to the two men who'd accompanied her. "You guys ready?"

The two burly miners nodded. "Yes, ma'am."

She activated her lapel mic. "Okay everyone, this is site one reporting in. We're about to hit the ready mark. I need confirmations from everyone that you're in position, because once we start, this'll all happen very quickly. One at a time, please. Site two, what's your status?"

"Ready and on site."

"Three?"

"We're ready."

Nwaynna continued through to site twenty-four. Everyone was ready.

And then she heard the words she'd been waiting for. *"Chrysalis is now on the far side of Epsilon."*

"Folks, a quick prayer before we start." She closed her eyes. "Dear Lord, please listen as I pray to you, and proudly defend the people of the colony. I will always serve you and our people, and be the best person that I can be. Amen."

A chorus of amens came across the comm.

"Okay, folks. It's go time."

Nwaynna clicked on her remote, and a video feed popped up in her viewfinder. It showed an open hatch high above the colony, out beyond the atmosphere, and a rapidly rotating spool spewing out what looked like a string of clear tape.

"Everyone, your viewfinders should now be showing a feed from a shuttle directly above your site. What you're seeing is a vehicle pulling a very long but thin sheet of graphene. That's the stuff I talked to you guys about. It's already been dropping for some time. We do this just like we drilled earlier, but if there are any questions, now's the time."

She was met with silence.

"Okay then. We're less than three minutes from the landers' arrival. Make sure the seal is tight. One person seals it, the other confirms that it's a tight fit. No mistakes. All of our families are depending on us."

One of the miners with her pointed up at the sky. "There it is! But it's not quite above us."

Nwaynna shielded her eyes from the sun. A dark object had

indeed broken through the haze. "The clouds probably shifted the homing signal a bit, but the rover will auto-center. Just watch."

The speck grew larger and its engines grew louder. She didn't see the graphene ribbon, and for a moment, she was concerned. But then the sunlight glinted off the nearly transparent material trailing above the descending lander.

They all had to cover their ears as the staccato of the lander's horizontal thrusters altered the course of its fall and slowed its descent. The landing was perfect, and the four-wheeled vehicle touched down right next to the thermal pipe. Above it, a graphene ribbon rose, as if by magic, into the sky. Over seven thousand miles long, and yet it just hung there as if immune to gravity. Nwaynna's mind had trouble wrapping itself around the sight before her.

"Amazing."

She activated her lapel mic. "The landers should all be down. If any are not, speak now."

Silence.

"Good. Just like we rehearsed. Let's do this."

One of the miners pushed the rover forward a few feet and pressed a button on its control panel. The graphene sheet with the metal bar attached spooled further out from the bottom of the lander.

The other miner removed the cap from the thermal pipe and applied a nanotube joining compound to the end of it. The first miner lifted the heavy bar and slid it horizontally into the slot at the end of the pipe while the other miner used a clamp to seal the connection. Both miners took signal measurements from both the pipe and the clean ribbon coming down from the sky, then conferred.

They looked to Nwaynna. "They're the same."

Nwaynna smiled and got on the comm. "Site one has a confirmed connection. Site two, report."

"Confirmed. We're good."

"Three is good."

"So is four."

Nwaynna's feeling of relief grew as the other sites reported in.

When all had reported successful connections, she said, "Great job, everyone. Let's go underground and meet up with our families. The rest is up to others to do."

As her two miner companions walked back to their transport, she hung back a bit, placed a call, and put her communicator to her ear.

The voice of the man who answered always sent chills through her. "Is it done?"

"Yes. All twenty-four are verified to have a sound electrical connection."

"Good job. Now go relax. Your family needs you."

Nwaynna knew that her job was far from over. The next step terrified her.

~

The governor spoke into her communicator. "Yes?"

"Madam Governor, it's Tina. I'm sorry to call, but I stumbled across something pertinent, and you did say to reach out if

there's anything about the colony I thought you might need to know."

"Go ahead."

"It seems that one of the reasons the UN guys are so keen on the colony is that they think you're hiding something. I just sent you the record I found—just in case there's something you want to move."

"Hold on, let me look." Welch pulled out her handheld PC. "I don't see anything."

"I only sent it a couple minutes ago. The bits might still be flying in your direction."

"Never mind, I just got it." She tapped on the file: a scanned UN record.

Date: 151.99 AE

Subject: Classified Briefing – colony concerns

GHD: We have intel from various sources that there's a secret level in the Chrysalis colony mines that none of the miners have access to.

SGNP: You think they're hiding something down there?

GHD: We have several working theories, but the one that we deem most likely goes back to the Exodus days. When Holmes died, the engine he developed was never found. If it's down there... well, it's not good for us. Our science team believes that what Holmes produced could be turned into a devastating weapon.

SGNP: A weapon that could be turned against us...

GHD: Exactly.

SGNP: If all they're doing is grubbing around in the dirt, then there's no reason for them to hide anything down there, especially from their own people. Okay, let's see what we can do about finding out what's down in this hidden level.

GHD: Yes, ma'am.

"Do you know who these speakers are?" the governor asked.

"It's safe to assume that GHD is General Heinrich Duhrer, head of UNIB, and SGNP is Natalya Poroshenko, secretary-general of the UN."

Welch laughed. "To think, that bitch is so insecure that she'd risk everything on something that could have been solved with a phone call. Those idiots could have just asked, because we have nothing to hide down there. Is there anything else, Tina?"

"No, ma'am."

"Thanks for the information. We're going to be going into lockdown soon, so if I'm out of reach, just send an email. I'll get it eventually."

As the governor hung up, Terry walked into her office with a duffel slung over his shoulder. "You ready?"

She stood, wearing fatigues for the first time in longer than she could remember. "Son, I've been ready for this for a very, *very* long time."

Priya's shuttle taxied past the gate and stopped amid controlled chaos on the tarmac. The hatch opened, an escalator was wheeled over, and moments later a half dozen armed colony security officers swarmed the cabin.

"It's fine," whispered Tom beside her. "They're just clearing the normals out of the way."

Once the Earth-based crew had been led off the ship and colony pilots had taken the helm, one of the men stood at the front of the cabin and made an announcement. "Per the orders of the governor, this shuttle will be acting as her security detail as we go planetside for the upcoming event. You'll want to remove your weight vests—you aren't going to want those on when we hit Epsilon's gravity. We're refueling, but we'll be taking off again in fifteen minutes. Be ready."

Priya's eyes threatened to pop out of their sockets.

"Epsilon?! Isn't the atmosphere poisonous? And it's like an oven! And the gravity is like half as much as Earth's. And—"

Tom squeezed her hand. He didn't seem fazed at all. "It'll be fine. I've been there a couple times. Yes, the gravity kind of sucks—it's about double that of the colony and forty percent more than Earth—but it's *not* like an oven and it's *not* poisonous. Average daylight temperature is about one hundred and thirty Fahrenheit, dropping to around ninety at night. Not comfortable, but not a killer."

An officer who'd taken the seat in front of them turned and smiled. "Hey, Chapper. Thought that was your voice." They clasped hands.

"Hey, Sanchez. Maybe you can clue me in on what's going on. I literally just got off mission from Earth. What's happening?"

The soldier shook his head. "It's sudden for us too—the governor *just* now made the call. Everyone on the colony is bugging out. Everyone. Going into the mines."

Priya looked out the window, past the refueling truck, to the hill in the distance that led to the mine she by now knew very well. There was a crowd of people in front of it. For her to be able to see them from here… there must be thousands of them.

"How is that possible?" she asked. "There are over three million people in this colony. And just like that, they're all going underground?"

"It's not ideal, but we've got no choice. According to the governor's announcement, Earth is heading our way with an armada of bombs. Enough to wipe us out. But evidently, this is a contingency she's planned for, and fortunately the people trust her. So when she ordered everyone to seek shelter, people sprang into action."

The refueling vehicle pulled away, and the soldier at the front said, "Buckle up, everyone. We're about to make history."

Thirty seconds later the shuttle was racing down the runway. Then they were in the air, and the G-forces pressed Priya back against the chair—hard. And the force was increasing as they rose. This was unlike any launch she'd ever experienced, and she held Tom's left hand in a death grip.

"This is a military launch," Tom explained. "It's a bit more abrupt than a cargo or civilian transport launch. We'll be fine in a few minutes."

Fine? She felt like an elephant was sitting on her chest. She focused on her breathing.

The speakers came to life, and a woman's voice projected through the cabin.

"This is Governor Welch, speaking to the soldiers on my shuttle as well as on shuttle two. I know that this is sudden for most of you—especially for the team that just arrived from Earth. I apologize, but we just didn't have the time to do things differently. I assure you that we made arrangements for your families' safety, and they'll be awaiting your return when we're done.

"After today, the relationship between the colony and Earth is going to be very different. The nature of that change is uncertain, but I hope this will be the beginning of a bright new era. In any case, over the next couple of hours you're going to be surprised by what we have in store. In the meantime, relax. It'll be about one hour before we enter Epsilon's atmosphere. I'll see you on the ground."

A timer appeared on the front wall of the cabin, counting down four hours and forty-five minutes. What was that for?

She tried to turn her head toward Tom. Given the forces still pushing on her, even that simple movement took everything she had.

"Try not to move," Tom said. His voice was strained, but he was clearly handling this much better than she was. "We're pulling about four to five Gs."

Priya managed a few words. "What's the timer for?"

"No idea. Seriously, just relax. If you fight the G forces, you'll be exhausted by the time we land, and you'll need your strength to walk around on Epsilon. Imagine you're melting into the seat."

Priya closed her eyes and again focused on her breathing.

What did I get myself into?

CHAPTER SEVENTEEN

When the shuttle landed on the surface of Epsilon, the higher gravity was obvious—but to Priya it didn't seem too bad, not after the G-forces she'd had to endure for much of the trip.

"Welcome to Epsilon," Tom said with a boyish grin. He stood, adjusted his belt, reseated his firearm, and offered Priya his hand.

"I swear," she said, "my butt is going to have a permanent mesh pattern from being pressed into that damned seat."

Tom chuckled. "That's something I'd like to see."

Priya gave him an accusing look. "Are you seriously flirting with me? Now, when your home, my new home, and millions of people's lives are at stake—*now* you choose to flirt?"

Tom began stammering a response, but Priya placed a finger across his lips and smiled.

"It's okay—I like flirting. But let's save it for when I'm in a frame of mind where I can return the favor."

Tom shook his head and smiled. "You're totally not the person I thought you were when we first met."

"I know. I tend to grow on you, like a fungus."

They followed the other soldiers to the front of the shuttle. Even before they exited, the temperature in the cabin had increased. Priya's clothes were suitable for summer in Florida, but the wave of heat hitting her now was unlike anything she'd experienced.

Actually, that wasn't entirely true. She'd been on level twelve in the mines. This place felt just like level twelve.

As they stepped through the hatch onto the stairs leading down to the planet's surface, she paused to take in the view of the landscape. It was bleak. They were in a craggy valley between two ridges, and everything was gray and dusty. A haze hung above them, obscuring any clouds.

"Be careful," Tom said behind her. "You're still not one hundred percent, and the first time I offloaded here, I ended up tumbling down the stairs."

"Well, I'm not a meathead." The phrase just popped out of her mouth, and she smiled.

"Oh no," Tom said dramatically. "You've been hanging around Steph for too long."

The other shuttle was parked about a hundred yards away. No, not parked—it was moving. Slowly. At a walking pace. Sideways?

"Tom… how is that shuttle moving?"

"Ah. That's alien tech. It's all over the place here."

Priya gasped as they reached the bottom of the stairs. Small silvery objects, thousands of them, were flitting across the ground toward their shuttle. They were like an ocean of skittering spiders. They gathered around the landing gear, and as soon as the stairs had pulled back, the shuttle began moving, carried by the sea of spiders.

"Where are they taking the shuttles?"

Tom pointed. "There are some caves over there where they'll be safe from the elements."

"Who programmed them to do that?"

A woman's voice answered. "I can introduce you to someone who can explain that."

Priya turned to see a blonde woman who looked vaguely familiar, though Priya was sure she'd never met her before. Beside the woman stood Terry, wearing fatigues and a sidearm, with a duffel over his shoulder.

The woman extended her hand. "Priya Radcliffe? I'm Jenna Welch—"

"The governor!" Priya gasped as she shook the woman's hand.

"Yes." She motioned to Terry and then Tom. "And you've already met my sons."

Priya looked at the two Chappers with wide eyes—and then a glare. "Why didn't either of you tell me your mom was the governor?"

Terry laughed. "What difference would that make?"

She narrowed her eyes at Tom. "And you?"

He held up his hands innocently. "You never asked."

With a laugh, the governor draped an arm over Priya's shoulders and began walking with her. "I can't begin to express how much you remind me of someone I knew a long time ago."

Before Priya could respond, the governor began giving her what was, apparently, a tour.

She pointed at a raised trail to the left. "You see that? That was the first indication we had of extraterrestrial life on Epsilon. When we spotted that, we *knew* it was manufactured by some form of intelligent life."

Priya scanned the length of the trail. "It's the straight lines. And the whole thing is raised above the ground. No riverbed would do that."

"Exactly. It turns out, that's what's left of a road built very much like the ones the Romans built millennia ago."

"Are the road's builders also responsible for the… alien tech that carried the shuttles? And"—her pulse quickened—"are those builders still around?"

"I'll defer the answer to the first question to someone else who we'll meet in a bit." The governor pointed to a cave up ahead. "As to the second question, I'm afraid they're gone. According to our best estimates, they've been gone for nearly two hundred thousand years."

Priya looked back at the road. It had survived for two hundred thousand years? That was unheard of.

When they reached the entrance to the cave, the governor turned to face the dozen men who'd accompanied them from the shuttles.

"I just got a heads up from the eye in the sky. It looks like we'll get storms late tonight, with possible flooding in the valley. So double-time it over to the shuttles, make sure they're squared away, and then hoof it back here. You don't want to miss the show." She turned to Terry and Tom. "But you two boys stay with me."

As she spoke, Priya noticed something odd about the governor. She was *young*. To be Terry and Tom's mother, she had to be at least in her late fifties, but she looked two decades younger than that. And then there was that strange sense of familiarity. Priya couldn't get over the thought that she'd seen this woman before.

But where?

It was surprisingly cool inside the caves. Unlike natural caverns with rough edges and dampness, these rock walls were smooth, rounded edges everywhere, and somehow there was a sterile sense to the air that seemed like it had been filtered. As they continued walking, Priya began feeling the burden of the gravity. After they'd gone down a smooth ramp for the fourth time, she asked Tom, "Did the colonists build this or was it here before?"

"Everything you've seen so far was already here. But you'll see lots of human touches soon enough. Or at least, I think so. I haven't been down here in a couple years, and the guy running it... well, he's got a mind of his own."

"The governor doesn't run this place? Then who does?"

At that moment they turned a corner, and Priya had to pause to take it all in. Directly in front of her was a fifty-foot-wide auditorium-style room with huge video panels arrayed all along the front, each displaying a feed from who knows where. And beneath those screens the floor was full of workstations, most of them manned. It looked almost exactly like the launch control facility back at Cape Canaveral. Above the main screens was a countdown clock, which currently read just over two hours.

"There's the man in charge," Tom said.

He was pointing to a tall, heavily muscled, dark-skinned man.

Priya gasped. "It can't be!"

There was no doubt about it. She'd seen the man's picture a hundred times before. This was one of the greatest scientists in history, the man her school was named after.

The governor greeted him, then they both turned and walked over to Priya, who had to concentrate to keep her jaw from hitting the floor.

"You... you're David Holmes," she stammered. "You're bloody dead!"

The man laughed. "I don't feel dead."

Stunned, Priya took two steps back and bumped into Tom. He put his hands on her shoulders and whispered, "It's okay. Calm down."

She shrugged out of his grasp and turned on him. "*You* calm down. I'm *rightfully* freaking out, damn it."

She turned back to Holmes, only to see him wiping tears from his eyes. Was he... crying?

"What the hell is going on?" she said.

It was Tom who answered. "Mom says you look and act exactly like Neeta Radcliffe. Neeta and Dave were best friends."

Holmes extended his hand. "I'm so glad to meet you. I thought Margaret had lost her mind when she told me about you, but she's right. You're just like Neeta. Even the British accent. It's unbelievable."

"Margaret?"

Holmes tilted his head toward the governor. "Margaret Hager."

Priya would have taken another step back, but she was already pressed up against Tom. This was too much impossibility coming at her all at once.

"You're… Margaret Hager. *The* Margaret Hager? First governor of the colony. President of the United States during the Great Exodus."

The governor winked. "Please. Just call me Margaret."

Minutes later, Priya found herself sitting alone in an office with David Holmes, the man responsible for saving all of humanity. Their knees were practically touching. It was surreal, and Priya said so.

"I can't believe I'm talking to the famous Dr. Holmes."

"And I can't believe I'm talking to a young Radcliffe. But call me Dave."

"Okay… Dave." That felt even *more* surreal.

Harold took the opportunity to climb into Priya's lap and transform into a cat. Dave smiled and nodded.

"Interesting. I've been wondering why some of the AIs around here have begun taking on the form of a kitten in recent years."

"AIs? You mean—there are other Harolds?"

"There are other AIs. There's only one Harold."

"But… you're saying when Harold turns into a kitten, they do too? So they're linked?"

"Well, they don't all turn at the same time, if that's what you meant, but they're capable of it. As to being linked, yes and no. I won't pretend to have a grasp of everything they do, but they have… well, not exactly a hive mind, but…"

"You mean like the Borg?"

Dave smiled. "Wow, I'm shocked you're familiar with that TV series; it was old when I was young. But no, they're not like the Borg either, and they don't share a mind. In fact, they have distinctly different personalities. But they do have a shared database of facts that contribute to the whole. So I suppose once the image of a kitten was introduced into their shared database, others picked it up."

Priya furrowed her eyebrows.

Dave laughed. "Wow, you even have the same expressions that Neeta did. And that expression means something's on your mind."

"A lot of things are on my mind, if I'm being honest. First and foremost… how are you still alive?"

"Yes, I thought you'd want to start there. But to answer, I need to roll back to a bit of history. I assume the government on Earth has hidden all evidence of the alien life we discovered on this planet?"

Priya nodded. "They have."

"Then here's the timeline, the best that I can figure it. About two hundred thousand years ago, this planet was very different than it is today. Lush grasslands, a bit cooler, with a civilization of insect-like beings who possessed the equivalent of 1950s technology. They had cities, farming, and a reasonably advanced manufacturing sector.

"But then a planetoid came. It struck Epsilon with only a glancing blow, but that was more than enough. The planet's surface became a furnace, and the impact sent a huge amount of debris into space. I believe that Chrysalis is a combination of what got kicked up from this planet's surface and the remnants of the planetoid that struck Epsilon. Epsilon had gained itself a moon.

"We found evidence of an observatory, so the inhabitants of Epsilon must have seen the asteroid's approach. They sent millions of their species underground, and amazingly, they survived. They were trapped—the surface was now uninhabitable—but they survived. In fact, they thrived for another one hundred thousand years, by our estimates, and their technology developed far beyond our own—such as Harold here, and other tech you've now likely been exposed to.

"But they eventually had a problem. Birth rates began dropping, and once it started, each generation got smaller and smaller. I suspect it could have been due to the background radiation that exists below the surface of most planets. Anyway, they eventually died out, all of them, leaving behind a wealth of unbelievable knowledge and technology."

"And then you arrived," Priya said.

"Yes. Then I arrived." He leaned forward, resting his elbows on his knees. "I arrived to find the remains of an alien civilization. But the government back on Earth... they weren't happy about it. In fact, they were deathly afraid. Afraid of the idea that an alien intelligence could have outpaced humanity. Perhaps afraid of how that intelligence and technology could disrupt their power structures.

"They agreed to the terraforming of Chrysalis. They agreed to the mining colony. But as for Epsilon, they wanted to pretend it wasn't there."

Dave smiled. "I disagreed."

"So… what? You faked your own death?"

"Nothing that dramatic. No, I simply ignored them, and visited Epsilon on my own. They threatened to nuke the place to stop me. And to destroy the 'aliens' I'd found. The AIs, that is. At the time, we weren't sure whether things like Harold were actually life forms, rather than the constructs they proved to be.

"Fortunately, instead of nuking the place, they sent two shuttle teams down to retrieve me and bring me back to Earth. I had warned them that if they tried to take me against my will, there'd be hell to pay. They didn't believe me." He grinned. "So when the first shuttle landed, I had the AIs start disassembling it."

Priya laughed. "No way. Really?"

"Really. And the second shuttle, after seeing what happened to the first, turned around and went the other way. Sadly, the crew of the first shuttle panicked, ran in the wrong direction, and ended up falling into a crevasse. It wasn't my intent that anyone die."

"Okay," said Priya, "that explains why you're on this planet, and why you didn't die the way the history books said. Come to think of it, it also explains why the government has told everyone that Epsilon is a poisonous hellhole—they don't want anyone else coming here. But what it doesn't explain—"

Dave cut in. "Is why I'm *still* alive all these years later."

"Yes." Priya nodded.

"It's the AIs. Think of them as fixers. From what I can tell, the early versions were originally designed to perform maintenance on computers and to aid in the assembly of CPUs and chipsets. They were in essence a solution the insect species had come up with for creating a computer factory of sorts. Subnanometer processes were child's play to these bots, and I'm still trying to figure out how some of this stuff works that they designed over 100,000 years ago. There are some examples of the earlier-gen AIs around here, and I assure you, they're nothing like the type you have purring in your lap. But they're good at their job—one hundred thousand years later, many of those computers are still working. The AIs have their instructions—think of it as their Prime Directive, since you're open to *Star Trek* references—and they perform it well, long after their creators have passed away.

"Anyway, back to my story. Epsilon became my home. It had to be my home, because I was persona non grata everywhere else. And perhaps I would have died here, if not for a fateful accident. I won't go into the details, but I managed to poison myself on something the aliens had left behind. And when I asked the AIs questions about the thing that had poisoned me, what they heard was that I 'needed repair.'

"Well, I didn't exactly know what that meant, but if the AIs knew how to cure the poison, I was all for it. Now, among the more recent generations of the AIs are ones that can cross porous boundaries like our skin, and that's exactly what one of them did. It was a tiny little thing, sat comfortably in the palm of my hand, and then it just melted right into me. I felt some pressure, but no real pain. I figured it would do what it needed to do, and then it would ooze its way back out.

"But… I don't think it ever did ooze back out. At least, if it did, I'm not aware of it. It took years for me to realize what had happened on that day."

"I suppose when you didn't die, you knew something was up."

Dave laughed. "True. I also didn't grow older. My guess? That little guy is still squirming around inside me, fixing things as they break. So here I am."

"And what about Margaret? Does she have one of those things inside her too?"

"Yes. As you know, she became the governor of the colony. She was sick of where the UN leadership was taking things, and there was bad blood all around. She too was poisoned, although in her case, it was intentional, done by a visiting UN official. She and I were still in contact—we always have been—and I got an AI up to her. Saved her life.

"But she had a better idea. Instead of surviving the attempted assassination, she decided to let the UN believe they had their victory. She went incognito. Has been running the colony, either out front or from behind the scenes, ever since."

"That's amazing. Absolutely amazing." Priya was struck by a sudden thought. "Wait—when I was up at the colony, I was attacked. I almost died. I'm told the only reason I survived was because Terry inserted something into my wound. Did he…"

"No, don't worry, you won't live forever. I later discovered that the AIs are able to produce repair nanites. They're just a few grams, not self-sustaining, and pretty much monotaskers. They fix the human body, stay in your system for about six months, and then become inert and get reabsorbed. I've provided packets of these repair nanites to the colony for medical use. That would almost certainly be what they used on you."

Dave glanced at his watch. "Looks like it's almost time to start the fun. Any more urgent questions before we get started?"

"Only one. What do you mean by 'fun'?"

He stood and smiled. "Come on. I'll show you."

~

Priya was still in a daze. *The* Dave Holmes led her back to the control room and had her sit in the center chair, right in the middle of the room. And then the famous astrophysicist clipped on an old-style lapel microphone and began the show.

An unknown voice broadcast across speakers around the room. *"Epsilon Mission Control, we are now at T-minus five minutes and counting for Warp Ring activation."*

Dave's voice carried loudly across the chamber as he spoke into his microphone. *"PAO, start the simulcast of the countdown along with the other telemetry readings and visuals we have in the control room. Let everyone on Chrysalis see what's going on. Their fate is most certainly linked to it."*

One of the men who'd arrived with the governor, presumably the public affairs officer, raced to a workstation and activated the external broadcast to the mining colony. When he flashed a thumbs-up to Dave, the scientist continued.

"For all within the reach of my voice, this is David Holmes, acting as mission director and broadcasting from the Epsilon Command Center. We are now approaching the four-minute mark before we activate the Warp Ring I've had installed around the Chrysalis mining colony."

Dave muted his mic and shouted to the PAO, "Can they see the contents of screen one?"

The officer nodded. "Sir, I'm broadcasting everything from all of the screens."

"I need mining comms up. Get me Nwaynna on the line. We need a direct link to her."

Only a moment passed before a woman's voice said, *"Hello?"*

Dave unmuted. "Nwaynna, Dave Holmes. You're my comms. Are you ready to rock and roll?"

"I am."

Dave motioned to the PAO, who returned a thumbs-up.

"Comms, what power level are you at on the ring?"

"We're at ten percent," Nwaynna replied.

"Signal quality?"

"We've got a clean sine wave without any indication of harmonics dirtying the signal. 4.325 terawatts are currently flowing through the ring. All systems are go for power-up."

Dave nodded and continued his announcement. "Chrysalis mining colony, by now you've been made aware that several shuttles are incoming from Earth, and that they intend to attack our colony. Let me reassure you: they won't succeed.

"It's my intention for you to relive what I experienced during the Exodus. We'll be playing a little bit of cat and mouse with our attackers. What they don't yet realize is that they're the mouse, not us. When the countdown hits zero, we will activate what I call a gravity bubble, and we'll begin moving the entire colony from its current position. Don't worry, when we're done, the colony will be back where it started.

"I know you've all gotten a proper colony education and are familiar with the Warp Ring, but it's one thing to read about it and another to experience it. Trust me, you won't feel a thing. Chrysalis will be accelerating, but you won't feel a change in momentum because of the gravity-isolated bubble.

"With the current settings, ten seconds after the Warp Ring is activated, you'll be traveling at nearly 1,750 miles per hour. After ten minutes, you'll be going over 100,000 miles per hour. And as for the shuttles incoming from Earth… well, I have a surprise waiting for them."

Dave gave directions to someone in the mission control room, and after a moment two of the screens on the wall showed new images. One looked like a cockpit view from a shuttle, and the other was from within a cargo bay.

"Chrysalis, on the upper part of the screen, you can see Epsilon's filtered view of the Chrysalis mining colony in orbit above the planet. Beside that is a view coming from the first of the Earth-based shuttles. They're now within visual range."

Priya watched the countdown unwinding its final seconds.

Dave called out, "Mining comms, commence with a controlled power-up sequence, maximum power output to stop at eighty percent of capacity and hold."

"Copy that. Powering up now."

Dave clicked off his mic and turned to Priya. "Having fun yet?"

"I just wish I understood what's going on. What's a Warp Ring?"

"We've set up a system with twenty-four thermal heat pipes buried deep into the surface of the moon above, and we've attached nanotube graphene sheets to them, forming a ring around the colony. We've been converting the heat energy into a power resource for decades in anticipation of something like this, and with that power reservoir, I'm replaying the formula that we used for the Exodus many lifetimes ago."

The screens flared brightly as a glowing hot ring of energy pulsed around the entire moon. The view from the shuttle cockpit showed the colony distort slightly, and then the entire moon began to recede.

Dave clicked on his lapel mic. "Chrysalis mining colony, you're on your way. Mining comms, go with the preplanned course."

He then picked up a communicator and spoke into it. "Go ahead."

The feed from the cargo bay shifted, the camera moving to reveal several bombs awaiting deployment. Then one of the bomb casings flashed brightly. Something was cutting into it.

"Chrysalis, what you're seeing is the cargo hold of one of the shuttles. Some of our devices found their way aboard, and they're currently disassembling the bombs that were destined for our colony."

The screen that had previously shown the mining colony

hovering above the planet flared brightly as four of the shuttles blew up in rapid succession.

Dave sighed. “It’s a pity that it came to that. Our goal isn’t retribution. In the end, we are all one people, one species, all from the same place. And hopefully, in the end, we’ll be one people once again.

“This is David Holmes, signing off. Get some rest, and we’ll be back to finish things in twelve hours.”

Dave clicked off his mic, removed it, and shouted to the room. “We’ve got an incoming storm up top, so let’s hunker down, grab a bite, take a nap, do whatever you want. I’ll see you all back here in twelve hours”

As Dave went to talk to the PAO, Priya felt a tap on her shoulder. The governor.

“How about having a meal with me?” the governor said. “The food here isn’t—” She paused. “Priya? what’s wrong?”

“It’s just… I know the colony has been moved, and the shuttles were stopped, so it’s safe for now. But the colony will have to come back, and at some point Earth will send shuttles that don’t have any alien tech on them. And then the colony is going to be a sitting duck. Won’t it?”

Margaret nodded. “That’s true. You’re absolutely right. But only if we stopped now.” She put her hand on Priya’s shoulder. “Dave is the smartest person I’ve ever met, and he’s had over a century to think about this problem. He hasn’t told me everything he’s planning, but I trust him, and you should too.” She laughed and shook her head. “I owe everything to that man. He saved all of our asses way back when, and even though I failed miserably at fixing the politics of the twenty-first century, and believe me I tried, maybe Dave has an answer for the politics of the twenty-third."

Priya took a deep breath and let it out. "Okay. I just hate not knowing what's going on. And not being able to do anything about it."

Margaret laughed. "Priya, you and me both. Come on. Let's go get something to eat."

CHAPTER EIGHTEEN

Twelve hours later, they were back in the mission control room, and Priya's neck and back ached from tension. It drove her insane to know they were within minutes of something huge, and she had absolutely no idea what it was. Was Dave going to pull out a magic wand and destroy Earth? Was he going to somehow talk reason to the Earth's government and have them leave the colony alone? Both ideas seemed about as likely as unicorns shooting out her butt.

As Dave put on his mic, he gave Priya a wink.

That's when she snapped. "Don't you bloody wink at me, David Holmes. I'm tired of the secrets. It's driving me bonkers."

He laughed. "I can't tell you how many times Neeta told me that same thing. Relax. You're going to enjoy this."

Priya huffed with frustration, yet she couldn't help but feel a small bit of relief that Dave was so calm and confident.

He yelled to the PAO, "I need Tina Polyudov on screen three

via the priority communicator. And switch all comms to the colony via the priority communication channels. I want them to see this real-time."

The screens came back online.

"Tina," said Dave. "Can you hear me?"

A woman on a screen in the upper left nodded. *"Loud and clear. I've got all of your stuff and I'm ready to rebroadcast across all the Earth channels when you're ready."*

Priya did a double take when she heard the voice. This beautiful woman spoke like a gruff male.

"Thanks, Tina," said Dave. "I'll be back with you in a bit."

Priya hesitantly raised a hand.

Dave clicked off his mic and turned to her. "Yes?"

"She's on Earth?"

"Yes."

"Then how are you talking to her in real-time?"

Dave glanced at the clock. "Are you familiar with quantum entanglement?"

Priya nodded. "It's when two particles are generated and their states remain identical no matter the distance between... oh!" Her eyes widened. "Are you telling me that you managed to get enough entangled particles that you're able to create a way of transmitting voice and data?"

"Exactly right." Dave fist-bumped with her. "There's obviously much more to it, but when we have time, I'll walk you through it. It's actually kind of cool."

As he went back to work, Tom appeared at Priya's side. "Hey, how are you doing? Getting over the shock of it all?"

"Sort of. Will you sit with me?"

Tom looked around. "I think all the seats are taken. But I'll kneel beside you."

"No, sit." Priya stood. "I'll park myself on your lap."

Tom raised an eyebrow. "Are we flirting now?"

Priya grinned. "Not yet."

Tom took a seat and she sat in his lap.

"Do you know what's going to happen?" Priya asked.

"Nope. I'm just along for the ride."

Dave turned his mic back on. "Chrysalis mining colony, we're back online, and welcome.

"Miss Polyudov, what's our status on the Earth satellite links?"

"I've slipped in back doors to their satellite control systems, and they're waiting for me to use them. I'm ready to transmit the moment you say. I'll have the world's undivided attention."

"Is Project Thor online?"

"Yes. I have the GPS coordinates for the two targets you asked for, and I have several live video streamers in place outside those locations for corroborating evidence."

"Good. This one is for Dr. Jerry Pournelle. Tina, go ahead with the launch of Project Thor."

"With pleasure."

~

The bright neon lights of Times Square flashed their advertisements for the latest Broadway shows and blockbuster movies. David Gatewood ignored them as he weaved his way through the crowds. He was a New Yorker, and the neon glitz was something only the tourists paid attention to. He had to get to work for the late shift. But as he pushed through the gawking tourists and street vendors, the lights suddenly dimmed, and it seemed as if the world had stopped.

Gatewood stopped right where he was and looked around at the blacked-out screens. And then, for the first time in his lifetime, he saw an unsanctioned transmission. Every screen was showing the same thing: a waving American flag.

The American flag was verboten, relegated to the same status as the old Confederate flag. But Gatewood knew the stories, the rumors of a time long ago, when the United States was an independent nation, under God, indivisible, and everyone enjoyed liberty and justice.

People whispered all around him. They all knew that to even look at what was on the screen was probably illegal. But that didn't stop them.

A logo appeared in the bottom left corner of the screens. "Ronald Reagan Presidential Library," it read. And then a voice spoke, booming loud and clear across the suddenly still streets of New York.

"Freedom is never more than one generation away from extinction. We didn't pass it on to our children in the bloodstream. The only way they can inherit the freedom we have known is if we fight for it, protect it, defend it, and then hand it to them with the well-fought lessons of how they in their lifetime must do the same. And if you and I don't do this, then you and I may well spend our sunset years telling our children and our children's children what it once was like… when men were free."

The crowd buzzed.

And then the flag vanished and a man appeared on screen. A man with a face everyone knew. From school. From history books. This man was the savior of the human race.

What is going on?

David Holmes stood proudly, faced the camera, and smiled.

~

Shinzo Watanabe stood in the center of Shibuya Crossing, one of the busiest crossings in Tokyo, along with thousands of others. But no one was moving or bustling about. They all stood still, looking up at the big screen that broadcast the face of a man everyone knew.

"Hello everyone. Your eyes are not deceiving you. I am David Holmes."

A Japanese translation scrolled beneath the image, but Watanabe understood the English.

This had to be a video trick by the government. But… why? What would be the point?

And then the face disappeared, although his voice continued to narrate, and the translation continued to scroll, as a series of videos played.

A UN shuttle landing on the planet Epsilon.

The shuttle being ripped apart by what looked like tiny robots.

The wing of a giant iridescent insect, and on its end, the potent poison that should have killed David Holmes.

Shape-changing alien creatures.

And through it all, Holmes spoke. He explained why he did not die on Chrysalis. He explained how it was that he was still alive.

It couldn't be true.

And then another video played, this one with a timestamp of less than twenty-four hours ago. It showed several views of what Holmes claimed was an attack by Earth against the colony. Watanabe watched with fascination as a ring glowed brightly around the colony, and with horror as the shuttles exploded.

Next up were pictures of classified UN Intelligence records. Holmes narrated the relevant sections, which indicated that both the secretary-general and the head of the UN Intelligence Bureau had been behind attacks against UN citizens.

Someone in the crowd yelled, "The UN has lied to us all!"

Others murmured in agreement or denial.

Shinzo Watanabe wasn't sure what to believe.

And then the man who claimed to be David Holmes reappeared. This time two women stood with him. One was light-skinned and blonde, the other was young and dark-skinned, with long black hair.

Watanabe couldn't tear his eyes away from the screen as this man from the past continued his message.

~

David Gatewood stood shoulder-to-shoulder with New Yorkers and tourists alike, all of them riveted to the screens above Times Square.

"Citizens of Earth," said the man who looked just like David Holmes, *"I want to introduce you to someone who is as responsible as I am for ensuring that we didn't all go extinct nearly two hundred years ago. A woman whose reward for her service was to endure an attempted assassination by the government that leads you today."*

He gestured to the blonde woman next to him. *"This is Margaret Hager, the last president of the United States, and the person who represented the United Nations during the time of the Exodus. I only wish she had been made secretary-general after the Exodus, as I'm confident the world would have been much better off."*

He then held out an arm toward the younger woman. *"And this is Priya Radcliffe, a direct descendant of Burt and Neeta, two people who were also very much responsible for the very survival of our species. Priya, Margaret, thank you both for being with me here today."*

Holmes faced the camera once more. *"I know I've shown you many things that you may find difficult to believe. Things you would rather not accept. Perhaps it would help if I showed you what your leadership is doing right... now."*

Holmes nodded to someone off screen, and the feed shifted to an entirely new location. The UN's logo was on a wall in the background, and Secretary-General Natalya Poroshenko was in the foreground, screaming at several people working furiously at computer terminals.

"Get this off the air now or I'll have all of you executed for treason," Poroshenko yelled. *"Now!"*

Gatewood cringed as the crowd around him bristled and became hostile.

"Fry the bitch!"

"How did this happen?"

"Traitors!"

"We need to march on the UN!"

Holmes appeared on screen once again, looking somber. *"I know that many of you still won't believe what I'm telling you. For those of you, I ask you to do just one thing for me. Look up into the sky."*

Gatewood, along with everyone else in Times Square, looked up—and gasped.

A glowing ball hovered in the night sky, growing larger and larger, brighter and brighter, nearly turning night into day.

"People of Earth, what you see above you is Chrysalis. Please welcome the colony as a temporary neighbor. I brought them to you to make a point. For too long, the people of the Chrysalis colony have been segregated from the people on Earth, and vice versa. But we are one people. Always remember that."

"Holy crap," someone shouted. "This is real!"

"Hager for Secretary-General!" shouted another.

"We need to wipe the UN out of existence!"

Holmes continued. *"Many of you might be thinking, 'Now what?' I understand how easy it is to let things just evolve on their own. It's easy to maintain the status quo and not make waves. I'm guilty of it myself. But like Ronald Reagan said oh so many years ago, the only way our children can inherit the freedom I personally have known is if we fight for it and protect it. My generation failed you. We didn't do what we should have done. Margaret and I and others should have fought harder for you all. But with these final words, I'll try to begin the fight that should have happened over one hundred and fifty years ago."*

The video went split-screen, showing two buildings. Gatewood recognized them both. One was the UN Executive Building, where the secretary-general worked. The other was on 66th, the headquarters of the UNIB.

And from up in the sky, two fiery streaks came down toward Earth. When they struck, both sides of the split-screen flashed white. The ground shook, and booms reverberated across the city.

Then the videos adjusted for the brightness, revealing that both of the buildings had been destroyed.

"Holy shit," someone yelled. "David Holmes just blew them to smithereens."

The crowd cheered.

The video switched back to David Holmes, Margaret Hager, and Priya Radcliffe.

"People of Earth. You've just now lost your secretary-general and the head of the intelligence agency. They were corrupt beyond comprehension. And now... you are free.

"But remember: freedom is what you make of it. I hope you make the right decisions. In the meantime," he smiled at the two women next to him, *"we'll be here to support you."*

AUTHOR'S NOTE

Well, that's the end of *Freedom's Last Gasp*, and I sincerely hope you enjoyed it.

I should note that when I finished writing the first book in this series, *Primordial Threat*, I didn't intend to have a follow-on.

Hear me out on this… I know I left an epilogue that strongly hinted at what could happen when humanity finally found a new home. At the time, I'd really debated with myself about whether to include that epilogue or not. I didn't want to write a scene that promised the beginning of a new story. I wanted to show Dave Holmes and others settling into their new reality, but with just a taste of what they'd encountered as a neat little bow on the story.

And maybe with that choice, I set myself up for the inevitable. Because in my mind, I didn't have plans to follow-up with a sequel. I thought the story in PT was tied up fairly nicely. The world had been saved, not everyone survived, and some people who we were sure were dead, ended up not being dead. It was a good end to a somewhat epic tale.

And then people began reading it. *Awesome!*

It landed on the USA Today bestseller's list soon after its publication. *Shocking!*

And I might note, that if I weren't as stubborn as I was, that book, nor its sequel would have come into being. Almost every publisher eventually turned PT down. However, there was one major publishing house, who shall remain nameless, that did consider purchasing the rights. But they asked for the main character to comply with a trend called OwnVoices.

At the time, I'd never heard of it, but simply put, the premise behind OwnVoices is that writers of a certain demographic should be allowed to tell the tales for that demographic.

Seemed reasonable, until I learned that the acquiring editor didn't believe they'd be able to get an approval for me writing PT. Why? Well, PT's main character was black, and I'm a first-born American of Israeli descent, and decidedly *not* black.

Evidently, David Holmes needed a race change, which I refused, and soon after I ended up self-publishing it. [I'd note that this is the first time I'm admitting this in "public" and primarily doing so as a middle finger to the establishment that wants to segregate authors into a specific lane. We have a diverse and beautiful society, and we should all be able to write who and what we want, with respect, and impunity.]

Well, I literally got 100's of emails asking when the follow-on to PT would come out. Each and every time, I backpedaled and said that I didn't have a schedule for it yet, but if readers demanded it, it would come.

Well, the readers spoke, and I responded. I hope you enjoyed it.

And I'm sure you'll be asking, if there's no epilogue in *this* novel, does that mean you have no plans for a follow-on?

Sigh…

I'll say what I always say: if the readership demands it, there's more that will be told. That is my way of hinting that if you enjoyed this story, tell your friends, create the demand organically.

As to there being more to be told, let's be realistic, there's a lot left to account for, isn't there?

Did Earth fix their governmental issues?

What happened with the mining colony and Dave Holmes, Margaret Hager, and now Priya? There's so many things those three are quite capable of doing as major roles for major plot-lines, don't you think?

What about the spaceship Earth was building, but was short on resources that came from the colony? You didn't actually think I forgot about that, did you? Why is that metal only found on the colony?

Is it a coincidence that level twelve has the same climate as the surface of Epsilon, or am I just noting it to distract you?

So, book three is currently not on my schedule, but readers ultimately influence what I write and in what priority. If many people are being introduced to this new Exodus Series, and the demand is high, trust me: I have many ideas already in place for where this will go.

Well, that's enough about this story at the moment, I usually leave the addendum for where I talk extensively about the current novel, the technology and what's real and not real.

In my Author's Note section, I talk to you directly about what I do, who I am, and why I do it, so let me say a few brief words.

Since this is book two of a series, I'll presume that I've introduced myself to you before and won't make you suffer through that sort of tedium again.

However, I did want to talk a bit about my contract with you, the reader.

I write to entertain.

That truly is my first and primary goal. Because, for most people, that's what readers typically want out of a novel.

That's certainly what I always wanted. Story first, always.

Now, don't get me wrong, there are all sorts of perfectly valid reasons to be reading, and in fact, I get a huge kick out of it when people tell me that they kept on having to look things up to see if they were real, and being shocked to learn that many elements in my stories are real.

For me, I take pride in trying to give people entertainment, while attempting to stay as true to science and technology as possible. And if the novel is inspired by real events in some way, I try to provide verifiable excerpts that allow readers a bit more insight into the facts of the subjects covered in the story.

When my stories contain topics that have possible controversy or ones with potentially polarizing opinions associated with them (e.g. GMO) I never take a position as the author. However, I don't ignore the fact that there is controversy. I let the characters play out their roles and make no advocacies. However,

I do endeavor to lay out the facts as they exist for the reader to ultimately draw their own conclusions.

So far, I've covered broken arrow incidents (See *Perimeter* for that), child sex trafficking (*The Inside Man*), and the dark side of medical research (*Darwin's Cipher*.)

Some have called my choices eclectic, unexpected, but the vast majority of feedback I've received to date has thankfully been positive. So, thank you for that. Posting reviews is, of course, the easiest way to let me and others know what you thought of this novel or any of my work. Word of mouth is precious to us poor authors.

However, even though I enjoy writing about events, history, science especially, my primary goal always circles back to entertaining.

As always, at the end of this book, I have an addendum where I cover certain details regarding the creation of this novel, the research that went into it, and of course, I go into the science and technology—mostly because I can't help myself.

I do hope you enjoyed this story, and I hope you'll continue to join me in the future stories yet to come.

Mike Rothman
March 20, 2020

If you enjoyed this story, I should take a moment to introduce you to another one of my titles that many of my science fiction readers have told me they enjoyed. It's best described as a medical techno-thriller (in the style of Crichton), but it does involve the intelligence community, espionage, and many of the things that readers of thrillers tend to seek. And yes, I nerd out quite a bit on the technical aspects of genetics, science research, and the realities of what can occur, thus bringing in science to what otherwise might be a simple thriller. This techno-thriller is called, *Darwin's Cipher*.

If you'll indulge me, below is a brief description of *Darwin's Cipher*:

Juan Gutierrez, a cancer researcher, has spent years studying the genome of animals that exhibit immunity to some types of cancer. Over the course of his study, Juan discovers a pattern that allows him to predict the course of a species' evolution across thousands of generations.

Using the algorithm he's developed from the pattern, Juan uncovers what he believes to be the key to conquering humanity's susceptibility to cancer.

Others are interested in using what Juan has dubbed "Darwin's Cipher," however, instead of cancer research, they see very different applications for the new genetic algorithm.

Nate Carrington, an FBI forensic analyst has been struggling with several cold cases when he's alerted to an incident at a nearby ranch. It's a case of a newborn calf who is found in the middle of a herd of dead cattle. It provides a single link to Nate's other cold cases: the DNA analysis of the calf doesn't match anything in the FBI's database.

Somewhere in a rural hospital in West Virginia, four hospital workers are dead and a newborn child has been transported to the NIH's level-4 bio-containment unit.

It's only when the NIH sends out an alert to all hospitals and law enforcement agencies that the world realizes the danger that faces them.

PREVIEW OF DARWIN'S CIPHER

Jon LaForce scrambled down the steep path leading into Tikaboo Valley and took a swig from the cheap red wine he'd bought from a nearby gas station. Almost immediately a flush crept up his neck and warmed his cheeks.

He'd just been fired for the second time this month.

He wasn't sure what had brought him out into the middle of nowhere in southeastern Nevada. When he was a kid, his friends used to talk about coming out here to spy on the military planes as they took off and landed. They used to whisper about secret experiments, mysterious clouds in the sky, and of course, UFOs. After all, this was supposed to be where they kept those aliens. Area 51.

Jon didn't believe any of that crap, and he doubted any of his friends had ever had the guts to actually sneak onto the grounds or even come out this way. And as he looked around, he had to admit they weren't missing much. Just acres of thick desert sagebrush.

Taking another swig from his bottle, Jon felt the buzz from the alcohol as he scrambled down the slope. Suddenly, something broke through the thick sagebrush at the bottom of the hill. Jon drew his Glock from its holster and took a shooter's stance. Bobcats sometimes prowled this area.

But it was just a stray dog. Dark brown coat, long tail, floppy ears—might be a chocolate lab.

Jon holstered his gun and whistled. "Hey, boy, what are you doing out here?"

The dog wagged its tail furiously and bounded toward him.

He screwed the top back on the wine bottle and held his hand out for the dog to sniff. As the animal huffed at his hand and ran its nose up and down the legs of his trousers, Jon noticed a bloody wound on its front right leg.

"Did something take a bite out of you, old boy?"

The dog whined and glanced back toward the scrub.

Jon scratched the dog's head. "Your coat's nice and shiny, and you look well fed." He shook his head and patted the dog on its back. "What are you doing out here? Someone's probably looking for you. Maybe I should get you to a shelter and see if they can find your owner. I sure as hell can't take care of you. I can barely take care of myself nowadays."

A rustle of movement sounded in the sagebrush about fifty yards away. The dog whined, took a few steps up the slope, and turned to Jon as if to say, "Are you coming?"

Jon drew the Glock once more and took a step toward the sound.

The lab darted in front of him and gave a low growl.

"Shh…" Jon stepped around the dog.

The dog whined, nipped at his pant leg and pulled hard on his jeans, trying to drag him up the slope, away from the sound.

"What the hell are you doing, mutt?" Jon yanked his leg away and gave the dog a sideways kick, which it easily dodged.

The dog backed away, whining, then yipped once and raced up the hill.

At the base of the slope, two dark animals burst through the sagebrush. Two more dogs, both nearly identical in appearance to the chocolate lab.

But very different in demeanor.

These dogs had neither wagging tails nor lolling tongues. They eyed Jon menacingly, lowered their heads, and stalked closer.

Jon aimed his gun and called out in a friendly tone, "Hey, boys, are you missing a friend of yours?"

As soon as he trained the Glock on the animals, they split, one going to his left, the other to his right.

His heart thudding, Jon aimed at the dog on his right. The animal immediately darted behind a boulder.

It was almost as if the animal knew the gun was dangerous.

Hearing the other dog's nails scraping on the gravel, Jon wheeled around and fired a warning shot.

The animal continued to advance, but it used a jerky zigzag pattern, making it difficult to aim.

A chill raced up Jon's spine.

His gun arm shaking, Jon focused on the approaching dog. For a split second his mind flashed back to his time as an artilleryman in Afghanistan. Back then, he'd shot at enemies he could barely see. Now, for the first time in his life, he was within spitting distance of his target as he squeezed the trigger.

The animal had just begun to leap when the bullet slammed into its shoulder. It fell to the ground with a whimper.

At almost the same moment, Jon felt over one hundred pounds of canine smash against his back. The second dog knocked him off his feet and clamped its vise-like jaws on the wrist of his shooting hand.

Jon struggled with the growling animal. He started to yell when his voice was suddenly trapped in his throat. The dog he'd shot had clamped down tightly on his throat.

He fell back onto the dirt, his windpipe closing under the crushing force of the animal's impossibly strong jaws. His vision wavered as he strained for breath.

His heart pounding with terror, he prayed. *My God, there's so much I could have...*

The world faded to black.

Hans Reinhardt stood at the top of the rocky slope and breathed in the acrid smoke of burning sagebrush. A half dozen men in fatigues spewed hellfire from their flamethrowers, and all across the burning landscape, stones cracked in the fierce heat.

The operation had been going well—until now. Now everything had turned to shit. A complete disaster. Despite the assurances from his bosses in the German Federal Intelligence Service, not to mention the US handlers in Langley, Hans knew it was time to reset. He needed to move the operation to a more remote location. One with less chance of… "incidents."

The base commander, an Air Force colonel, walked up and stood beside him. "His name was Jonathan LaForce, Marine artilleryman, ten years out of Afghanistan with an honorable discharge."

"What the hell was he doing here? I thought this base was secure."

The base commander shifted his weight nervously. "The base *is* secure. However, we'd underestimated the containment measures needed in the kennel. I reviewed the security tape myself, it seems one of the experiments figured out how to open the latch to its stall. Once it escaped, the others managed to copy its actions. And before anyone could stop them, the animals had dug a hole under the perimeter fence."

Hans kicked a stone off the rocky escarpment and ground his teeth with frustration. "A dead Marine is the last thing we need. How big of a problem is this going to be?"

The colonel's discomfort increased. "The good news is, he was one of those disaffected types. No family, and it looks like he was out of a job. A wanderer who probably won't have anyone searching for him, at least not for a while. We'll deal with his remains."

"And the experiments? Have they all been tracked down and decommissioned?"

"We tracked five of the animals through the signal coming off their PIT tags. We captured and disposed of them." The colonel blew out a deep breath. "Unfortunately, we have not yet been able to locate the sixth. I've sent out the drones. They're programmed to run grids across the terrain, looking for the animal's signal. We'll find it."

Hans silently wondered how such an incompetent ass had come to be the base commander at a supposedly high-security location. "We don't have time for a lengthy search, Colonel. We cannot have one of our experiments encountering civilians."

"We'll track the dog down—"

"That's not a fucking *dog*, you moron!" Hans snapped. "It's a specially bred nightmare with enough strength and intelligence to escape your so-called 'secure' kennel and take out an armed ex-Marine who got in its way."

The colonel's eyes narrowed and his jaw tightened.

"Listen to me," Hans continued. "Both my neck *and* yours are on the line if any of this gets out. We can't risk our arrangement being exposed. And let's face it, your government has already proven itself incapable of keeping things out of Wikileaks."

"Mr. Reinhardt," said the colonel, "believe me, I know exactly what's at stake. You do *not* need to remind me. This is a black operation, and it's staying that way. I'm overseeing the cleanup personally." The colonel pointed toward the nearby slope. "We found some blood that we believe is from the missing animal. It's wounded, which will limit its ability to elude us. Between the contractors on foot and the drones in the air, we'll find it."

Hans glared. "You damn well better."

Frank O'Reilly poured a few inches of pea gravel into the fence-post hole he'd just dug. He glanced over his shoulder at Johnny, one of the ranch hands he'd recently hired.

"Make sure you get at least three inches of these rocks into the hole and tamp it down good, like this." he said, tamping the rocks down with a large wooden pole. "We need a solid footing for the fence posts. Them cattle will rub up against just about anything, so these here posts need to be sturdy, you understand?"

"Yessir, Mr. O'Reilly. And you need them posts eight feet apart so them sixteen-foot planks can span two openings, right?"

"That's right. Make sure them posts are square with the ground and space them evenly."

Frank handed Johnny the post-hole digger and smiled. The ranch hand had just turned eighteen, and Frank couldn't help but remember when his Kathy was that age. Johnny had that same lively spirit and energy that reminded him of Frank's baby girl when she graduated high school and took off for the world.

He patted Johnny on the shoulder. "You got this?"

"Yessir, but if'n you don't mind my asking, why all of a sudden you taking on help? You fixing to retire?"

Frank laughed and shook his head. "Johnny, I might be fifty-three, but I've still got quite a bit of life left in me. Just get the job done, and you best be minding what I said about doing a quality job. I'm going to check all your work, so don't take no shortcuts, you hear?"

"Yessir. Don't have to worry about that." Johnny hefted the post-hole digger and walked to the next flagged spot.

As Frank turned away, he nearly tripped on a dog that was sitting on its haunches right behind him.

"Damn it, where the heck did you come from?"

The chocolate lab just sat there with its tongue lolling. A beautiful animal. Shiny coat, heavily muscled body, and obviously well-fed. Not a stray.

Frank held out his hand. "Are you friendly?"

The dog stood, and its tail became a blur. It sniffed at Frank's hand, then lowered its nose and sniffed at his boot and up along his jeans. Finally, it sat back on his haunches, licked its lips, and whined. Its bright brown eyes stared up at him, glanced at his trousers, and then back up at his face. It whined again.

Frank tilted his head, unsure what the dog was trying to say. Then it hit him, and he laughed. "Ah! I know why you're so interested in me." He pulled a folded-up piece of homemade beef jerky from his pocket and tossed it gently to the dog.

The animal snatched it in midair and chewed contentedly.

"Well, I best be off, pup. I'll get a tongue-lashing if I'm not home in time for supper."

Frank walked the roughly half a mile to the modest white ranch-style home he'd built almost thirty years ago. As he drew near, he heard paws padding along behind him. *Figures. I know better than to feed a strange dog.* He purposefully ignored the animal and started up the steps to the front porch.

The aroma of roasting beef was in the air.

Megan stepped out onto the porch. "Oh good, you're back. Dinner is almost ready. Go get washed up."

He gave her a peck on the lips. "Smells good."

She looked past him with a puzzled expression. "You made a friend?"

The lab now sat at the bottom of the porch steps, looking hopeful.

Frank shook his head. "I made the mistake of giving him some of the beef jerky."

Megan pushed her shoulder-length auburn hair behind her ears, knelt, and patted the wooden deck of the porch. "Here, boy, did you like the jerky?"

The dog bounded up the stairs and lay down in front of her, its belly up and its long tail sweeping back and forth over the wooden planks.

Megan giggled as she rubbed the dog's belly. "You're such a good boy." She looked up at Frank with that sheepish smile he knew so well. "Do you think anyone owns him?"

"No idea. He just wandered up. He's obviously been cared for, but he's not wearing a collar or anything." He hesitated. "I thought after Daisy died, you swore—"

"Oh, you poor thing!" Megan exclaimed. She was examining the dog's front right leg. "It looks like he got into a fight or something."

The dog whimpered as she fussed over his injury.

"I'm sure he'll be fine," Frank said.

"No." Megan stood and wiped her hands on her apron. "We're going to take him to the vet and get him looked at."

Frank wondered how much the vet would try to gouge him for. "He's not even our dog."

Megan turned and gave him that look that said her mind was set. "Then we can have the vet check him for one of them chips they put in dogs nowadays."

Megan was five feet tall and built like a pixie, but once she set her mind to something, she was immovable. If thirty years of marriage had taught Frank anything, it was that.

He raised his hands in defeat. "What about dinner?"

"Dinner will keep." Megan walked into the house and motioned for the dog to follow, which it did. "I think we still have Daisy's old bowls. I'll see if this boy is thirsty while you go call the vet and tell him we're on our way."

~

The examination room doors opened and a blue-smocked veterinary assistant with a long black ponytail stepped out. "O'Reilly?" she called.

Frank waved. "Right here."

Her gaze shifted to the chocolate lab lying between Frank's and Megan's feet. "And what's your name, gorgeous?"

"He doesn't—"

"Jasper," Megan announced, as if that had always been his name.

Frank groaned inwardly. He hoped she wasn't getting attached. This animal belonged to someone. No way would a stray look as healthy as he did.

"Well, let's get Jasper weighed and see how he's doing."

"Jasper" stood the moment Megan did, and he obediently trotted after her into the examination room. Frank, shaking his head, followed.

The veterinary assistant—the name "Sherri" was stenciled on her scrubs—stopped beside a large metal scale. "Let's see if we can coax Jasper on here."

Before Megan could even nudge the dog in the right direction, Jasper walked over and stepped on the scale.

"Hah, what a good boy," Sherri said. "Wow, 125.8 pounds. I'd never have guessed it." She scribbled the weight on a sheet of paper and slid it into Jasper's chart.

"Do you have one of those chip scanners?" Frank asked. He ignored Megan's severe look. "Jasper just wandered onto our property today, and he has no collar or tags. We don't know anyone who's missing a lab in our area. But we wanted to do the right thing and see if he'd been chipped or not."

"Oh, of course. Be right back." Sherri disappeared through another door while Megan began fervently petting the top of Jasper's head. Moments later, Sherri returned with what looked like a thick stick with a small loop on its end.

Megan grabbed Frank's hand as the veterinary assistant approached Jasper.

Sherri passed the wand back and forth over Jasper's back. "Hmm. Most vets inject the chip between the animal's shoulders, and I'm not seeing anything there."

Megan squeezed Frank's hand tighter.

"Let's just make sure there isn't one anywhere else." Sherri slowly moved the wand over Jasper's hindquarters and then back toward the front again. As she neared the right front leg, the dog whined.

"It's okay, Jasper," Megan said soothingly. "She's not going to hurt you."

The veterinary assistant paused over the dirt-encrusted wound. "Poor baby, you've got an ouchie. Dr. Dew will make it all better." She finished dragging the wand over Jasper and shook her head. "No chips that I can find."

Frank sensed Megan's smile without even having to look. He sighed wistfully with the realization they had just adopted a dog. "Okay," he said. "In that case, in addition to tending to that wound, let's get Jasper a full workup."

"Okay. Dr. Dew will be in to look at Jasper in a bit. And since it looks like Jasper is favoring his right front leg, we may need to take x-rays and sedate him to treat the wound. It'll be at least four hundred dollars." She raised a questioning eyebrow.

"Just fix him up," Megan said quickly. "We'll pay whatever is necessary."

Frank kissed the top of Megan's head. There was no arguing with Mrs. O'Reilly over such things.

Frank spent nearly an hour in the waiting room, with Megan fidgeting the whole time. And when at last the vet appeared—without Jasper—Megan grabbed Frank's arm and held it tightly.

The vet was a huge man with a bodybuilder's physique, yet his voice was soft, almost effeminate. He gave Frank and Megan a wide smile. "Jasper will be coming out of sedation in about twenty minutes, but he'll be fine. It looks like he must have gotten into a fight, and the wound got infected. Luckily, the x-rays showed no breaks. However, it's fortunate that we did that x-ray, because I probably wouldn't have seen this otherwise."

He pulled a clear plastic baggie from his lab coat and handed it to Frank. It contained a four-inch-long metal wire.

Dr. Dew showed his arm and pointed at a four-inch length above his wrist. "That wire managed to lodge itself between the skin and muscle just above the wound. I have no idea how it could have gotten in there, but it came out without any problems."

"So… he's okay?" Megan asked.

Another broad smile. "Jasper's still a little loopy at the moment, but he's just fine. All stitched up. He's on antibiotics, which he'll need to take twice a day, and I'm also going to give you guys some ointment that needs to go on the wound on a daily basis."

Barking sounded from the back, and the exam room doors burst open. Jasper came bounding into the waiting room, his gait a bit awkward, one foot wrapped up like a mummy. He raced straight to Megan and spun rapidly with excitement as if he'd expected to never see her again.

Sherri came in right behind him. "I'm sorry Dr. Dew, but Jasper woke up way early and began frantically pawing at the door. I didn't want him to pull any of his stitches. It looks like he really wanted to see his mommy."

Megan scratched Jasper's head. Clearly the two had already formed a bond.

"Well, we can't have this big guy breaking down any doors," said Dr. Dew, laughing. "I'm quite sure he's the heaviest *healthy* lab I've ever encountered, and it's not even close. It's odd, because he doesn't look like he'd be any heavier than seventy-five pounds or so, which is still heavy for a lab, but this boy has got some incredibly dense musculature. And judging by his teeth, he's still young. He might grow a bit more yet."

Frank groaned. "I'm already tired just thinking about how much work it'll be just keeping him fed."

Jasper walked away from them, grabbed a doggie blanket that was tucked under one of the waiting room chairs, brought it back, and laid it on Frank's lap.

Megan smiled. "Aww, he heard you're tired and he brought you a blanket."

Dr. Dew patted Jasper on his head. "You're one smart dog."

Jasper sat up a bit straighter and woofed in agreement.

Frank couldn't shake the feeling that something wasn't right about this animal. But as he watched Megan fawning over Jasper, he knew that what he thought no longer mattered.

ADDENDUM

My formal background has kept me fully immersed in the world of science for decades. Given my science background and my access to some folks in academic research, it shouldn't be a surprise that I've found ways to draw from both my background and theirs to produce stories that involve technology in some way or another.

Many might label this novel as a hard science fiction tale, and I suppose they'd be correct. The funny thing is, Larry Niven, one of the grandmasters of the genre, he read *Primordial Threat* and labeled it science and adventure fiction, mostly because it carries many elements of an action thriller, and that could just as easily apply to *Freedom's Last Gasp*.

One might ask, "What is hard science fiction, and is it something that I can read?"

To me, the key thing that differentiates hard science fiction from "soft" is that in the former, science is not just an ingredient of the story, but a key part of it.

However, in my honest opinion, that shouldn't mean you need advanced degrees to understand what is happening. All you should need is a love of good stories that contain science and technology. It is up to the author to make the science portion accessible to all that would read it.

Like all my stories, I strive to maintain some level of scientific accuracy with the things that a reader is exposed to. Certainly, there will be elements in any tale of fiction that are impossibilities today. However, built upon a solid foundation of science, I attempt to venture forward with some predictions of what could be, and from that, construct a tale that should hopefully be entertaining and maybe somewhat enlightening.

Since many of the concepts I use in this novel stem from scientific elements I introduced in Primordial Threat, I'll review some of that referenced science at the end of this addendum so that people can also get up to speed on some terms that maybe aren't as extensively described in this novel.

I should note that the purpose of this addendum is to talk about technical elements that I've used in this story, and give you, the reader, an insight into how some elements of hard science might relate to them or serve as inspiration. For example, I talked about a "priority communicator" that allows real-time communication across great distances, seemingly violating some of the laws of science what we know today. I'll admit that the concept itself is not new to science fiction, but in this addendum, I'll separate for you the real vs not real and actually talk about how elements of known science could achieve some rather remarkable things, while employing minimum handwavium (nonsense). In this addendum I also talk about something called the Kinetic Bombardment Project (KBP) and in the end of the story, it comes into play as a means of asserting some bits of justice. This is a totally real thing conceived in the 1950's and I'll talk about what was known as Project Thor. Much like when I used it in Primordial Threat, I'll cover again the concept of a Warp Ring, and even though there are absolutely no such things in today's science that exhibit such properties, such a thing isn't in the realm of complete and utter fantasy; there's actually reasonable physics behind it!

All these things have a basis in academic research and history. Let me hopefully tantalize you with the possibilities, as I point out things in the book that might have initially seemed like works of fantasy, but have real science behind them.

As I give very brief explanations of what may be very complex concepts, my intent is to only leave you with sufficient information to give a remedial understanding of the subject. However, for those who want to know more, it's also my intent to leave you with enough keywords that would allow you to initiate your own research and gain a more complete background understanding of any of these topics.

Well, that's enough of my babbling, let's get to the science of science fiction.

The Tube Network:

In this story, we introduce a new transportation system that has become the primary means going from point A to point B in very little time. It seems somewhat fantastical that a trip from New York City to Los Angeles might only take an hour, whereas a flight today usually is triple that, at minimum.

The elements of such a transport method have been talked about already in popular culture by Elon Musk with a project called the Hyperloop. The premise for the tube network is really no different.

The biggest problem today in high-speed transport is friction. Not so much the friction of tires on the road, but air friction. Even a plane suffers from a tremendous amount of drag associated with having to push through air, which is rather dense at high speeds. Think about the devastation a hurricane causes when 200 mile-per-hour winds blast against most buildings.

Now imagine 700, 1000, or even 2000 mile-per-hour winds. We don't have many materials that can deal with that type of friction. However, under what conditions do we not have any friction?

A vacuum.

Much like in the vacuum of space, things can move practically as fast as they want and suffer no ill effects because the ship, train, whatever, is pushing through emptiness. Well, the tube network (much like Musk's proposed Hyperloop) has two key elements that must be in place for it to work. No friction under the vehicle. This is addressed by existing technologies associated with magnetic levitation. In essence, high speed trains would move forward not on wheels but on a magnetic cushion with nothing touching between the train and the rail underneath.

The second element is the need for a vacuum. By creating a tube and sucking the air out of it, the train in essence becomes a self-contained space ship on Earth. It moves without friction and has the potential for amazing speeds.

To give you a practical example, let's imagine that you're in one of these tube pods that I described in the book. And to ensure we aren't overly stressing anyone out, the maximum acceleration will be about .3 G, which is about the same force you experience during takeoff in a commercial jet.

Let's assume you start from a standing position, at 0 miles per hour. After one minute of acceleration you'd be going nearly 400 miles per hour. After five minutes, you'd be going almost 2000 miles per hour.

Amazing, isn't it?

The technology to do this exists, but the reason it isn't yet practical is that there is a huge cost for developing a means to maintain a true vacuum across long distances. These things are likely addressable over time and as technologies and power sources evolve.

So, if I was asked whether or not I believe we'd have a tube network in the next 100 or so years, I'd give it a fairly decent chance. It can be done.

Real-time Communicator:

The real-time communicator. This is a trope of sorts in science fiction. How does Star Trek communicate with star fleet across the galaxy and have a back-and-forth conversation? It should be impossible, and here's why…

Let's imagine you want to talk to someone one light minute away. (A light minute is the distance light travels in one minute.)

Well, imagine you pick up the phone, and start the conversation. It would look something like this:

Me: "Hi there."

Friend: hears me say "Hi there" a minute later and then they say, "You owe me $5."

Me: After waiting two minutes total, I hear, "You owe me $5."

Not exactly riveting TV nor conducive to convenient conversation. So, to address this problem, we need to science up a solution. Well, in many science fiction novels they wave hands and say they're using quantum entanglement as the means by which to solve such a problem. Which is fancy-speak for there isn't a clean way to address this issue, and I'll get into why, and dive deep into how it might actually be done with as little nonsense as possible.

First, what is quantum entanglement?

Briefly explained, quantum entanglement is the idea that through a variety of methods a single item can be split into two parts where each of the parts end up sharing an unseen link even though they may have a relatively great distance between them.

Let's for a moment imagine I take a jelly bean and split it in half with a very special knife. The result is two pieces of jelly bean, but they have this weird property. If I turn one of the jellybeans over, the other jellybean flips over as well. Seems like magic – and trust me, for most, it is a bizarre piece of voodoo.

The amazing thing is that quantum entanglement has already

been experimentally verified both at the subatomic level as well as at the macroscopic level using two small diamonds.

So, given that, you can imagine if someone had an entangled phone, one is located with you, and the other is on the far side of the galaxy. You might be able to have a nice conversation without delays.

For most of you, the description should end there. But, I can't leave well enough alone, because even though everything I've said above is true, what I described is also nonsense.

The following is only for the brave at heart, I'll start explaining at a graduate course level:

There's a fundamental flaw in this scenario, but before I even go into it, let's describe what a practical communication protocol even looks like.

When I send somebody a message, we've always heard about 1's and 0's, and that's true, but in a practical sense, we send messages we can read, like "Hello there."

Let's just focus on the "H" of hello there, I'll walk us through a rudimentary encoding exercise.

An "H" numerically would be equivalent to a 01001000 as an eight-bit ASCII encoded character. For basic computer scientists, that's the equivalent of a decimal 72, or a hexadecimal 48. But, again, 1's and 0's, our "H" is known as a 01001000. It is known as an eight-bit encoding because each bit (the 1 or 0) occupies one space and to encode one of our human-readable characters, let's say it takes upwards of some combination of eight 1's and 0's.

So, if I had a device that was quantum entangled, I'd need eight different bits to be entangled with each other, and if someone sets up the correct pattern, I can remotely read the "H". That's awesome.

There's a but coming, and you know it.

Every time you read one of those entangled bits, it becomes unentangled. So, basically each end gets one shot to write or read. And once you did, those bits aren't talking with their sisters or brothers anymore, and you're done. And what makes matters even worse is that if you read something before someone sent the message, you'll never get the message.

Okay – now that sucks. And that's also why I said the use of quantum entanglement is kind of nonsensical without a lot of forethought. Especially as a eureka moment in the novel, and the writer simply says, "I used quantum entanglement" to solve the problem. I like to go deeper.

So, what to do? Remember folks, I like to present you with things that could be, as much as I possibly can.

I noodled on this a long time and here's a possible scenario where such a thing could work given what we know of quantum entanglement.

Imagine you had a [gun] magazine full of sets of these entangled eight bits. Once you use a set, the next one comes up, etc. Since we're talking about particles that could easily be subatomic in size, in a practical sense this magazine could hold a ridiculous number of these entangled sets of bits. I'd even assert you'd have two magazines, one for reading, and one for sending. Well, fine, now what?

Imagine you had a synchronized high accuracy clock on both communicators. Basically, the premise would be that each communicator would on a regular basis, let's say every millisecond, read a set of bits and send a set of bits. If the communicators were idle, they're basically spitting blank messages at each other and reading blank messages. After each message, the unentangled bits are tossed, and the next set are used, on both devices. This way, they're always synchronized and talking via the correct set of entangled particles.

So, when a message is sent by someone, it's immediately received. And that would form the basis of the real-time communicator.

Think of the magazines as a battery of sorts. Each communicator may only be good for n-number of years before they run out of entangled sets of bits.

And obviously I only covered the transmission of a single character. Ultimately, that same method can be used to transmit text messages as well as audio and video.

Are we anywhere close to making one of these? Absolutely not… and then there's the question about whether it's possible to explicitly force (write) the setting in the first place - but the science is "close enough" that it could be possible, with a wink and a nod.

Project Thor:

I talked about the KBP, the kinetic bombardment project, as a concept where telephone-pole sized rods of tungsten were lifted up into space and in effect were dropped onto unsuspecting targets. It may seem somewhat fantasy-like, and has certainly been used before in science fiction as a weapons system, but the reality is, the concept was actually developed in the 1950s by

Doctor Jerry Pournelle while he was working at Boeing, doing analysis of proposed new weapons systems. He'd nicknamed the idea behind such a weapons system as Project Thor.

The science behind it is actually pretty simple. The metal rods were made of tungsten, which is a very dense and heat resistant material. Its melting point is over 6,000 degrees Fahrenheit, whereas things like steel melts at around 2,500 degrees. It may not seem like it would be all that destructive, but if you are in essence taking a very tough and dense material and throwing it at very high speeds, you'll end up with impacts that could mimic small nuclear explosions, but without the radiation and fallout.

The initial estimates by the Air Force were that a roughly 20-foot-long rod of 12-inch thick tungsten weighing approximately 19,000 pounds would slam into the Earth at ten times the speed of sound, and be the equivalent of twelve tons of high explosives. This alone would devastate a couple city blocks, and utterly destroy well-built concrete buildings. It would also likely blow out the windows upwards of half a mile from the site of impact.

And taken to further extremes, if you imagine a small engine pushing the rod along its way, increasing the speed, and if the rod were a bit bigger, you could have impacts at upwards of 30,000 mph and the equivalent of 500 tons of high explosives. Easily leveling a city block, destroying most buildings in a half mile from the impact site, and blowing out the windows of everything within a mile of the impact.

Much of what the novel covered is true. Small engines to push these rods, the ability to aim based on a GPS coordinate would be relatively trivial with known technology, and it would be very hard to detect before it smacked into its target, largely because it'll have almost no radar cross section. There won't be a launch detected, because it's simply a dropping object from above the atmosphere.

The thing that makes it impractical is that it's very expensive to get these rods up into orbit.

Might there be some up there now?

Very hard to know, but I'm sure if there are, it's classified.

Nanites:

Though the specific applications of nanites in this novel are fictional, nanites themselves are not a thing of fiction. The engineering world has had the ability to create things at the molecular level for quite some time.

The best example of this is in computer CPU manufacturing. Today, we are mass-manufacturing electronics with processes dealing with trace widths as low as seven nanometers. That's more than a thousand times smaller than the width of the finest hair. An atom averages anywhere from 0.1 to 0.3 nanometers wide.

We've even been able to manufacture tiny machines at the nano-scale. Think of a nanite as a tiny robot. A nanorobot, if you will. Molecule-sized robots have been the promise of medicine for quite some time. The concept used in Perimeter, where these "tiny doctors" are able to repair the body (within reason), and fend off sicknesses, is not really as ridiculous as it might seem.

Today, it is already possible to synthesize nanites that can determine where they are, and deliver minute units of a medicine to the correct locations. For instance, if one of these nanites was carrying a drug meant to treat a specific form of cancer, it would also carry a sensor that would help it identify its molecular target.

The advantages of such a precision approach are obvious. Chemotherapies, by contrast, blast the entire body with poisons, damaging healthy cells along with the cancerous ones. Nanites could be "programmed" to target only the unhealthy cells.

Yet today we are not using nanites as tiny doctors. Why?

Many challenges exist—among them, the ability to manufacture these nanites in a sufficient quantity to do clinical testing. This is hugely expensive today, and frankly, that's the biggest technical hurdle.

But once that hurdle is crossed, the field is open for what could be a revolution in medicine, generating entirely new methods of treating cancer, other diseases, and even possibly halt the aging process.

Warp Ring:

In this book I describe what Doctor Holmes called a Warp Ring, and oftentimes I refer to the phenomenon it creates as a gravity bubble.

The concept is simple to imagine, inasmuch as you wrap something (e.g. a ship, Earth, etc.) in a bubble, and it is the bubble that travels at tremendous speeds while everything within the bubble doesn't have any relative sense of motion whatsoever.

Definitely sounds like something out of pure space fantasy, but would it shock anyone to know that there are scholarly papers discussing the topic? I used one of these papers in particular to form some of my model of what this warp ring could do.

I refer you to a paper produced by Miguel Alcubierre called, "The Warp Drive: Hyper-fast travel within general relativity."

For purposes of research on practical experiments to some of Doctor Alcubierre's work, I would also refer you to Doctor Harold "Sonny" White, working out of the NASA Johnson Space Center. He had an excellent paper titled "Warp Field Mechanics 101".

I'll admit that for many folks, this is where the explanation should probably stop, but I'll just briefly touch on more advanced topics.

One should note that Doctor Alcubierre mentions general relativity in the title, and he does so for very specific reasons. There's a difference between general relativity and special relativity.

For special relativity, observers from different reference points will measure mass and speed differently, because space and time will expand and contract so that the speed of light in a vacuum is constant to all observers.

Sometimes these things are best explained with an example. For instance, I may turn on a flashlight and the light pouring forth will be traveling at 300,000 kilometers per second, usually denoted as the symbol "c". If I'm on a spaceship traveling at .5c and I turned on that same flashlight, the light pouring forth is also traveling at c.

I know for some of you, you're scratching your head and asking the following question. If you were standing on Earth and could see the light from the spaceship rushing by, wouldn't the light be going 1.5c, and if it isn't, why not?

For the person in the space ship, all seems to be going normally, when in fact, time and space have warped around them. Time is moving slower for them, and distances are contracted. That's what allows the person in the spaceship and the person watching the spaceship to both observe things comply with special relativity.

I'll leave the reader to stew on that for a moment, and I offer a good-natured apology if it is confusing, it *is* a complicated topic.

However, special relativity is actually a subset of general relativity. General relativity is describing spacetime itself. Spacetime is actually a model in which space and time are woven together to simplify talking about the four dimensions that would normally involve space and time. Here, Einstein determined that large objects cause a distortion in spacetime, and that distortion is known as gravity.

Anything that proposes traveling at arbitrarily high speeds would need to take advantage of this warping of spacetime.

The Warp Ring leverages this fact in the same way that Doctor Alcubierre's paper does. It harnesses the expansion and contraction of space itself and in so doing, envelopes the object in a bubble of sorts. The object (e.g. ship, Earth, etc.) isn't moving, but space itself is moving around it.

In the case of this story, the Earth is riding on this distortion, kind of like a surfer rides a wave.

I'd also suggest reading up on inflation theory. It does

provide some good background reading if you're inclined to learn more about faster-than-light movement.

As an aside, I will note that things like time dilation have been experimentally verified. I'll refer you to the U.S. Naval Observatory experiments by Hafele and Keating, which documented what happened when four incredibly accurate atomic clocks were synchronized and two of them were flown around the world while the other two remained stationary. When the clocks were brought back together, the time had shifted ever-so-slightly for the clocks which had been traveling at jet-like speeds. For them, time had slowed ever-so-slightly.

The explanations I give in the book are actually congruent with the concept of the Warp Drive that Doctor Alcubierre mentioned.

The only things we're missing are a substantial (ridiculous amount) of energy and the still theoretical concept of negative mass.

In attaining some of these things, you could imagine our ability to wrap an object (e.g. ship, Earth, etc.) into a bubble of sorts. This bubble is gravitationally isolated and when the bubble itself moves, the contents within it don't even sense the movement.

Kind of cool, don't you think? I'm waiting for Doctor Holmes to be born, so he can fiddle with things and we can make it so.

Space Elevator:

Space elevators have been written about for quite a while in the science fiction realm, but there isn't that much fictional about them.

First of all, what is a space elevator?

Simply put, imagine if you could put an object high enough up in space that it would maintain geosynchronous orbit. We do that all the time when we launch satellites. Such an object could act as an anchor for an elevator of sorts.

Imagine if you could drop a rope down from such a height and tie it down wherever it lands on Earth. You could conceivably build something that climbs up and down that rope and easily bring objects into space.

Why bother?

Well, with today's technology, it is very resource expensive to bring things into space. You could easily imagine that if the Earth had a myriad of space elevators, it would be much easier to assemble large objects (e.g. spaceships?) in space.

So what's the issue, let's get started!

The issue has always been, and still largely is, the material that you'd make this hypothetical rope from.

I like to use examples when explaining things, so let's do that.

You need to be roughly 22,000 miles above the Earth to maintain geosynchronous orbit. That's the height where the gravity pulling you down and the centrifugal force that makes you want to fly away are effectively even.

That means we need rope that is 22,000 miles long at a minimum. So how much does such a thing weigh?

I'll take for an example the lightest climbing rope I could

find. This rope weighs 48 grams per meter and has a rather impressive 1660 pounds of carrying capacity.

Well, how much does 22,000 miles of that rope weigh?

With my handy calculator in hand, it turns out that it comes to about 1,699,467 kilograms, or about 3,746,683 pounds just for the rope. That basically means that the rope isn't strong enough to even hold itself up nor any payload.

That illustrates the biggest problem space elevators have faced: what to make them out of.

In this story, I talk rather extensively about graphene. I'll leave it to the reader who is interested to read up more about graphene and its capabilities, but let's just say that if the mass manufacturing of graphene can be achieved (which is not an impossibility), then that would make something like a space elevator extremely practical.

I'll further note that graphene has rather amazing physical properties such as electrical and thermal conductivity that surpasses those of many of the known "best of" types of conductors.

ABOUT THE AUTHOR

I am an Army brat, a polyglot, and the first person in my family born in the United States. This heavily influenced my youth by instilling a love of reading and a burning curiosity about the world and all of the things within it. As an adult, my love of travel and adventure has allowed me to explore many unimaginable locations, and these places sometimes creep into the stories I write.

I hope you've found this story entertaining.

- M.A. Rothman

You can find my blog at: www.michaelarothman.com

I am also on Facebook at:
www.facebook.com/MichaelARothman
And on Twitter: @MichaelARothman

Made in the USA
Monee, IL
19 June 2023

717c9fa5-f064-43d5-9ff8-2df34bb2bd86R01